Praise for

A Family Daughter

"A beautifully told saga."

—*W* magazine

"Dazzling . . . riveting and engrossing . . . Meloy's tale of a family struggling with guilt and forgiveness spans decades and crosses continents, proving her status as one of the best literary observers of contemporary American life."

—*Booklist* (starred review)

"Rich, moving, and full of human comedy. [Meloy is] an enormously empathetic writer."

—*The New York Times Book Review*

"Meloy has written a broadly imagined intergenerational novel that reads like a funny, quirky bildungsroman. She writes like a woman who can't resist her passionate interest in how families work."

—*Newsday*

"A thoroughly original and undeniably brilliant companion piece to Meloy's debut novel, *Liars and Saints*. Each novel stands alone; together they pack a seismic wallop."

—*Kirkus Reviews* (starred review)

"[Meloy] sounds like no one except herself. And that's cause for rejoicing. Like all the best fiction, *A Family Daughter* tells us something about ourselves, and something about the world."

—*Buffalo News*

"Clear-eyed, well-written . . . You'll ache for [the Santerres] as if they were your own family—then thank God they're not!"

—*Marie Claire*

"'Dazzling' is a word perhaps too promiscuously employed by book reviewers, but in this case, I think it entirely applicable. . . . More than a writer to watch, Maile Meloy is a writer to read."

—*The Globe and Mail*

Praise for

Liars and Saints

"Maile Meloy combines the meticulous realism of domestic fiction with the witchery of a natural-born storyteller."

—*The New York Times Magazine*

"Upends popular notions of American fiction . . . a spectacular first novel."

—*The New York Times Book Review*

"Meloy's Santerres may just be the most fascinating, engrossing American family since the Louds."

—*Los Angeles Times*

"[Meloy] may be the first great American realist of the twenty-first century. . . . The Santerres aren't real but they feel like they are, and the reader will not soon forget them."

—*The Boston Globe*

"Breathtaking. . . . Leaves us with characters we'll still feel we know thirty years from now, when we pull this book down off the shelf once more."

—*Esquire*

A FAMILY DAUGHTER

✦ A NOVEL ✦

MAILE MELOY

SCRIBNER

New York   London   Toronto   Sydney

The author wishes to thank the John Simon Guggenheim
Memorial Foundation and the Santa Maddalena Foundation
for their generosity during the writing of this book.

SCRIBNER
1230 Avenue of the Americas
New York, NY 10020

SCRIBNER and design are trademarks of
Macmillan Library Reference USA, Inc., used under license
by Simon & Schuster, the publisher of this work.

For information about special discounts for bulk purchases,
please contact Simon & Schuster Special Sales:
1-800-456-6798 or business@simonandschuster.com

Designed by Kyoko Watanabe
Text set in Berthold Garamond

Manufactured in the United States of America

1   3   5   7   9   10   8   6   4   2

Library of Congress Cataloging-in-Publication Data
Meloy, Maile.
A family daughter : a novel / Maile Meloy.
p. cm.
I. Title.
PS3613.E46F36 2006
813'.6—dc22   2005051574

ISBN-13: 978-0-7432-7766-2
ISBN-10:   0-7432-7766-X
ISBN-13: 978-0-7432-7767-9 (Pbk)
ISBN-10:   0-7432-7767-8 (Pbk)

And Nature in her perplexingest mood would not of herself cast me as a family daughter.

—MARY MACLANE

PART ONE

1

IN THE SUMMER OF 1979, just when Yvette Santerre thought her children were all safely launched and out of the house, her granddaughter came to stay in Hermosa Beach and came down with a fever, and then a rash. Yvette thought it might be stress: Abby was seven, and her parents were considering divorce, and she must have sensed trouble. At bedtime she cried from homesickness, and Yvette asked if she wanted to go home. Abby said, "I want to go home, and I want to stay here."

The rash got worse, and Yvette's husband said they should tell Clarissa her daughter was sick. But Clarissa had gone back to Hawaii, where she had lived in Navy housing before Abby was born. She said it was the last place she had been happy, and she was staying somewhere without a telephone. So Yvette called Abby's father, up in Northern California.

"Oh, man," Henry said, when he heard.

"Was she exposed to anything?"

"I don't know," he said. "Let me talk to her."

"I think she has chicken pox."

"No, she can't have chicken pox," Henry said. Yvette imagined him on the other end, big and sandy-haired and invincible. It was

3

one of the infuriating things about Henry: he thought he was immune to bad luck, and by extension his daughter was, too.

"Has she had it before?" Yvette asked.

"I don't think so," he said.

"Well, then, she *can* have chicken pox."

"Did you take her to the doctor?"

"I raised three children, Henry," she said. "I don't need a doctor to recognize chicken pox." Mrs. Ferris next door had already quarantined her own daughter from Abby. Yvette hadn't heard anything about an outbreak in Los Angeles.

"Put Abby on," Henry said.

Yvette gave the phone to the child, who held the receiver to her ear with both hands. Abby nodded, in answer to some question of her father's.

"You have to say it aloud," Yvette said. "Say *yes*."

"Yes," Abby said, into the phone. She turned toward the kitchen wall to have the conversation on her own.

Yvette washed Teddy's breakfast dishes and thought her husband seemed annoyed to have a sick child in the house again. It took her attention and drained her energy. She didn't want a divorce for her daughter, she wanted a time machine. There would be no Abby, without that dominating Henry, but there would be some other child—a happier child—and a marriage that wasn't doomed from the start. Her older daughter, Margot, had a husband who was kind and stalwart and patient: if only Clarissa had found a man like that. Yvette tried to accept that the way it had gone was God's plan.

Abby said good-bye to her father, and Yvette took the phone.

"I want you to take her to a doctor," Henry said.

"He'll want to know when she was exposed."

"Well, I don't know that," he said.

"Do you know where I can reach Clarissa?"

"Clarissa won't know."

"It's not going to be a very nice summer for Abby."

"Look," Henry said, "if she has chicken pox, it's not my fault. Kids get it sometime, right? And if she got some mystery rash at your house, it's *really* not my fault. Just please take her to the doctor and find out."

Yvette said tightly that she would.

Dr. Nye, in his office with poor Abby sitting shirtless on the white table, confirmed that it was chicken pox. He was a white-haired man in a clean white coat, who reminded Yvette of a parish priest back in Canada when she was a child. He wanted to know when Abby had been exposed.

"At least ten days ago," she said. "The only child she's seen here is Cara Ferris."

"Can I play with her yet?" Abby asked. Cara lived next door, and had blond ringlets, and had marched at the head of the Fourth of July parade, twirling a baton, as Miss Hermosa Beach Recreation. Abby worshiped her.

"Not until you're better, sweetheart," Yvette said.

"But Cara's *had* chicken pox," the doctor said.

"Her mother said it was such a slight case she could get it again."

Dr. Nye made a little scoffing noise. "Just keep Abby home," he said, "and use calamine. I'll pronounce her not contagious as soon as I can, and she can play with Miss Recreation."

The next day a heat wave started that broke Los Angeles temperature records, even in the beach towns. The air was stifling, the sky was pale with smog, and poor Teddy left for work, miserable in his dress shirt and tie. The best refuge was the pool, surrounded by cool sycamores, where the children played Jump or Dive, shouting at the last second what the child launched from the diving board should do and squealing with laughter at the midair scramble to obey. Abby lay on the living room couch, banned from the pool, staring miserably out the window as Cara pranced to the car in her blue swimsuit and her yellow curls, a rolled-up towel under her tanned little arm.

They still didn't know where Clarissa was. Yvette talked to Teddy about it in bed, but he was too tired to be worried. He had too much work, and was ready to retire. She stayed home with Abby on Sunday, and Teddy went to Mass alone. She knew it was dangerous to compare sisters, but Margot wouldn't have sent a sick child without warning. She had devoted her life to raising her two boys, and she would never be unreachable about them.

On the fourth day, Clarissa finally called. Polka-dotted with dried calamine lotion, Abby told her mother she couldn't go to the pool and then went back to doing puzzles in a book. Yvette took the phone.

"I think one of the neighbor kids might've had it," Clarissa said. "I forgot."

"She's your child. She's your first obligation."

"Don't start," Clarissa said. "I've been so unhappy."

"Everyone is unhappy sometimes."

"I didn't know—" Clarissa began and trailed off.

"What?" Yvette snapped. "That there were responsibilities?"

"That my marriage would fall apart. That there would be such killing boredom. That I wouldn't get to do anything *I* wanted to do. I didn't know!"

Yvette stood at the kitchen counter wondering what part of her daughter's selfishness was her fault. Had she not given Clarissa enough attention when she was Abby's age? Had her other children distracted her—Margot, who was older and perfect, and Jamie, who was younger and troubled? Yvette took a deep breath. She would love her daughter as God loved them both, with all of their flaws. "Are you finding what you want, there?" she asked.

"No," Clarissa said. "I'm in the most beautiful place in the world, and the first time I call, my kid has chicken pox. So I feel guilty and *horrible*. And I've felt guilty and horrible all week just in anticipation of *something*. I knew there was going to be something like this."

"You sound like you think it's my fault," Yvette said.

"No," Clarissa said, unconvincingly.

"I'm not asking you to come back," Yvette said. "She'll get better."

"I didn't think she'd get sick. She has to play with someone. That time alone is my sanity."

When Yvette hung up, she took a fresh glass of juice to the living room, where Abby lay on the couch reading a comic book. She was at the age to have communion, and she wasn't even baptized.

"Your mom said good-bye and to tell you she loves you," Yvette improvised.

"Where am I going to live now?"

Yvette pushed Abby's hair from her face. "I think you'll live with your mom."

"In Hawaii?"

"No, I think at home," Yvette said.

Abby looked at her pink-splotched knees. "With just my mom?"

Yvette sighed. "I don't know, sweetheart," she said.

Yvette kept the drapes drawn to keep the house cool, and the dimness increased Abby's gloom. Yvette tried to teach her to crochet, but Abby got frustrated with the yarn. They played Boggle and Go Fish. Sometimes, in bored wanderings through the house, Abby took pictures off the master bedroom wall and lay on the bed looking at them. She liked Yvette's wedding picture, with Teddy in his pilot's uniform during the war. And she liked a picture of the two girls: Clarissa with her dark hair coming out of its curls, and Margot standing behind her, polished and serene. Abby would study the pictures and then hang them back on the wall and turn on the TV. In the heat wave they were airing Coke and Pepsi and 7UP commercials, and Abby had memorized them all. She sang the jingles absently in the bath. It was killing Yvette.

At the end of the week, Yvette called Jamie, her youngest, who was in college in San Francisco. She begged him to come home.

"I'm taking a summer class," Jamie said.

"You should see her," Yvette said. "She's so miserable. Mrs. Ferris won't let her play with Cara. I could just wring that woman's neck."

"My car might not make it."

"I'll send Triple A," Yvette said.

He was home by late afternoon, with a duffel bag full of laundry that he dropped on the kitchen floor. Her handsome, mischievous boy: he had caused her so much trouble over the years, but now he had come when she needed him. She kissed his cheeks out of gratitude, as Abby sidled into the kitchen.

"Where's my favorite niece in the whole world?" Jamie asked.

Abby wrinkled her nose at him. "I'm your *only* niece."

Yvette noticed that Abby had washed the calamine off her face and arms, in honor of Jamie's arrival. She still had spots, but she didn't look like she was dying of a pink plague.

"Oh, yeah," Jamie said. "Well, if I had others, you'd still be my favorite. Want to hit the beach?"

"People might think I'm contagious," Abby said, solemnly.

"Are you?"

She shook her head no.

Jamie shrugged. "So who cares what they think?"

"I can't go in the waves alone," Abby said, more hopeful.

"I'll carry you in," he said. "Let's go, get your suit on."

Abby turned and nearly danced down the hallway to her room.

"Thank you," Yvette said to Jamie. "I can't tell you—"

"No biggie," he said, opening the refrigerator. "That class was a drag anyway."

"Was it? I'm sorry."

"It's pretty much your fault," he said, but she could tell he was joking.

"You can take another class later."

"Sure." He closed the refrigerator.

"I'll go shopping."

"Looks good, Ma," he said. "I was just checking. Here she is, let's go."

He lifted Abby in her blue swimsuit onto his hip, as if she weighed nothing, and carried her out to the red Escort that used to be Teddy's.

Yvette followed with a twenty from her pocketbook. "After the beach, you can bring back ice cream for dessert."

Jamie snapped the bill for Abby. "Score!" he said.

Two hours later they came back, Abby sandy from the beach, with a tub of Dairy Queen ice cream and some Dilly bars that they rushed to the freezer. Abby chatted happily all through dinner, and it seemed to Yvette as if her cheerfulness were a wheel that Jamie had gotten spinning. Now he just needed to give it a push every so often, to keep it going.

"Thank you, Jamie," Yvette said, when she got her son alone. She couldn't remember when she had last thanked him for anything but Christmas presents, and now she couldn't stop.

Jamie moved into his old room and took Abby to the beach every morning. In the afternoons, he taught her five-card stud, sitting at the kitchen table with piles of unshelled peanuts.

"No eating your chips," he told her, "or we won't know who wins."

"You'll win," she said.

"I might not," he said. "I think you have a real talent for the bluff."

"No, I don't."

"You do!" he said. "Or you will when I get through with you. We can go on the road and win big—you'll be the perfect hustler."

Abby laughed. Anything Jamie said was funny; anything he did was fun. He played guitar for her, making up songs with her name in them, and he made chords and let her strum. He listened to records in his room, and Abby sat on the floor, her dark head bent over the album covers.

One afternoon, Yvette was collecting laundry from Jamie's room, and his new Bob Dylan record was playing. Abby was studying the cover. Jamie lay on the bed, reading his old paperback copy of *Dune*. Bob Dylan sang:

> *You may be living in another country, under another name*
> *But you're gonna have to serve somebody.*

"Why would you have another name?" Abby asked. Yvette took a towel off a doorknob.

"I guess if you did something wrong," Jamie said.

"So they wouldn't find you?"

"Right," Jamie said.

"But if they saw you, they would know you."

"That's why you live in another country."

Yvette bundled Jamie's clothes under her arm and said, "I live in another country, under another name."

Abby looked at her, astonished, and whispered, *"Why?"*

"I married Teddy, when he was a pilot in the war," Yvette said. "And I moved here from Canada and changed my name to his."

"That's not the same thing," Jamie said. "She didn't do anything wrong."

But it had felt wrong, leaving her father, who hadn't wanted her to go. "I did leave my family and my country," Yvette said. "And I never went back. I always thought I would."

Jamie shrugged in grudging acceptance. "Okay," he said to Abby, "so the song's about your grandma. It's about Canadians getting married and moving to California and serving the war effort and the holy Trinity."

"Oh, *Jamie*," Yvette said, and she laughed, embarrassed, and took the wash to the machine.

Yvette cooked Jamie's favorite meals—enchiladas and chiles rellenos for dinner, poached eggs and toast soldiers for breakfast—and they became Abby's favorites. When Clarissa or Henry called, Yvette was careful not to praise Jamie too much and make them feel they were being replaced, because she didn't see any benefit to their reclaiming their daughter yet. Abby was blissfully happy, and Jamie had a devotee and a life at the beach. If Henry was working, and Clarissa was off finding herself, then they were all where they wanted to be.

2

HENRY DIDN'T WANT the divorce. Clarissa was his wife and he loved her, even if she wasn't all *there*, all the time.

There was the time, for example, when Clarissa wandered away from the kitchen sink, where she was washing nursing bras with the baby lying on the drainboard. While she was gone, Abby rolled with a splash into the soapy water and had to be hauled out wailing. Or there was the time Clarissa left their daughter, at three, strapped in the backseat next to a roll of insulation for the house while she ran some errand. By the time Clarissa got back, Abby had hives all over her wrists from playing with the pink fluff. "Fiberglass," Abby announced; it was written in big letters on the roll, and was the reason Clarissa reported the story proudly to Henry.

"I hadn't said it in front of her," Clarissa said. "I know she *read* it. Isn't that amazing?"

"Clar, you can't just leave her in the car!" he said. "Someone's going to call the cops!" People in Santa Rosa paid attention to their neighbors.

"Well, we'll just show them she can read, at three," Clarissa said, getting sullen. "At least I had her seat belt on. And it's none of their business."

Henry had grown up in Santa Rosa, and buried his parents there. He had goodwill there, people who had known him all his life. It was only an hour north of San Francisco, a good place to start a law practice, a good place to raise children. When he got out of the Navy in Honolulu, it was only natural that he would go back.

But from the moment they had unpacked their books and hung some pictures on the walls, Clarissa—already pregnant—started complaining it was too small, too restrictive, too provincial. She wasn't able to fulfill her potential. Henry thought she should be busy having his baby, but he didn't say so. The complaint came up again, in those early years, but Clarissa's only decisive act was to go to Hawaii and leave Abby with her parents with the chicken pox. During an argument after she came back, when the separation was still just an option, Henry had asked what exactly she imagined her potential to be, but that was a mistake—she left him the next day, and moved to San Francisco to take classes at the university. She said it would be better for Abby to stay in a house she knew. Henry found himself suddenly a single parent.

A friend told him, "Get family to help you. There's nothing like family, you can't trust anyone else." But Henry's parents were dead, and he had no siblings. He couldn't go to Clarissa's parents for help again, and they lived eight hours away.

So Henry hired a woman named Maricruz, who seemed kind and intelligent, and had been a teacher at home in Honduras. He told her he didn't want a lot of Catholic hocus-pocus around Abby, but the babysitter seemed fine with that. When the neighbor's cat died, Maricruz helped bury him and told Abby that now the cat was helping to make the flowers grow. She took Abby to every lesson they offered in town—piano, tennis, swimming, jazz dance, Drawing on the Right Side of the Brain—but what Abby learned best was Spanish from Maricruz.

When his caseload and his household were under control, Henry took Abby to Hawaii for her eighth birthday, just the two of them. He wanted to show it to her before Clarissa did, to claim it for his own.

By the end of the first day of airports and taxis, and making sure Abby had books to read and food to eat, he was exhausted, and had new respect for Maricruz. The next morning they had breakfast on their balcony at an old beach hotel, and then he helped Abby catch the little waves at the beach.

After lunch, before going back into the water, Henry led his daughter into a deserted changing room to use the old-fashioned medical scale. Abby was getting taller, and he wanted to know what she weighed; it seemed like something a parent should know. A man came into the empty room with a towel around his waist and said, "What's she doing in here?"

"We're just using the scale," Henry said, sliding the big weight to 50. He felt Abby's big eyes looking up at him.

"She's not supposed to be in here," the man said.

"It's no big deal," Henry said.

"I mean it," the man said.

"She's *eight*," Henry said sharply, and Abby flinched.

"I don't care!" the man said. "It's the men's dressing room! What the hell are you thinking?"

Henry tapped the little weight up the bar until the needle swung free and balanced. "Fifty-eight pounds," he said. "That's amazing."

"I'm telling you," the man said. "Get her out."

Henry helped Abby off. He checked that the scale zeroed out correctly, to prove a point about his unhurriedness, and then he led Abby slowly toward the doorway to the pool. She clutched his hand and took two quick steps for each of his.

"What were you *thinking*?" the man yelled at their backs. "Jesus Christ!"

Henry lifted Abby carefully to his hip and turned, at the door. "Don't be crazy," he said. "She's eight."

He could feel her heart racing against his chest and could feel his own pounding as he carried her out. He realized then that they were going to be two alone in the world.

3

AFTER THE DIVORCE, Abby went to visit her mother in the city every few weekends, riding the bus south from Santa Rosa. Clarissa lived in a single room with a Murphy bed, near the university. The kitchen was in a closet, and everything was playhouse-sized: a half stove, a small sink, a cube refrigerator. There was a little table by the window, and when the bed was folded up, there was room to move around. Clarissa had a new boyfriend, a homeopath with round glasses, who showed up in the morning with muffins from the organic bakery down the street. On Saturdays, Abby went to yoga class with her mother, and her mother bought her a yoga book for children: *Be a Frog, a Bird, or a Tree*. Then they went to hear drums, or singing, or poetry. On Sunday mornings they went to a meditation class and lay on the floor visualizing a path through a green forest, and a white light expanding in their hearts.

After two years, Clarissa finished her degree and came back to a rented bungalow in Santa Rosa, and they arranged for Abby to switch houses every month. Clarissa said Henry was wrong in not letting Abby experience a wider world, but Henry said there was plenty of time for the wider world, and it would be nice to let their daughter have a childhood. Abby moved each month with a duffel bag of books and clothes.

At dinner at her father's house, it was just the two of them. He talked to her about work and his day, and he asked about school. For a while, he called her "princess" and "pumpkin," but by the time she was twelve he had stopped. She missed the names but guessed that he had decided she was neither a princess nor a pumpkin, and it wouldn't help her to think she was.

At her mother's house, the boyfriends came and went. Abby played jump rope at school, on the asphalt playground, and one of the songs went

> *Rich man, poor man*
> *Beggarman, thief*
> *Doctor, lawyer*
> *Merchant, chief*

The one you missed your jump on was the one you were supposed to marry, but in Abby's experience of her mother's lovers, you could have the whole list. There had been her father—that was the lawyer—and a paramedic who could be the doctor. There had been a real estate investor, a cabinetmaker, a Buddhist guitar player with no job, and a writer who borrowed money from Clarissa and never paid it back. There had briefly been a handsome Navajo horse trainer who held tribal office and could count as the chief. *The Joy of Sex* was on her mother's bookshelf, and her friends spotted it and demanded to see the pictures. Abby dutifully showed it to them when her mother was out, but felt a vague horror at the hairy grown-ups in the illustrations.

When she was thirteen, Abby found a letter lying open on the kitchen table, and read it in the automatic way she read anything lying out on the table. It was a letter to her mother, about wanting to make physical love to her again, and how and why, and it was signed by a man Abby knew to be married; his son went to her school. Abby left the letter there, and by dinnertime it was gone.

"I was thinking," Abby said, making waffles for dinner, "that it might be better if I lived in one house again, all the time."

"Is this because I didn't make dinner?" Clarissa asked.

"No," Abby said. "I was reading something in a magazine. They did a study and decided that joint custody isn't as healthy for kids as they thought."

"So you want to live with your dad?"

Abby forked a waffle off the iron and brought it to her mother's plate. "It would be easier for him," she said. "He has Maricruz to come cook sometimes."

"He has Maricruz because he has money," Clarissa said. "I'm not going to let my daughter be raised by a babysitter."

"I think the raising part is sort of over," Abby said.

Clarissa looked hopeless and bereft, and let the waffle sit cooling on her plate. "You were always your father's," she said. "He wanted a girl. And then when you were born, you looked so much like him, you were clearly just *his*."

"All babies look like their fathers," Abby said. "We evolved that way so fathers would stay and help."

"But you were like him, too," Clarissa said. "You would always go to him, when you started to crawl."

"If I started with you," Abby said, "then he was the only other person there to crawl to."

"No," her mother said. "There was always this bond. When you started talking, I could really tell."

"I was a *baby*," Abby said. "You're saying I talked like a lawyer?"

"See, you're still like him," Clarissa said. "You're trying to prove me wrong, just to do it."

Abby poured her own waffle and let the subject drop. There were advantages to her mother's house anyway, in that there weren't really any rules. Sometimes she had a curfew, but mostly she didn't, and she could see how that would become useful.

She wrote letters to Jamie during those years. He loved his sister, but he understood what she was like. He came to Santa Rosa sometimes, between jobs and girlfriends, and showed up at Christmas with mix tapes for Abby. When her mother started going to a Reiki healer, who put his hands on Clarissa's chakra points through her clothes and visualized her healing, Abby wrote to Jamie about it. "She says that Western medicine is so limited," she wrote.

She says there's incredible research and that she knows her own experience with it. But that's what she said about the psychic who channeled her past lives (pioneer woman, French peasant). She doesn't seem very "healed" to me.

In high school, she brought boys home, and there wasn't any awkwardness about it. They went up to her room to kiss and joke and fumble, saying *hey* to Clarissa on the way. At Henry's house, she couldn't do that. He didn't like any of her boyfriends, and he terrified them. He was polite enough, but the politeness was a sign of not taking the boys seriously, which made it hard for Abby to take them seriously. There was one her father called Archie, because he thought he looked like an Archie, and after a while she could only think of him as Archie, too.

When she was living at her father's house, he stayed in and read at night, and she did, too. He had a girlfriend in Sausalito but he saw her only when Abby wasn't there. The dinner dishes ran in the dishwasher and her father read thrillers and biographies on the couch. Abby lay sideways in the overstuffed armchair and read paperbacks off his shelves—*The Electric Kool-Aid Acid Test* and *Helter Skelter*—until he started bringing books home so she would read something else.

"How come you get to read Robert Ludlum and I have to read *Wuthering Heights*?" she asked him once.

"Because I read it already," he said.

Eventually he would close his book and put his hand on her head and go up to bed, leaving her reading under the lamp in the dark, quiet house.

4

YVETTE KNEW THERE had been lapses of attention in the raising of Abby, and she volunteered to go with her to look at colleges. Abby, to her surprise, wanted to go to San Diego to see where Henry and Clarissa had met in the registration line at UCSD.

"Why?" Yvette asked.

"I just do," Abby said. "They must have been happy there. I want to see what it looks like."

Yvette remembered trees on campus, but not as many as they found there: the university was a vast eucalyptus grove. In the brochure Yvette read that the trees, with their peeling papery bark and their finger-long leaves, had been planted by the Santa Fe Railway, for use as railroad ties. "None of this was here when your mother was here," she said. "I don't remember any of these buildings." The central library looked like a blocky flying saucer resting on its landing gear.

The student center curved around an outdoor stage, and there were student activities posted on one of the walls—Bi-Gay-Lesbian Movie Night, Life Drawing Class, a kosher barbecue: "Schmooze with the Jews." A group of girls who looked Chinese spilled out of one of the doors, laughing. The students everywhere were talking and happy.

It was an intensely bright day, and Yvette wanted to rest on a bench in the shade, so Abby went to the admissions office alone. As she walked away, she looked just like one of the college students, and Yvette was amazed that this was her little Abby, grown up. A boy smiled as Abby passed, and Yvette remembered what it had been like to be at the beginning of things. But she also wanted to protect her granddaughter. The school seemed so vast—it was a place a girl could get lost in.

When Abby came back with an application packet, Yvette said, "Let's go see the University of San Diego."

"Isn't that Catholic?"

"I remember it being so beautiful," Yvette said. "It isn't far on the map."

Abby agreed—she was in such a good mood Yvette thought she would agree to anything—and Yvette spotted the university before they arrived; the creamy white Spanish buildings took up a whole hilltop, with towers and arched windows above the trees. They parked and walked through a silent courtyard, and a redheaded girl in a yellow skirt came out of a building.

Yvette said, "Excuse me, do you go here? My granddaughter is applying."

The girl sized Abby up frankly. She had freckles and a turned-up nose, and Yvette guessed she was Irish.

"It's a great school," the girl said.

"Are the teachers priests?" Abby asked.

"It depends on the subject. One of my favorite courses was Logic, which I took from a priest. He was wonderful."

Abby turned away to study the elaborate stucco at the tops of the buildings. Yvette asked a few more questions and then let the girl go.

"Why did you say I was applying here?" Abby asked when they were alone.

"It was just a way to ask the questions," Yvette said.

"I really liked UCSD."

"Don't you think it was too large?"

"I'm going back to the car."

"We could find the admissions office."

"I'm not going here. You said you just wanted to *see* it."

They went back to the car, and Yvette wished she had gotten Abby into confirmation classes, that summer of the chicken pox. She thought of the Jesuits: "Give me a child before the age of seven . . ."

Abby drove back down Marian Way, into the traffic.

"You know," Yvette offered, "I was an adult a long time before I found my God. It wasn't even when I was your age, it was much later. He came to me through my children, and my struggle to be a good mother. He knew I would have to be won over through my emotions; that was the only way I would come in."

Abby ran a yellow light. On the other side of the intersection, she said, "Then he'll know he's not going to get me through a Logic class taught by a priest."

Yvette decided to let it go. It would take longer for Abby to see that everything didn't depend on logic and reason. It wasn't her time.

5

"I'M GOING TO UCSD," Abby wrote to Jamie in the spring.

I was reading about Freud and the primal scene, about people being fixated on the scene of their own conception, and maybe it's that. When I think about college, I see myself on that campus. My teachers keep asking why I don't go to some east coast school. My mother thinks that's a great idea, but then why didn't <u>she</u> do it? Those schools are all cold and expensive. You had that girlfriend from Sarah Lawrence— she was cold and expensive. I'm staying west.

When it was time to go, her mother warned her not to end up with the boy she met in the registration line. "That was such a mistake for me," she said.

"Thanks a lot."

"I don't mean having you was a mistake," she said. "I just mean marrying your dad was."

"Isn't that the same thing?"

"I was so young," Clarissa said. "I was right out of Catholic girls' school. The only boyfriend I'd had was Jimmy Vaughan."

"I'm not getting married, and I didn't go to Catholic school," Abby said. "So I think I'm safe to register."

"You're never getting married?" her mother asked sadly.

"I just mean not now."

"I was so young," her mother said. "I was your age. Isn't that strange?"

In the registration line, a boy asked Abby where she was from and if she knew what her major would be. His name was Leon, and whenever she saw him in the cafeteria, carrying a tray of food and a glass of milk, there was a dangerous thrill about saying hello to him. She described the feeling to her new roommate, Miranda, who laughed.

Miranda had rich, inattentive parents in Newport Beach and long, shiny black hair from her Japanese mother. She thought Abby's virginity was adorable and her relationship with her parents was quaint. She loved Henry; when he took them to dinner she linked arms with him, tossing her hair. It made Abby self-conscious.

"He's so proud of you," Miranda said. "And you never enjoy it, you never tell him anything."

"I don't have to," Abby said. "He knows."

"I don't mean telling him that you *love* him. I mean like *things*. You're so lucky, you have a dad you can be close to, and you don't take advantage of it."

"Yes, I do."

"No, you *don't*. You take him for granted."

"Who can you take for granted, if not your parents?"

"You'll see," Miranda said. "Wait'll you meet my parents, and then you'll see."

Time went by imperceptibly on the unchanging, eucalyptus-grove campus. There were riots in Los Angeles, and Abby called her grandparents, who were fine. Iraq didn't pull out of Kuwait, and the war started in grainy bombing footage on the TV in the common room. Protest posters went up at the student center, and then it was over. When Sinéad O'Connor tore up the Pope's picture, Yvette called to ask what young people thought about it, but Abby hadn't heard it had happened.

She met Miranda's mother, who was a plastic surgeon, and her father, who bought a hundred-thousand-dollar Hummer the week they became available to civilians. It gleamed in their driveway like a tank. He liked to say that Arnold Schwarzenegger had one, too.

They kept on as roommates; Abby couldn't afford to move off campus, and Miranda liked the crowded friendliness and distraction of the dorms. Boys came to the room chasing her, and some of them gave up and turned their attention to Abby. The first one was on the swim team and Miranda was sure he was gay; it didn't last long. The second was a premed who was skilled and instructive, and dispatched the virginity before leaving for Johns Hopkins with a decorous sadness and reluctance.

The last one, in Abby's junior year, was a visiting student from the University of Palermo. His father was a Sicilian baron with no money, who hoped Gianni would find a rich American wife to shore up a crumbling house and an unlucky family. He had sent his handsome son to California to find an heiress.

"Why aren't you a rich girl, bella?" Gianni asked, lying in Abby's narrow dorm bed.

"I think you should tell your father you're not cynical enough to pull this off."

"Miranda is rich," he said. "I could marry her, and we could all live together, like now."

"That won't work."

"The rich girls here don't even *like* me," he said. "Miranda laughs at me."

"Not really."

"I'm happy here," he said. "In this terrible bed. But then I think of my father."

"Maybe you could *make* the money."

He shook his head patiently, as if she would never understand. "We need much more than that," he said.

He was uncircumcised, which was alarming at first, and he was against condoms. "This is like going to swim in your *stivali di gomma*," he said. "How do you say this?" He mimed pulling them on.

"Rubber boots."

"Rubber boots," he said. "Exactly."

But it seemed to be Safe Sex Week all the time on campus, with an earnest student handing out pamphlets in the cafeteria, which were even more alarming to Abby than Gianni's unexpected foreskin. So they found ways not to fuck, to avoid the rubber boots and the horrible diseases. What Gianni wanted most was to watch Abby make herself come.

"I can't do it if you're watching," she said. "I'm too shy."

"*Shy,*" he said with disgust. "Pretend I'm not here."

"Then I wouldn't be doing it."

"You should do it for your*self.*"

"Maybe," she said. It took so much concentration, and boys did it for her so easily.

"You say this to tease me, because you know I want to see it," he said. "I'll give you fifty American dollars."

"You need that money in your hope chest."

"My *what?*"

"For when you get married."

He shook his head. "When I get married," he said, "she will be so rich I can spend all my money so you will do this little trick."

In November of her junior year, Abby was tired of not fucking. She went to Student Health and got a prescription for birth control pills, just in time for Gianni's announcement that he was leaving for England. He hoped his chances for marriage would be better there.

"Don't be sad, bella," he said. "We had this nice time."

Abby was more depressed, after he left, than she had expected to be. She went home for Christmas, and everything seemed bleak and colorless. Her mother was at a yoga retreat in Peru. Her father asked why she seemed down, but she deflected the question. There was nothing she could tell him: Gianni's feelings about rubber boots? His desire for an English heiress? Everything was about sex or the pursuit of money, and her father would hate hearing about it.

*

In February, her father called to ask her to go skiing. He had just won a case that had taken all his time, and there'd been six inches of new snow during the week.

"I don't want to drive all that way to ski," she said.

"You can fly to Reno," her father said. "I'll meet you there."

"I don't know if I can get a flight."

Miranda was pulling on a tight black minidress in front of the closet mirror and said, "If you're flying to ski, go to Utah."

"Miranda says we should go to Utah."

"Well, Miranda's a rich kid," her father said. "Anyway, the snow's better here. It's been raining all week, and snowing in the mountains."

Miranda considered the dress in the mirror, then turned around and considered it over her shoulder. The boys upstairs, one from Colombia and one from Bolivia, were having a Putita party on Friday, at which everyone had to dress like a little slut. Miranda thought it would help Abby out of her mood.

"I have work to do," she told her father.

"You can bring your books," he said. "The lifts close at four."

"I have to work at the café, too."

"Get a sub," he said. "Don't they have library jobs for girls like you?"

Miranda peeled the dress off. In heels and black bra and underwear, she looked through the closet again.

Abby said, "You should wear that."

"Wear what?"

"I was talking to Miranda."

"I'll get the plane ticket," he said. "It can't be that much."

"I have a paper due," Abby said, though it wasn't due until Thursday.

"Okay," he said. The disappointment in his voice almost made her change her mind. But she'd just been home for Christmas. Miranda pulled another dress over her head, a red one with fringe that made her look like a sushi bar hostess. Abby shook her head.

"What's the paper on?" her father asked.

"It's a close reading of a poem, but I haven't picked one yet."

"How about 'There once was a man from Nantucket'?"

Abby laughed. "I don't think that's on the syllabus."

"Well, what then?"

"Maybe one by Auden."

"What's it about?"

"The sadness of people getting old, I guess."

"Auden would want you to go skiing, while you're young," he said.

"I don't think he would."

"Shakespeare would."

"Dad, I can't. I'm sorry."

"Okay," he said. "You sure I can't convince you?"

"I'm sorry," she said. "Next time."

"That was *so* sad," Miranda said when Abby hung up the phone.

Henry loaded up his old skis and went alone, as the police reconstructed it later, leaving after work to drive up over the Donner Pass. While Abby was at the Putita party, with her shirt tied up like Daisy Duke's and the Colombian boy's hand on her bare waist, and while Miranda danced on the windowsill in the tight black dress and slingbacks, Henry Collins hit a patch of black ice. The car spun out of control, broke through a guardrail on the highway, and landed upside down sixty feet below.

The next morning, Abby got back to the dorm room first. She took a shower and then stood in a towel checking messages. There were two for Miranda, from boys she had stood up. The third was one of the waitresses asking Abby to fill in at the café. The fourth was her mother, crying, and before she said it, Abby knew.

6

CLARISSA HAD NEVER expected anything to happen to Henry, so she had never considered the burden on Abby if something did. Even if she *had* thought about it, she could never have predicted the way Abby fell apart.

Clarissa had already gone to the police morgue to identify the body. She was led into a little space like a closet, where someone pulled open a curtain. Henry was on a gurney on the other side of a window, with only his face visible under a sheet. He was still and blue and badly bruised, with a star-shaped contusion on his forehead. She stayed a few minutes, feeling emptied out. Her therapist said she had defined herself in opposition to Henry since the divorce, like she had defined herself in opposition to her sister growing up, so it was natural that she would feel that a part of her was missing. She was glad she had seen him, and when her daughter came home from UCSD, Clarissa asked if Abby wanted to see him, too.

"I can't," Abby said.

"Maybe you'll want to have seen him."

"Don't tell me what I want!" Abby said and shut herself in her room.

For a week, Abby didn't go outside. She alternated between panic and fury, and wouldn't let Clarissa touch her. Then the babysitter, Maricruz, brought food to the house and sat on the couch while Abby cried in her lap.

Henry, who had drawn up dozens of wills for other people, had died without one of his own. One of his friends, a lawyer named Jason Katz, offered to help with the estate, but Abby stalled. She didn't know what to do with the house she had grown up in, and she wouldn't take the phone or answer questions. She started wearing Henry's watch, which had survived the accident, and she lived in pajamas and refused meals, eating crackers out of the box. When Clarissa suggested once that she do some restorative yoga, Abby started crying again.

"Why don't you give Jason power of attorney, and go back to school?" Clarissa finally asked.

"If you want me to leave, just say it."

"I don't," Clarissa said. "I just think it would be good to have something to do."

"I don't want to go back to school," Abby said. "It's so stupid."

"You're young. You're supposed to be stupid."

"What would I do there?" Abby said. "I can't do a close reading of a poem. I can't eat in the cafeteria, when my hands shake all the time. I can't go to parties, and stand around by a keg, and dance to the YMCA song."

"Maybe there's a poem that would help you."

"I don't want help from poems," Abby said. "Fuck poems."

Two months passed. Clarissa doubted that Abby would have been so destroyed if *she*, Clarissa, had died instead of Henry. She was jealous, and felt robbed of the consolation of consoling her daughter.

Jason Katz started to come by the house after work, to see how things were. He understood how hard it had been. Clarissa would pour him a beer, and he would drink half. Some days he rode his bicycle from work, with his pant legs clipped around his ankles. She started to look forward to his coming, and to think about him during the day.

He was in the kitchen one afternoon, and Clarissa was telling him how Abby had barely spoken to her all week, when her daughter came in, wearing one of Henry's old plaid shirts over jeans, and the too-big watch.

"Stop *talking* about me," Abby said. "Stop pretending this is something that happened to you. You left him thirteen years ago."

"You're my daughter," Clarissa said, trying to keep her voice steady. "And you're suffering."

"So what? You can't make that your drama!"

"I had to talk to someone."

"If you want to fuck Jason, that's your business, but don't you *dare* use me as an excuse."

Jason flushed and looked at the floor. "I think I should go," he said, and he was out the door before Clarissa could stop him.

"Why did you do that?" Clarissa demanded.

"Why did *I* do that?"

"There's nothing between Jason and me."

"There will be," Abby said. "There would be. I have to leave this house."

"No, you don't."

"I keep thinking," Abby said, "about how you always said I was like my dad. But part of me must be like you—that's how it works. So now part of me is dead, and I don't want the other part. I don't *want* to be like you!"

She left the room, and Clarissa sat numbly at the table, feeling as if Abby had struck her. She tried to remember that her daughter was in pain. She tried to imagine how she would feel if her father died, but it was impossible; she couldn't make herself believe it enough to imagine the feeling. Then she wondered if she was half Teddy and half Yvette. She didn't think she was like her mother. She was more like her father. Margot was more like their mother.

Abby came back with two duffel bags, got a toothbrush from the bathroom, and took the bags outside to her car.

Clarissa followed her. "Abby, don't do this." It was cool out, and she didn't have a jacket. "Don't go."

Abby put the bags in the backseat. "You wanted me to move on, right?"

"I don't now," Clarissa said. "Wait a while."

"Don't worry," Abby said, getting into the car. "You'll be fine."

When her daughter had driven away, Clarissa went back inside and looked around. The house was silent. The power must have gone off and come back on, because the digital clock on the stove was blinking. She hadn't noticed it before.

She had spent so much time wanting to be free of Henry and Abby: the husband she had followed at the expense of her own experiences, and the child who had chained her to a confining little town until it was simply her home and she couldn't imagine leaving. But she had stayed, and now her captors had left her, and what did she have?

7

J AMIE WAS LIVING IN San Francisco when Clarissa called him about Abby. He was taking a class called The Bible as Literature, as a misguided attempt to understand his parents, and was thinking in Bible talk. *Honor thy sister when she calls thee with another crisis.* He was thirty-three years old, still hadn't finished his bachelor's degree, and had moved out of a girlfriend's apartment onto a friend's couch. His friend was a bassist and mellow about the arrangement, and Jamie had a job in a guitar store. It wasn't a terrible life.

Five months had gone by since Henry died, and Clarissa told Jamie she thought her daughter was still dangerously depressed. Abby had moved back to San Diego, but school was out for the summer; her friends would be gone. She was waiting tables. Clarissa asked Jamie to call her.

"Why don't you call her?" Jamie asked.

"She doesn't want to talk to me."

"I'll don't know that she'll want me," Jamie said. "But I'll try."

He called the number his sister gave him, but the phone just rang, and no machine picked up. He thought he had a good sense, from his dating life, of the hours when waitresses would be home, so he kept trying, but he couldn't catch her. He guessed she was there but not answering. Finally, someone picked up the phone but didn't say hello.

"Abby?" he said.

"Jamie." She sounded relieved.

"I've been trying to call you."

"Sorry," she said.

"How's the job?"

There was a pause. "I like it," she said. "It's sort of hectic and constant. You clear the table, someone sits down, you take their order, they eat the food, they leave and you clear the table again. It's beautifully mindless." She sounded as if she hadn't talked to anyone in a while, as if she'd been saving this up, waiting for someone to ask.

"What if you forget what they ordered?" he asked.

"I write it down. That's what keeps it mindless. Some girls memorize everything to show off."

"Do you have a place?"

"A sublet," she said. "I use one little room. I don't even use the kitchen, I eat at work."

"I was thinking of driving down to Baja," he said. "Maybe I could stop on the way, if you're around." He didn't have anything better to do.

There was a long pause. "Did my mother tell you to do this?" she asked.

"No."

"You swear?"

"Yes," he said. "She gave me your number, that's all."

There was another long silence, and then there was a choking sound at the other end of the line, and a high muffled sound, and he realized Abby was crying.

"Ab?" he said.

"Oh, God," she said, sobbing. "It hurts so much. It hurts."

When he got to San Diego, his legs stiff from the drive south, he went to Abby's restaurant and took a table by the window. It was a big place with orange walls, turquoise trim, and vaguely southwestern food; there was a blackboard with the specials written on it. He looked for his niece among the cute waitresses, wondering which ones were the show-offs. When he found Abby, she looked shockingly grown-up, with the short white apron tied around her hips. She had composed herself since the phone call, and she came to his table with her pad and pencil.

"Can I getcha something?" she asked, mock folksy.

"I'll have one of them there waitresses," he said.

"Which one? We have the redhead, the brunette, and the little tattooed lesbian blonde."

"One of each, please."

"Coming right up." She tucked the notepad in the front pocket of the hip apron. "Seriously, you want a sandwich or something?"

"Shouldn't you write it down to keep it mindless?"

"Yours I can remember," she said.

"What's good?"

"The turkey avocado with chipotle sauce. With sweet potato fries."

"Sold."

"Are you going to stand up and say hello?"

Jamie took his newly grown-up niece in his arms. Her notepad pressed against his thigh, her arms wrapped tightly around his back, and her soft hair brushed his chin. He felt suddenly nervous.

"I'm so glad you're here," Abby said, her voice muffled against his chest.

"I am, too," he said.

The fiction of the Baja trip dissolved without comment, and Jamie stayed. He had left nothing solid behind: he had no apartment, just a few boxes in his friend's garage, and the guitar store had divvied up his shifts. The kitchen had a breakfast table by the window, and Jamie learned how to use the shiny silver coffeemaker Abby had never bothered with. They had coffee at the table in the mornings, Abby in a white bathrobe, and she talked about her father.

"I feel responsible," she said. "I should have gone skiing with him."

"Then you'd be dead, too."

"They think he might have fallen asleep on the road," she said. "If I'd been there, he wouldn't have fallen asleep."

"You don't know any of that."

"He wanted me to go. I should have gone."

"Abby."

"He could have flown into Reno to meet me. Then he wouldn't have been on that pass. We'd have been coming from the east."

"Have you seen anyone about this?" Jamie asked, feeling awkward about it.

"I went to a counselor at Student Health, but I only went once. She told me to try writing things down. And I do some. Sometimes it helps me figure out what I think."

"That seems good."

"But what I think isn't good." Her face crumpled. "It's been five months, and it's still *all* I think about. My mother's all lightness, and he was the solid part of me, the—I don't know, the *integrity*. I feel like I was on a tether that kept me safe and it was cut."

"Maybe you can be your own tether."

"I can't," she said. "It's my fault that he died. The shrink said kids who are young when their parents divorce think they're responsible, and have delusions of omnipotence. But I could have made it different. And instead I went to this stupid party where you had to dress like a slut. Jesus, it hurts."

"I'm sorry, Ab."

"Oh, fuck," Abby said, blowing her nose.

Jamie had brought his guitar, and he practiced in the mornings after Abby left for work. Then he walked over to campus, where the pretty summer school girls were in shorts. He bought used books at the bookstore and read them at lunch, sometimes at Abby's restaurant. Then he walked home. He read the Bible sometimes—skimming past the boring parts for stories like Lot and Job—as if he were still in his class.

"I'm like a crazy homeless guy," he told Abby one day when she got home from the café. "People are starting to look at me. I'm becoming a fixture, wandering around."

"Hang on a sec," she said, kicking off her shoes. "I smell like that place." She disappeared into the bathroom, then reached back around the door to toss her jeans and her T-shirt into the hamper in the hallway. The T-shirt fell to the floor.

"I'll get it," he said.

She disappeared again, leaving the bathroom door open two inches, and Jamie heard the shower come on. From behind the door, over the sound of the water, she called, "I never want to *see,* or *smell,* or *taste* chipotle sauce again, as long as I live."

He picked up the T-shirt and smelled it. It smelled like sweet potato fries and Abby's peppermint soap. He dropped it in the hamper. The shower curtain rings rattled along the rod, and the sound of the water changed, hitting Abby's body instead of the tub.

Jamie sat on the floor in the hallway, just outside the door, in case she wanted to say more. That was his job now, to listen to Abby. It was at least as important as selling guitars. Peppermint steam started to come out of the bathroom. He adjusted his jeans and thought it was time to admit to himself that he was hot for his niece. It wasn't a noble thing to be, but it felt human. She was so pretty, and she loved him, and she was naked in the shower six feet away, behind an open door. The healthy thing to do was to accept that it was human, and not to act on it. That was all.

She came out in a towel with wet hair. "Why are you sitting on the floor?"

"I could hear you talking from here."

"Thank you," she said. She leaned over and kissed his temple. Her wet hair fell against his face, and the tuck of the towel over her breasts was at eye level. The important thing was not to act on it.

She sat on her heels and looked him in the eye. "Someday you're going to have to do something besides take care of me," she said.

"But it's the only thing I'm good at."

She studied him for a long second, and then she did something he hadn't expected: she kissed him, not on the temple, but on the mouth.

"Abby," he said, when she drew back, but then he was kissing her, too. She kneeled on the floor, and he took her face in his hands. He pushed the wet hair behind her ears and ran his hands down her arms, which were smooth and strong. Then he stopped. "Wait," he said.

He was going to say they shouldn't do anything more, but she waited like he said, watching him. He picked her up in the towel, with an arm under her knees and one under her back. He groaned a little, which made her laugh. Then he carried her out of the hallway into the bedroom and laid her down on the sublet bed, no excuses about how she had led him into it. He untucked the end of the towel and pulled it aside, and there was half of her, the soft breast, the smooth hip. It was right there in the Bible, as literature or not: *Do not uncover the nakedness of your sister's daughter, for she is your niece. It is a depravity.* He pushed the other side of the towel away.

"Oh, Abby," he said.

8

LEILA TIRRETT WAS a psychologist with a Ph.D. and problems of her own. Her daughter had become clinically depressed after an abortion, and her husband was being investigated for business fraud. She went to work every day, but she didn't know whom she was more reluctant to see: the hard cases who seemed ready to pull her under with their own despair or the college students who cried over getting a B and the white university professors who moaned over tenure applications and real estate woes.

Once she had loved her job. She had been engrossed in the stories her patients told, and energized by the clarity with which she saw their lives. She gave them strategies and tools. She loved them in an expansive-feeling, empathetic, but dispassionate way, expecting no love back from them. She was good at what she did.

But lately, as her own family had buckled under stress, she had started to resent her patients. She still saw their problems clearly—*more* clearly, now that she had lost her muddying compassion. But she also saw herself turning against them, and none of her strategies seemed to pull her out of it. Her father, a career military man, had wanted her to be a medical doctor. "That's the way people can be *helped*," he said. She had started to think he was right.

Her impatience extended to everything in her life. She had always straightened her hair and worn it shoulder length, but one morning she cut it short with the kitchen scissors. Then she had to beg for an emergency salon appointment, so her clients wouldn't think she had lost her mind. Her hairdresser, when she saw the mangled cut, said, "Leila, my *God*," and Leila had to fight back tears in the chair.

Abby Collins, the undergraduate who'd lost her father, called when Leila was feeling worst. She didn't really want to see the girl, who was just grieving and needed time to pass, but Abby's voice was insistent on the machine.

On the scheduled afternoon, it wasn't Abby who came to her office but a young white man in his early thirties, dark-haired, nice-looking, in faded jeans. He looked at her sheepishly as she stood, confused, in the open doorway.

"Abby sent me," he said. "I'm Jamie. She thought I needed this more than she did."

Leila frowned at him. "She made the appointment for you?"

"She made it for herself, but then she changed her mind. I think she left you a message."

"I haven't had time to check them," Leila said. She looked past him to the waiting room. "Is she here?"

"No. She thought about coming, too, but decided not to."

It wasn't normal procedure, and Leila had every right to send him away.

"Please just let me talk to you," the young man said. "It's about Abby, too."

She didn't have the energy to say no, so she sighed and let him in. He looked at the two chairs and the couch in her room, and he hesitated.

"You can sit on the couch," she said.

Jamie sat on the edge of the cushions, as if he might get up any second. Leila sat down in her own chair.

"So—how do you know Abby?" she asked him, when he didn't say anything.

There was a long pause. "She's my niece."

Leila tried not to assume anything. "You're very young to be her uncle," she said.

"Her mother, my sister Clarissa, is older," he said. "I'm closer to Abby's age than hers."

Leila nodded.

"Abby says you can't tell anyone what I say here," the young man said.

"That's true."

"Can you tell the university anything I say about Abby?"

"No."

Jamie took a breath and leaned forward, with his elbows on his knees and his hands clasped. "I took care of Abby for a while when she was a kid," he said. "At my parents' house when my sister was getting divorced. Then recently my sister, her mother, wanted me to come visit Abby, after— I think she told you. Her father died."

"Yes."

"So I came, and I was really happy to see her. I hadn't in a few years. She's having a hard time, but she's this really cool young woman now, you know? She's not a kid anymore. And I was sitting in the hallway the other day when she was taking a shower, thinking how I shouldn't have a boner for my niece—or if I did I shouldn't act on it—and then she came out and kissed me." He stopped short.

"And what did you do?"

"Well." He looked at his hands. "I kissed her back."

Leila waited. People were so slow telling about sex, as if they thought you didn't know how it went.

"It sort of went too far," he said.

"How far?"

"As far as it could. I know we shouldn't have."

"How did you feel afterward?"

"Weird," he said.

There was another long silence. Leila waited.

"Sometimes, after sex," he said, "you're not that excited about hanging out with the girl anymore. That's sort of how you can tell, you know, how you feel about her. With Abby, I do want to hang out with her, but after I come, she's my niece again. I want to hang out with her as my *niece*. But that's until a little time passes and I see her pull on her jeans and then I want to fuck her again. Oh, Jesus." He put his head in his hands. "I know we're going to have to be at the same family things for the rest of our lives," he said, "and that's—I mean—it would just *suck* if this went bad, but it has to go bad. I mean it can't go on."

"You've had sex more than once?"

He shrugged, embarrassed, and Leila understood. Once could be an accident. More than once was deliberate, in full knowledge of what was on the other side.

"Did you use birth control?" Leila asked, thinking of her daughter and the abortion and the misery.

"She's on the pill," he said. "All those college girls are on the pill."

Leila nodded.

"In my day," Jamie said, "there were side effects or something, girls wouldn't take it. And that wasn't even that long ago. Abby says all the girls in the dorms have those little plastic compacts on their bureaus. Now, when they're *supposed* to use condoms."

"Did you use a condom?"

"No. But I know I don't have anything."

"How old is Abby again?"

"Twenty-one," he said.

"And you?"

"Thirty-three."

"You like the fact that she's young."

"Of course I do."

"What else do you like about her?"

Jamie thought about it. "I like the way she's like me," he said. "I taught Abby what was funny, when she was a kid. That sounds arrogant, but I did. I taught her music—she'd still be listening to Air Supply without me. It's like I *made* her, a little bit, but not for any evil purpose. And then I show up at a time when she's lonely and single, and she's all grown-up, wearing this waitress apron tied around her waist, and how can I not think she's sort of wrapped up for me? And then she kissed me first, my God, I swear she did. I was going to resist all temptation."

They stared each other down, for a long minute. It wasn't true that Leila kept all secrets from the university. If she was particularly alarmed about a student, there were channels to go through.

"How's Abby doing?" she asked.

Jamie looked down at his hands. "At first she was fine," he said. "At first she just seemed kind of sweet and charged up, you know— the early stages. But two nights ago she had a total breakdown, cried for two hours straight. We stopped doing anything then, and I said she had to see someone, and she left you the message. But by this afternoon I was feeling worse than she was, and she wanted me to take the appointment."

"She should come see me," Leila said. It was the first time she had wanted to see a patient in months.

"I know," he said. "She will."

Leila looked at the clock on the wall behind him. "We have some time," she said. "Tell me about your family."

The young man sat back on the couch, and stretched his arms, and looked around the room as if the answers might be there, and then he started to talk.

9

JAMIE TOLD THE shrink things he hadn't thought about for a long time. He was glad Abby had told him Dr. Tirrett was black; he would have been thrown if she had just opened the door. He wondered, even as he was talking, if black shrinks usually had black patients, and if they got annoyed by white people's problems. But then he got caught up in his own story. He told her about his parents, about how they'd been fighting before he was born, maybe over Yvette's pregnancy. They'd never kept it a secret that he wasn't planned.

His mother had gone to stay in a convent, to rest during her pregnancy. Dr. Tirrett seemed surprised at that. But his mother had wanted to make a spiritual retreat anyway, and she'd been afraid of losing the baby, and Teddy was unhappy about the burden of another child. He felt, as the shrink watched him, that this sounded like too many reasons.

His oldest sister, Margot, had been in France that year, having her junior year abroad. Margot was the perfect sister, the one who stayed Catholic and never did anything wrong. The nuns at school loved her. She was well behaved and good at school, and after that year spoke perfect French.

Clarissa was wilder, but she and their father had forged a real relationship while they fended for themselves at home: an enviable connection. Jamie had no real closeness with his father; Teddy had always seemed to suspect him of something. And Teddy was so straightforward, military, strict, and morally sure. Jamie was none of those things. He didn't even look like his father.

He told Dr. Tirrett all this, trying to gauge her reactions as he went. She seemed smart and somehow motherly, with her short hair, but she looked unhappy. He couldn't tell if it was his situation that was making her look that way.

"How long was your mother in the convent?" she asked.

"Until she had me. But first she went to visit my sister in France. She went into labor there."

Dr. Tirrett seemed startled. "In France?" she said.

"Yeah," he said, surprised by her surprise.

"Was that expected?"

"No, I was early."

"How long had your sister been in France?"

"For the whole school year," he said. "Nine, ten months."

The shrink just looked thoughtfully at him.

"What?" he said.

She shrugged.

"Hey, don't check out on me here," he said. "I've told you all this. So now what?"

She sighed. "Did your sister have boyfriends?"

"I don't know," Jamie said. "But I told you, she was the good girl in the family."

"And your father was strict."

"Yeah. We all went to Catholic school, but I got kicked out. He went nuts about that."

"Nuts?"

"Yeah."

"Do you want to talk about that?"

"No."

Jamie thought about his father's disapproval and flushed with shame.

The shrink said, "So he had angry reactions to problems with his children."

"Sure."

"Was your mother on your side?"

"Yeah, but he was in charge."

"I see," she said.

"Why did you ask about Margot's boyfriends?"

The shrink shifted in her chair, rearranging her gray skirt. "I had a patient once," she began. Then she said, "No, never mind."

"What?" he said.

"I was just reading somewhere," she said, "that half of all pregnancies in this country are unplanned. I don't know how the statistics have changed since you were born."

"I told you I was unplanned," Jamie said cautiously, unsure what she was getting at. "My parents used the rhythm method."

The shrink nodded.

"I know that seems kind of stupid now. When I was still in Catholic school, they said we would have to learn it with our wives. I know—it's embarrassing."

"Do you think the nuns taught it to your sisters?"

"No," he said. "I think they taught them to say no."

"And did they? Say no?"

"I don't know." He tried to back away from the idea that had started to form.

"Where exactly did you say you were born?" she asked.

"In a French hospital," he said. "Because my mother had gone to see my sister. Oh, God."

"What are you thinking?" she asked.

His first thought was that if they had passed off Margot's baby as Yvette's, and Margot was really his mother, then Abby was only his cousin. Not his niece. That wasn't so bad. His second thought was that the ground had opened beneath him and everything he knew was a lie.

He put his hands over his eyes so he wouldn't have to see the shrink anymore. "Oh, man," he said.

10

ON THE DAY JAMIE went to see Dr. Tirrett, Abby was working the lunch shift, trying not to think about what she had done with Jamie, when a feeling of doom came over her like a dark wave. Her breath was short, and the room seemed to be spinning. She reached for a countertop, and held it tight so she wouldn't fall. After a long minute, she let go of the counter and found one of the other waitresses watching her. Sandi was the tattooed blonde, barely five feet tall.

"You okay?" Sandi asked.

"I don't know," Abby said. But she wasn't. She had wanted it, too, in the hallway and the bedroom. What kind of girl *did* that? It couldn't be okay.

"Did you feel dizzy?"

"I guess," Abby said. "My chest hurt."

"I get that sometimes. The best thing is just to hold on to something and wait it out."

"I think there's something really wrong," Abby said.

"How do you feel now?"

"Okay."

"It's a panic attack," Sandi said. "If you go to a doctor they'll just put you on drugs that make you fat. It's better to ride it out." She looked around the restaurant to see how crowded it was. "I'll take your tables. Go home and feel better."

"That's okay. I'll stay."

She finished her shift and walked out into the afternoon light, feeling dazed. She thought about going to Student Health, but she didn't want to be told that something was wrong with her body, and she didn't think they could fix what was wrong with her head.

She walked home carrying sandwiches for dinner. It was August, and the days were getting shorter already, and school would start soon. She felt less and less like she would be able to fit in again, and fake her way through, pretending to worry about papers and midterms.

She had hoped Dr. Tirrett would be compassionate and helpful, and blame Jamie less than he blamed himself, but he came home shaken and subdued, and wouldn't tell her what was wrong. She didn't press him, because he didn't seem to want to be pressed. They ate the sandwiches in silence, and then Jamie went out on the patio with his guitar, but he didn't play it, he just sat there. Abby left a message asking Dr. Tirrett to call her, and picked up the phone when it rang.

"Jamie is really upset," she said, hoping the doctor would give her a clue. "I know why he went there, but this seems different."

There was a silence on the line. Dr. Tirrett wasn't going to let anything slip.

"I called because I had this thing today at work," Abby said. "This feeling came over me, and I thought I was dying. I felt completely doomed, and so dizzy I was afraid I'd fall over."

"Are you okay now?"

"I think so. Another waitress said it was a panic attack."

"That wouldn't be an unusual response to the kind of stress you've had lately."

"Can I make it go away?"

"You can think about the reasons for the stress," she said, "and the history of how you've responded to it. There are visualization exercises you can learn."

"I was dragged to too many yoga classes as a kid," Abby said. "I'm not into visualization."

"Have you thought about going back to school?"

"No," Abby said. "Yes. Sort of."

"Is anything absorbing to you, besides this relationship?"

"No. The problem is I'll *always* have a relationship to him, I can't change that."

"I know," Dr. Tirrett said. "Go talk to him. But just *talk*, okay? Don't do anything that lets you avoid talking."

Jamie was still on the patio, not playing his guitar, so Abby went outside to try.

11

JAMIE LAY IN BED with Abby in the dark, in the quiet lull that always came before the guilt returned. He had a hand on her bare hip, where it curved down to her waist.

"I was thinking," he said.

"What?"

"I don't know. That we're the same people we were before, but we've done this thing that people would think is really wrong, but it didn't feel that wrong as it went along."

Abby said nothing.

"It's interesting," he said. "Don't you think?"

"I guess."

"I think you should write a book about it."

Abby laughed.

"Not a true account," he said. "But like a novel. You used to write me those letters about high school, and life with your mom. I think you could do it."

"I don't know how."

"Just write down what happens."

"That's not a book."

"It could be, though. It could have Dr. Tirrett's plot: a Catholic mother raises her teenage daughter's baby as her own. And then he—the son—finds out that everyone has lied to him."

"Because they were trying to give him a normal, stable life."

"But it can't be normal."

"Okay, so what does he do?"

"I don't know. If you wrote it, you could tell me. It should have sex in it, and a murder. People like books about murders. It can be set in California."

"Then people would guess about this."

"You just tell them it's a novel."

Abby laughed, and they lay there for a while in silence.

"You do think I look like Margot, right?" Jamie asked.

"Of course. She's your sister."

"But I don't look like Teddy."

"Not much."

"So you think it's possible."

"I don't know. Maybe."

"It does help if we're cousins," he said. "Cousins get married all the time."

"But I grew up as your niece," she said. "And we're not getting married."

"Here comes the groom," he sang, to make her laugh.

He thought about confronting Yvette with the question: *Are you my mother?* It was the question the baby bird asks the steam shovel in the children's book he had read to Abby when she was a kid.

He had taken care of Abby when she was a kid. That was what made lying here in bed with her so unforgivable, more than whatever blood relation they had. When she was asleep, she looked like she did at seven, sleeping on Yvette's couch: all the years fell away and the muscles went slack, the lips soft and open. She could still sleep through anything, like a kid, and watching her brought his transgression home. The guilt crept back, like the tide moving up the beach. How could he summon the moral force to ask his mother if she had lied to him, when he was sleeping with her granddaughter?

"Abby?" he said finally.

"Yeah?"

"I don't want to say this, but I think I should probably leave, don't you?"

Abby didn't say anything, and lay very still.

"You don't have to write a novel, but you do have to go off and have your twenties."

Still Abby was quiet.

"I'm giving you weird attacks and I'm going to give myself an ulcer. This can't be good for either of us."

"I don't want you to go," she said.

"I don't want to either," he said. "But I don't think we can keep this up."

12

YVETTE WENT TO VISIT Clarissa up north. She knew Abby had kept her at a distance, after Henry's death, and it had hurt Clarissa deeply. It was so hard to see your children in pain. Yvette was in pain because Clarissa was in pain because Abby was in pain. Did it never stop?

Yvette put her suitcase in Abby's old room, and Clarissa said they were meeting her friend Del for dinner.

"Is Del a boyfriend?" Yvette asked.

"She's a friend," Clarissa said. "She's a woman."

"Oh," Yvette said. "What an unusual name."

"Her name's Delilah. But she won't let anyone call her that."

Del already had a table at the restaurant, which had a brick front and large glass windows, and Yvette thought idly that the woman reminded her of poor Henry. She was big and sandy-haired like him, and shook Yvette's hand with a strong grip. Yvette wondered, with a start, if Del was a lesbian.

"What a nice place this is," she said, to hide her shock at the idea. "Do you come here a lot?"

"Sometimes," Clarissa said vaguely.

They sat on three sides of a square table, with Clarissa in the middle, and ordered wine from a slim young waiter. There was a faint sound of clanking dishes from the kitchen. After a moment, during which Yvette tried to think what to say, Clarissa asked, "Do you remember the photographer who took our picture for Dad?"

"What photographer?"

"It must have been when Dad was in Korea. Someone took our picture."

Yvette flushed, unprepared for the question. "Oh. Yes, I remember that."

Clarissa waited, frowning, while the waiter set the wineglasses on the table. "Did you maybe"—she cleared her throat—"have an affair with him?"

"Oh, no!" Yvette said, remembering the kiss she hadn't wanted, the cut lip when she twisted free.

"You see?" Clarissa said to Del.

"What did happen?" the big, strange woman asked.

"Nothing," Yvette said. "Nothing. Why?"

Clarissa hesitated again. "Remember how I wouldn't eat, as a kid?" she asked. "And you would make me sit with my plate after everyone left the table?"

"Oh, honey, I thought you were going to starve."

Clarissa glanced at Del and seemed to gain confidence. "Well," she said, "I was trying to figure out when that started, and what I keep thinking of is the photographer."

"He took our picture for your dad."

"But then he came back."

"To deliver the pictures."

"He came back more than once."

"He *did*?" This was news to Yvette.

"He had a white and green car, and he would drive by our house when Margot and I were outside."

"I don't believe it."

"Was the photographer's car white and green?" Del asked.

Yvette thought it had been but said nothing. Who was this bullying woman?

"The man, the photographer, wanted to talk to us," Clarissa said. "Margot wouldn't go near him, but I thought it was exciting. He would call me over to the car, and I would stand by the rolled-down window, and he would ask me questions."

"About what?" Yvette asked.

"I don't know. About our family, I guess. About you."

"And you *told* him things?"

"I was five!" Clarissa said.

"I'm sorry, honey. I'm just trying to understand."

"I thought he was very romantic," Clarissa said. "Once when we were talking, he reached out and touched my hair." She touched her own hair, as if remembering.

"Oh, no," Yvette said.

"That's all he did," Clarissa said. "I think I had fantasies about him coming to be our father, because Dad was away."

"Oh, honey."

"Margot couldn't stand him, and threatened to tell on me. I can't believe she didn't. But there must have been something going on between you, right? Or he wouldn't have come to the house. And then Dad was so different when he got home, and I stopped eating—*something* was going on. I can't just be making this up."

"Oh, honey, I'm so sorry."

"So what happened?" Del asked.

Yvette considered telling the woman to mind her own business. But then she took a deep breath and told them the story she should never have told Teddy, and hadn't told since.

The photographer had taken their picture, and then Yvette had made him a drink—"We did that back then," she explained—and then he wouldn't leave, and he grabbed her and kissed her. "You and Margot were playing outside," she said. "I can't tell you how terrible I felt. I felt eaten up by guilt."

She had gone to confession in a church where she didn't know the priest, and he had said she must tell Teddy. Teddy had responded badly. He had hated leaving her alone, when he was in the service, and the photographer had confirmed his fears.

"But I didn't have an affair, sweetheart, I promise you I didn't."

Clarissa said nothing.

Yvette sensed that her daughter was disappointed. Clarissa must have wanted her mother's infidelity to be the source of all her problems. Yvette felt almost sorry that she couldn't give her daughter that satisfaction; Clarissa's shoulders had sunk a little, and a discouraged frown made her look older than she was.

"My parents had problems in their marriage," Yvette said. "My father was a—a *roué*, you know. When I started to have my own family, I thought that as long as you children knew that Teddy and I loved each other, everything would be all right. I thought that was the important thing, and that was what I tried to do. I never would have had an affair. My mistake was in telling your father about a thing that meant nothing."

Clarissa nodded, vaguely.

The waiter came back. "Are you ladies going to want something to eat?"

"I'm not hungry," Clarissa said.

"Neither am I."

"We'll have a large mushroom pizza," Del said. "If you two don't recover by the time it comes, we can take it home."

Yvette took up her wine, feeling sad. It was sweet and cold, the glass slick with condensation. That poor, lustful photographer had done nothing more than kiss her once and touch her daughter's hair. Not terrible things, in the catalog of human villainy. But they had used him to make each other unhappy, and were using him still.

13

AFTER JAMIE LEFT TOWN, Abby started school again. She moved back into the dorms with Miranda, with some apprehension. The other students were cheery and suntanned, at the end of the summer: they wore flip-flops and toe rings, and cried out with happiness at seeing friends. They had no responsibilities; even midterm exams felt years away. So they threw Frisbees, they planned parties. Outside her window was a beach volleyball court, where girls in bikinis played two-on-two. Abby felt like a dark presence, carrying her private sense of disaster and chaos through an ad for light beer.

She wasn't sleeping well, but Miranda stayed at her boyfriend's, so Abby could keep the lights on at night. Sometimes she wrote letters to Jamie, but she didn't send them. She was taking a class on the eighteenth-century novel and read *Robinson Crusoe* and *Pamela* until it was light outside. In the morning, to keep herself awake in class, she wrote out the lectures verbatim. The professor spoke slowly. He was a tall, deliberate man with a beard, who never smiled.

One day, as she was putting her notebook away, the graduate student who led her discussion section sat next to her. He had called on her unexpectedly the week before, and she hadn't forgiven him.

"You missed section," he said.

"I'm sorry."

"I'm Peter Kerner," he said. "I'm your TA."

"I know." She had just been on the point of remembering his name.

"Are you okay?"

"Fine."

There was a pause, and she surveyed him for signs of gayness—Miranda would want to know. He had nice, curly brown hair, which would be a warning sign for Miranda, but that was all. He was clean-shaven and wore a checked shirt that had been washed a lot.

"I was watching you taking notes today," he said. "I was sitting over there."

Abby waited.

"Have you missed any lectures?" he asked.

"No."

"I've skipped a few this term. He tends to improvise, and I'm not sure what he's covered, and I have to put the midterm together."

"Okay."

"I have a feeling your notes are pretty—complete," he said, "and I wonder if I could borrow them. Just to make sure what should be on the exam."

Abby flushed. "I do it so I won't fall asleep," she said.

"Do what?"

"Write everything down."

"Don't you sleep at night?"

She wished she hadn't said anything.

"I could have the notes back to you on Thursday, if I took them today," he said.

Abby slid the notebook across the little folding desk. It had nothing but class notes in it, no thoughts for Dr. Tirrett, no letters to Jamie; she was careful to keep things separate.

He took the notebook, watching her. "Thanks," he said.

*

On Thursday, Peter Kerner caught up as she walked to class.

"You can have this back," he said, out of breath. "It was really useful."

She took the notebook.

"You really write *everything* down."

"That way I don't have to process it," she said.

"You can process it later," he said. "What will your paper be about?"

"I don't know yet." She had tried to finish *Joseph Andrews* the night before but fell asleep, and slept until morning. The sleep seemed to have made her more tired.

"You never talk in section," he said.

"I'm sorry."

"Where did you grow up?"

"Santa Rosa. North of San Francisco."

"What do your parents do?"

She hesitated. "My mother's done a lot of things," she said. "My father was a lawyer, but he's dead."

"I'm sorry."

Abby said nothing. They had reached the building and went inside.

"I was going to guess they were divorced," he said.

"Do I look that wounded?"

"It was something about the quality of your shyness."

"They were divorced, before," she said, then wondered why she had told him.

At the top of the stairs, outside the lecture hall, with a crowd of students moving past, Peter Kerner said, "If you want to talk about the paper, you can call me. I mean, that's true for everyone."

"Okay."

"Okay," he said, and they went to their usual seats.

During the lecture, which was about the novel *Joseph Andrews* as a response to Richardson's *Pamela,* she thought about Peter Kerner sitting behind her. Then she thought about Jamie's idea for a novel and how he was like a Fielding character, directionless and likable.

He had gone to San Francisco to put distance between them. He still hadn't asked Yvette whether Margot had been pregnant in France.

The class ended, and Abby looked for the TA as she left, but he wasn't there. She had taken hardly any notes. There was a rock band setting up in the flat concrete square outside the building; Abby skirted the backs of the amplifiers and walked toward the dorms. It was a sunny day, and girls lay on the grass with their shorts rolled up, reading. A boy fumbled a football, so it bounced toward one of the girls. He touched her arm in apology, and she smiled forgivingly over her sunglasses.

There were folding tables set up, with petitions to sign, and cookies for sale by a Korean sorority. Hanging from the cookie table was a handmade poster with pictures of each of the girls, and their names in curly handwriting. Near the dorms, a girl was leading pairs of dancers through a dance to Spanish music on a boom box, the girls skillful, the boys awkward but willing, shuffling their big feet.

Inside, her room was cool and silent, and Abby felt relieved. She had inherited a laptop computer from her father's law office, and she waited while it booted up and then typed a heading:

Abby Collins, Paper 1
The Rise of the Novel: Defoe, Richardson, Fielding, Sterne
November 3, 1993
Peter Kerner, TA

Then she stopped. He had said she could call. But she hadn't even started the paper yet; what would she ask? She opened her notebook to the notes she had taken that day.

Richardson's Pamela, or Virtue Rewarded. Richardson was writing letter-writing manual, then switched to epistolary novel. Maidservant Pamela Andrews tells story in letters to parents: she refuses approaches of employer, then marries him when he proves himself worthy.

Fielding's <u>Joseph Andrews</u> 1742. (Joseph A. in Fielding's novel is Pamela's brother.) Joseph chaste, like his sister: dismissed from job for resisting female employer's advances, thrown out in hypocritical world. Joke of male chastity → criticism of Eng. society and its imagined virtues.

(Fielding's <u>Tom Jones</u> a response to Richardson's <u>Clarissa</u>? Tom Jones not evil, just easily seduced.)

<u>Jamie</u>.

Why Yvette sends Margot to France.

That was the end of the notes; then she had spaced out completely. She wouldn't be able to lend these to Peter Kerner.

She went back to the cursor blinking under the paper heading. She typed, "In Fielding's *The History of the Adventures of Joseph Andrews*," and watched the cursor blink. Then she picked up *Tom Jones* to try to read herself to sleep.

14

JAMIE HAD PLANNED badly and left San Diego in the middle of weekend beach traffic, as if leaving Abby didn't feel bad enough already. A million cars crawled up the 5 in the relentless sun, which had sunk just low enough to blind him as he drove. His car felt like the torture box in *The Bridge on the River Kwai*. His shirt, wet, stuck to the upholstery. On his left were endless strip malls; on his right were housing developments with fake Italian names.

He could, he knew, stop in Hermosa Beach to ask Yvette if Margot was his mother, but he couldn't face her right now. She would ask how Abby was, and he couldn't deal with that. So he stayed on the slow freeway through all of Los Angeles, wondering where everyone was going, and why they had to do it *now*—what was so fucking urgent?

North of Los Angeles, the traffic finally slackened, and the sun went down, and Jamie could drive unimpeded and think about what to do. He stopped for gas in a desert town and called his bassist friend in San Francisco, to ask if he could have the couch again. His friend had a new girlfriend but said a week was okay, and Jamie drove into the city in the middle of the night, with the vampires and addicts and the wandering homeless. The closest parking spot was six blocks away. He still had a key and let himself into the second-floor apartment.

When he woke at noon on his familiar old couch, the new girl-friend, Dena, made him pancakes and coffee. She had freckles and played the accordion. Jamie wondered why he'd never found a girl like her, and told her so. She laughed, a sweet laugh, and seemed pleased. They were going to play poker that night, and Jamie went along.

The poker game was at the house of the guitarist for Blind Melon, and it had expensive-looking leather couches, two felt poker tables, and wraparound windows overlooking the water. A girl at one of the tables was shuffling her poker chips with one hand. She was tall and blond, and looked bored.

"Who's *that*?" Jamie asked Dena.

"Oh, don't be so predictable," she said.

"Am I?" he asked. "Is it? Who is she?"

Dena rolled her eyes, but she told him: the girl was called Saffron, and she was a few years out of Stanford and had never had a job. Her father had made a lot of money in Silicon Valley and had bought her a house in the city. Her mother was some kind of socialite, but they were divorced.

"She thinks it's vulgar to ask people what they do," Dena said, "because she doesn't do anything. She hates most people."

"Would she hate me?"

"Oh, Jamie," Dena said. "Her name's *Saffron*. She's proof that too much money is bad for the soul."

Jamie figured Dena was right, but there was no harm in looking at Saffron. She had the luminous skin of rich girls, the healthy, glossy hair: everything about her looked carefully tended. She crossed one long leg over the other. It felt good to be longing for someone who wasn't related to him.

The buy-in was a hundred dollars, more than Jamie spent on food in a week, and he sat down at Saffron's table with his chips. He nodded to the others at the table, two men and a girl. They all looked at him with wary friendliness.

Saffron won the first hand and shuffled expertly. The fear of saying something wrong had paralyzed Jamie, and he didn't know how to shake it off except by doing exactly what Dena had told him not to do:

"So what do you do?" he asked.

Saffron gave him a quick disapproving glance. "Right now I'm shuffling cards."

"And the rest of the time?"

"I do other things."

"Like?"

She looked at him, incredulous.

"I don't really know what I do either," he said. "I play the guitar a little."

"That's what the guy who lives here does."

"Yeah, but he does it for giant piles of cash. I do it to meet girls."

She gave him the deck to cut. "You should do it for giant piles of cash," she said. "That would help you meet girls."

He laughed—she had won the point—and he thought she was softening, knowing she'd won. He concentrated for the rest of the game on making her laugh, without seeming jokey. A few times it worked.

By the time they stopped playing, Jamie had lost all but six dollars. Most of it had gone to Saffron. The others got up to cash out, and he was left alone with her.

"Do you always play like that?" she asked.

"Like what?"

"You were playing every hand. You should fold more."

"I was distracted. Do you live here?"

"In this house? God, no."

"I meant in the city."

"Most of the time."

"Can I call you?"

She studied him. "I don't think so."

"Why not? You can call me."

She gave him a funny smile. "Thanks."

He wrote down his name and the bassist's number. "For when you get tired of whatever it is you do," he said. "Shuffling cards."

"I'm tired of that already."

"Then call me."

She slipped the piece of paper into her pocket without looking. "It isn't likely," she said.

Two nights later, when Jamie knew he was getting on his hosts' nerves but wasn't ready to leave a city Saffron was in, she called, after dinner.

"I don't know why I'm doing this," she said.

"I'm glad you are."

"I guess I got bored."

"I was counting on that."

"I was telling a friend about you, and they're here."

"Okay," he said. He felt there was something to pause and think about.

"Why don't you come over?"

Jamie could have run through the streets, but he took a cab; he didn't want to break a sweat.

The address Saffron had given him was a narrow three-story house in Pacific Heights, painted yellow. Jamie rang the doorbell and was greeted by a tallish young man in his late twenties. This was the thing he should have thought about. Saffron's "friend" was not a cute brunette sidekick. He looked like a match for Saffron: handsome and rich. Even his handshake felt rich.

"I'm Martin Russell," he said. "You must be the fascinating Jamie."

In the entry of the house, there was a low yellow bench and a wooden table with a vase of flowers on it. Jamie took off his jacket and left it on the bench, and he saw that on the wall there was a painting of the room, with the bench and the flowers on the table, as if in a mirror.

"Saffron loves things like that," Martin said. "There's another one upstairs. We're in here."

Jamie followed him to a room where Saffron sat in a low chair by the fireplace. She was wearing a pale blue slip dress, and Jamie's heart sank further. Why had he gotten his hopes up about a girl this hot? He should have listened to Dena. He should have asked her to find him another Dena. He took an armchair, in what he hoped was a casual way, and Martin said they had almost gone out to Saffron's place in the wine country for the weekend.

"It's her mother's house," Martin said. "Her father keeps it up even though they're divorced. It's architecturally kind of interesting, it's been added on to so many times."

"He keeps it up for *me*," Saffron said. "We're having negronis. I'll get you one."

Jamie watched the dress go. He tried to remember what they were talking about. "My sister lives in the wine country—well, in Santa Rosa," he offered, feeling how inadequate it was.

"Oh?" Martin said politely.

They sat in painful silence. Of course there could be nothing interesting to Martin about Jamie's sister's house. He felt old and poor, and was grateful when Saffron brought him a dark red drink in a tall glass.

"They're kind of awful-looking," she said. "My parents used to drink them."

"I've never had one."

"Oh, good!" she said. "We're corrupting you."

The drink tasted like wine spiked with gin. He set the glass on the side table.

"Last year," Martin said, "I decided that each month, I would try one totally new thing. But I had to stop after five months. I ran out of things I hadn't done."

"Show-off," Saffron said.

"It's true."

"Did you try fucking a man? Or piercing your scrotum? Or getting shat on by Japanese girls?"

"I mean things I hadn't done that I *wanted* to do."

"Well, that's a whole different thing," Saffron said. "You don't need to set yourself an assignment for *that*."

The conversation went on like that for an hour, with little help from Jamie, and finally Martin got up to leave. Jamie stood to shake his hand but didn't move toward the doorway. He thought he saw an amused look on Martin's face, but he might have imagined it. He wondered what Saffron saw in that guy, then remembered that he was good-looking and rich.

"Is he your boyfriend?" he asked, when Martin was gone.

"No, just a friend." She yawned behind her hand. "Are you going, too?"

"Do you want me to?"

"Is that a proposition?"

"Yes."

She laughed. "You were so quiet tonight."

"I didn't know what to say."

"You seemed very earnest and serious and direct next to Martin," she said. "I liked that."

"Really?"

"Yes."

There was a silence, and then he said, "So can I stay?"

She stretched her long arms over her head and looked up at her hands, as if she were alone and thinking about something else, and then she dropped her arms and shrugged and said, "Okay."

He couldn't call it an enthusiastic invitation, but still Jamie felt he had won the lottery, the sweepstakes, the long-shot bet.

15

CLARISSA HAD STARTED thinking seriously about what she had wanted to *do,* before she had a husband and a child. Her mother never expected to be anything but a wife and mother, so Clarissa had no role model. What had she really *wanted,* aside from proving to the nuns, and then to Henry, that she was smart? She couldn't remember—it seemed just out of her memory's reach. She had been a teacher, a guidance counselor, a nursing home ombudsman, and a gardening consultant. She liked the gardening best, but it was hard to live on it.

Del, who had moved into Clarissa's little bungalow in Santa Rosa, was a contractor and made money by putting roofs over people's heads. It was straightforward work, and she was good at it. Clarissa envied her clarity and the pleasure she took in her career. Del moved her power tools into the garage and a TV into the living room for sports, and Clarissa wondered why, if life was going to throw her this curveball, she had to fall in love with a woman who was so much like a man. Why not just a *woman*—why this half measure? Her friend Rae said she wanted Henry back, without a penis. Clarissa said she had liked Henry's penis fine; it was the rest of him she divorced.

Some days, Clarissa thought the answer to her emptiness was to have another baby. She was forty-four; it wasn't too late. She and Del could raise it together. She sized up her male friends as sperm donors and finally floated the idea to Del.

Del, sitting at the kitchen table after dinner, looked at her with sadness and said, "Don't do this, Clar. Don't toy with me when you aren't serious, it cheapens the things that I want."

"I am serious."

"Clarissa, don't."

Clarissa took another piece of bread—she was gaining weight, eating as much as Del did—and thought how little Del trusted her.

"You can be ambivalent," Del said. "I know that's true, and honest. You can have the 'Am I really a dyke' crisis, because that's real, and maybe you aren't. I'm happy to be with you anyway. But you can't pretend you want things you don't want. You can't pretend you'll stay with me for all the years it takes to raise a kid, because Clarissa, you *won't*. I'm not stupid. So don't fuck with me."

After a long silence, during which Clarissa carried dishes to the sink and tried to decide how angry she was, she said, "Maybe I'll go back to school."

"You did that already."

"In the wrong thing, though," Clarissa said. "I got a teaching certificate so I could show a piece of paper to Henry. But that wasn't where my heart was."

"And where was your heart?"

"I don't know. Abby's doing English. Maybe I should have done English."

"Would you go back to USF?"

"I don't know," Clarissa said. "There's probably someplace better. I don't think I could get into Berkeley. But Abby seems to like UCSD. It's so different now, from when I was there."

There was a long pause.

"Clarissa."

"What?"

"There are thousands of universities in America, and you want to go study Abby's major at Abby's school?"

"It was *my* school first. We'd hardly overlap at all."

"Clarissa."

"What."

"I'm not your shrink, and I'm not your daughter," Del said, "but neither of them would think this is a sane thing to do."

Clarissa ran water in the sink, frowning. "Why should Abby stop me from doing what I want?"

"Because it isn't what you want," Del said. "It's what *she* wants, and you'd be landing on top of her."

"Well," Clarissa said. "Then maybe I'll study something else."

16

ABBY WAS LYING in bed in the dorm at noon, having missed class, looking at the outline of daylight against the white vinyl roll-down shades. The second phase of whatever was happening to her was that she *slept,* finally, but slept too long, and didn't want to get out of bed.

The phone rang, and she watched it ring three times—it didn't vibrate or dance in the cradle, like in the cartoons—and then she picked it up and listened.

"Abby?" a man's voice said.

"Yes."

"It's Peter Kerner, your TA," he said. His section was one of the classes she had missed. "I have your number from the contact sheet."

"Hi."

"You don't say hello when you answer the phone."

"Sorry."

"Where were you during section?"

"Here."

"I have your *Tom Jones* paper. I handed them back today."

"Okay," she said, embarrassed that he had even seen it.

"You got that kind of character really well," he said. "How everyone likes and roots for him without any real reason to."

Abby was relieved but said nothing.

"Will you be at the lecture tomorrow?"

"Yes," she said, though she hadn't been planning on it.

"I'll see you there," he said. "I can show you what I mean about your paper. Don't skip again."

"Okay."

She was going to get up and go to lunch, but instead she lay thinking about Peter Kerner. He wasn't gay. He didn't wear a wedding ring. The section was in a stuffy trailer, but people showed up for it, and seemed to like him. He said things about the books that seemed true once he had said them. She had once caught him watching as she packed up her books, but pretended she hadn't seen him. He hadn't hated her paper. She ran out of things she knew about him and fell back asleep.

17

JAMIE STARTED SPENDING his nights at Saffron's house. He loved the expensive sheets, the woman who came to clean, the food ordered in from a fancy market on Union Street. He thought maybe he had found his calling, as a kept man. He didn't worry about things he had worried about, when money was always an issue. He didn't ask his mother about Margot, and he didn't even worry about Abby very much; he knew she was resilient, and he managed to keep her out of his head.

One night, in the middle of a card game with Martin Russell, Saffron suggested they play strip poker.

Martin said, "Oh, Saffron, grow up."

"Spoilsport," Saffron said. "It'll be fun."

"We've both seen you naked already," Martin said, "and I think I can safely say that we don't want to see each other."

Jamie was startled. "When has he seen you naked?"

"Uh-oh," Martin said. "Was that a secret?"

"We went to high school together," Saffron said.

"Saffron was voted Most Likely to Take Off Her Clothes."

"That's not true. Never mind. It was just an idea."

"What was that about?" he asked, when they were alone in her yellow bedroom. The other painting Martin had told him about faced the vast bed: it looked exactly like a reflection of the room, with a maned lion sleeping on the floor.

"I don't know," she said. She lay on her back on the bed, still clothed, and stretched her legs up to the ceiling. "I was bored."

"It was kind of a high school suggestion," he said.

"I was playing strip poker in junior high."

"No wonder you get bored. Did you want some kind of two-on-one?"

"No," she said. "But sex does get boring, doesn't it? This isn't a complaint, I just mean it in a general way."

"What's up with you and him?"

"Nothing."

"What *was* up with you?"

"I've known him since I was fifteen," she said. "Something had to happen, at some point. There's nothing now."

"Except that you just offered to strip in front of him, because you were bored."

"Who was offering to strip?" Saffron asked. "I play to win."

"When I was your age," Jamie began.

Saffron laughed. "I'm twenty-seven."

"When I was your age," he said, "I was happy with a hand job in the dark."

"And you slogged through the snow to school?"

"With no shoes."

"Poor Jamie," she said, touching his face. "But—and don't take this the wrong way—weren't you an unemployed, aging college student at my age?"

"Yes," he said. "I still am."

"So you were lucky to get the hand job. You still would be. Everything else is a bonus."

"*You're* starting in about unemployment?"

"Girls don't need jobs for men to want to fuck them."

"Well, someday they won't want to fuck you anymore," he said.

Saffron looked shocked for a second. But she had hurt his feelings—she had taken the gloves off first.

"Don't say that," she said, in a small voice. "I'm so afraid of being my mother."

Saffron's mother lived on a ranch in Argentina, where she had adopted a Romanian orphan through an exiled princess she had known in her socialite days. The princess had since become a nun, involved in good works. When the child arrived, still an infant, Saffron's mother remembered how much she disliked babies and handed him off to her staff. He was now four. The situation made Saffron livid.

"Are you thinking about the kid?" Jamie asked now.

"She got old and bored, and men lost interest in her, so she adopted a refugee and ignores him," Saffron said. "It would've served her right to get one of those psycho toddlers."

"He'll be all right."

"They're all alone out there."

"With the maids and the cooks and the gardeners."

"Don't be sarcastic."

"I'm not," he said. "I'm serious."

"People with money have problems, too."

"I'm beginning to see that."

Saffron slid a leg across his body, then sat up, straddling his hips.

"When I was seven," she said, "my mother told me that sex was the most beautiful thing that could happen between a man and a woman. Then my cousin Nell told me there was a thing called a prostitute who had sex for money. I put those facts together: The most beautiful thing that can happen between a man and a woman, and you can get paid for it. That was the job for me. I told my mother I was going to be a prostitute."

"If this is a demand for cash, I can't afford you," Jamie said.

"Wouldn't you do whatever it took?" she asked. "Pawn your watch?"

He held up the black plastic band on his wrist. "It cost twenty-four dollars new."

She pulled her shirt over her head, and there were her round, honey-colored breasts, the small nipples already hard. "Would you sell your car?" she asked.

"Yes," he said. He reached for her breast, but she leaned back out of reach, which pressed her pelvis against him and stretched out her torso, the flat stomach disappearing into her jeans. He gave up on her breasts and unbuttoned the jeans, but she stopped him.

"Would you steal?" she asked.

"Yes," he said, and he thought he would.

"Would you sell your blood?"

"Ugh," he said. "But yes."

"Okay," she said brightly. "What do you want me to do?"

"Take off your jeans," he said.

She stood and peeled her jeans and underwear down over her hips. "Like this?"

"Turn around. Let me see your ass."

She turned, and slid the jeans further, looking over her shoulder, then bent over to slide them down her legs, so that he could see the mauve asterisk of her asshole, and a hint of the pink slide beneath it. She stepped out of them and turned, naked. "Now what?" she asked.

"Put a finger inside your cunt," he said.

She slid her hand down her stomach to the dark blond patch of hair and pressed her middle finger inside. "It's so wet," she said.

"Taste it."

She put the finger in her mouth. "It's salty."

"Come here," he said. He was caught. She could say anything she wanted, be shallow and spoiled and easily bored—he couldn't blame her. He just wanted to have her. He pushed his pants off his hips so she could impale herself there on his cock: his Saffron, his whore.

18

TEDDY WAS READING *The Wall Street Journal* one morning over breakfast, and the story in the center column was about a man who embodied the principles of hard work, responsibility, and care for his fellow man. This man had built a business up from nothing and now had a thriving charitable foundation. Teddy read the paper through his glasses—he had to hold it at just the right distance as his cataracts got worse—and then clipped the story for Jamie. Even as he folded it up to send, he knew the article would have no effect on his son.

Teddy didn't understand what he had done wrong with Jamie. He had tried to teach him the value of hard work. He'd given Jamie chores to do, so he could learn the pleasure of earned rewards. He had paid for all of his children to go to college, but Jamie had never finished. It was as if his son had started to tear open a gift and then abandoned it without taking it out of the box.

Teddy blamed California, in part. He and Yvette had grown up in hard times, in northern climates, in cold houses and families racked by the Depression. They knew how to appreciate California's abundance and warmth and beauty. Children who grew up with it couldn't appreciate it. They took everything for granted, and time seemed to flow past them; they had no sense of urgency. Nothing was difficult

for them, not even the weather. They floated through school and went to the beach in all seasons. When he passed these young people on the street, he saw a blank, entitled, sunstruck look in their eyes.

He had heard that Jamie was in San Francisco, and when Yvette called there, a girl said Jamie was staying with a rich new girlfriend. But what kind of life was it for a man, to live off a woman? He would never have the respect of his children—assuming that Jamie could keep this one long enough to make her his wife and have children.

Teddy unfolded the newspaper clipping again and thought he would send a copy to Margot's husband, Owen, too, although Owen didn't need it. He was just the kind of man the article was talking about: hardworking, successful, generous.

It didn't seem right to send it to Clarissa. It wasn't easy to be a divorcée, and she still hadn't found another man. She'd bet on a bad horse, he supposed, though he had always liked Henry. He sat at the table with his cut newspaper and his breakfast dishes and felt paralyzed with sadness. Two of his three children were lost.

Their children would be lost, too; it stood to reason. Abby was a good girl, but she'd been raised with no God, and now had no father.

Yvette came inside. "Why are you moping in here? It's a beautiful day out there. You can fix the fence."

His wife was a blur since his eyes had worsened, but he knew she was still beautiful. People commented on it all the time, and she took their admiration as it came.

"I planted that lobelia," she said. "Oh, Teddy, are you clipping inspirational things?"

He smoothed the folded piece of newspaper.

"Don't send it to Jamie, honey. He'll think you're disappointed in him."

He thought about it and then said, "I am."

"Oh, Teddy, don't say that."

"Why not?" he said. "I am."

"Oh, Teddy."

He got to his feet on his stiff knees and took his dishes to the sink, and got ready to go fix the fence.

19

IN JUNE, JAMIE and Saffron moved into her place in the wine country. It had been in her mother's family for a hundred years, and her father had given it a new roof and a shored-up foundation. It had cornices and gables and things Jamie didn't know the names of, long upstairs hallways that led to other hallways, and two staircases, one grand and one for the servants who weren't there anymore. A housekeeper, around sixty and skittish, came in the afternoons and kept her distance from Saffron.

The key to Saffron's personality, Jamie thought, was her enormous capacity to be bored. He was happy to make her laugh and make her come, in every way he could think of, and the big house had its own novelty, but he could sense her mind wandering. Without work to keep him busy, boredom stalked him, too. He read books off the shelves: an old thriller called *Mayhem in Greece* and *Prize Stories: The O. Henry Awards 1982*. He played guitar on the covered porch, and backgammon with Saffron. The housekeeper came at noon, made lunch, cleaned up, and left cold things for dinner. One day ran into the next, and on an afternoon when Jamie thought he couldn't stand the creeping restlessness anymore, he asked Saffron to marry him.

"Really?" she said.

It was a good question, under the circumstances, but he said, "Yes." He meant it. An engagement was a tangible change. Maybe marriage would rekindle things. That suggestion, made by someone else, would have made him laugh, but it seemed like a possibility for Saffron. Who knew how she would respond to marriage? It would be a new game. And Saffron was beautiful and depraved—he would be crazy to give her up, and he would be lost if kicked back out into the world.

To his amazement, Saffron agreed, and they searched the house until they found an old square-cut garnet ring in a drawer. Saffron put it on her left hand and kissed him, which led to a very straightforward hour in one of the baroque beds.

Afterward, wearing nothing but the ring, Saffron rolled toward the nightstand and picked up the old black rotary phone. Jamie sleepily admired the curve of her ass and thought she was going to call her parents, but instead she called Martin Russell. She told him she was engaged, and asked him to come visit.

Martin arrived from New York with gifts for Saffron and a congratulatory handshake for Jamie; Jamie searched his face for skepticism, but it was kept hidden. His clothes seemed to fit better than Jamie's ever would. He went for an effortless-looking swim in the pool and settled into his old banter with Saffron.

After dinner they played Botticelli, and Jamie fell asleep on the carpet. He had meant only to rest his eyes for a minute, but when he woke it was morning, and the room was light. Saffron was in the kitchen making coffee, in a short yellow flannel bathrobe that showed off her legs. Jamie shuffled in, groggy from sleeping on the floor, and sat at the table. His fiancée put a cup of coffee in front of him. The robe made a deep V in the front.

"Hello, floor sleeper," she said.

"Why did you let me stay there?"

"You were dead," she said. "What was I supposed to do, carry you upstairs?"

He drank some coffee. Saffron's hair was wet. She didn't usually wash her hair in the morning, because they would be swimming later.

"You could have woken me up," he said.

"Easy for you to say."

"Where's Martin?"

"He's still asleep."

"You've seen him?"

She shot him a look. "I'm guessing. His door is closed."

"Why'd you take a shower?"

"Why the inquisition?"

"You never take a shower first thing."

"It was hot last night. I felt sticky."

"Look, I might've fallen off the turnip truck yesterday," Jamie said, "but we learned a thing or two back at the turnip farm."

He wasn't sure, though, what exactly he thought. To believe she had actually fucked Martin would put him in a blind rage; he could feel himself at the edge of it but didn't want to be pushed over. He had to be careful. If he kept calm, he might still prevent her doing it.

"What's this about?" she asked.

"Wake me up next time."

"Next time what?"

"I fall asleep first."

"I don't know what you're talking about," she said, and she left the kitchen with her coffee, the yellow flannel brushing the backs of her smooth brown thighs.

20

ABBY SIGNED UP for a poetry class in the spring, and when the sections were assigned, she found herself on Peter Kerner's list. She wanted to ask if he had done it on purpose but was too embarrassed to suggest that he had. Miranda had seen them walking after a lecture and demanded to know facts.

"He's writing his dissertation on Poe," Abby said.

"So he's attracted to craziness," Miranda said. "That's good. But I mean real facts."

Abby told what she knew. He was thirty, and had grown up in Philadelphia. His parents were philosophy professors. His Jewish grandparents had been furious when their only son eloped with a halfhearted Lutheran, and his mother's parents had warned her that she'd never get her new husband into the tennis club. So Peter and his sister had grown up without religion or the tennis club, but with long arguments at the dinner table about philosophy. He'd been kicked out of college for a year and said it was the good thing about being in your early twenties: that you could afford to waste time.

"You're blushing like crazy," Miranda said. "Are you going to sleep with him?"

"No," Abby said.

"Why *not*?" Miranda was dying to have an affair with a teacher, but she was a design major and her TAs were all women or gay. Professors were harder to land; she didn't want to be obvious about it.

"I'm just not," Abby said. She couldn't go from her uncle to her teacher; she would start having attacks again. But she couldn't explain that to Miranda.

"Can I have him, then?" her roommate asked.

"No!"

"How fair is that?"

Abby had started trying to write a novel, which she kept in a computer file called "English 199a" so Miranda wouldn't read it. One Sunday night she was in the basement computer lab in the Central Library printing out two chapters—one from the point of view of a woman like Yvette, and one from Teddy's—when Peter came in. She turned the printed pages facedown.

"Writing a paper?" he asked.

"No," she said, then wished she had thought to say yes.

He sat without looking at her screen, and she ejected the disk.

"What are you printing?"

"I don't know."

"You don't *know*?" He laughed, watching her. There was one other student in the lab, a boy at the other end of the long basement hallway, typing away. "Do you think he'll leave soon?" Peter asked.

"He looks busy."

"You're wearing a skirt."

She shifted in the chair and felt her bare knees rub against each other. The skirt was pink: Miranda's. "It's my roommate's."

He nodded and waited. Finally he said, "Do you wish he were gone, too?"

She nodded, and they sat looking at each other. She could feel her heart beating and tried to slow it down.

"There's a room," she heard herself say. She had found it while looking for the bathroom. It had industrial carpet, temporary shelving, and some overhead projectors.

"Show me."

She slid the printed pages into her bag and wondered if she were creating a diversion to lead him away from them. But she wanted to go. She found the door, which opened, and let it close behind them.

Peter looked around. He plugged one of the overhead projectors into the wall and turned it on, and switched off the fluorescents. The room went dark blue, with a square of light on the bookshelves and the sound of the fan cooling the machine. He put his hand on the back of her neck, under her hair, and she shivered. She had gone off the pill so she wouldn't do things she hadn't planned to do, but he wouldn't be expecting to fuck, not the first time.

She watched the whole thing as if at a distance. He was interested and reverent: he knew that girls like to be praised. It was the first time since Jamie left, and she wondered how long it would be before she stopped thinking of Jamie when someone took off her clothes. He went down on her as soon as she would let him, and he was good, he knew how to draw out the end. She lay thinking about the shape of the orgasm, and then she did the same for him. It seemed to cost her nothing.

Peter took her face in his hands and said, "What if I had let you go by?"

She lay with her head on his chest, on the tight-napped carpet, listening to the overhead whir. She had his section on Tuesday, and one more paper to write for the class.

"I've never done this before, with a student," he said.

"Good."

"Have you done this with a teacher?"

"God, no."

He laughed. "I love that indignation. I was just asking. Let's go somewhere with furniture."

They dressed, and he left first, to see that the coast was clear. She turned off the overhead and smoothed down her hair and her skirt before following. The typing boy was gone, and everything seemed quiet.

"Come home with me," he said.

"I can't. I should go." She felt dizzy.

"Then I'll walk you home."

They got outside in the cool air, beneath the concrete legs that held up the top-heavy library, and Abby wanted to sit down on the steps. She kept walking, with Peter beside her, and tried to think the dizziness down. He didn't say anything, and neither did she. She smelled the eucalyptus trees overhead, and tasted his come in the back of her throat, and she couldn't stop shivering. Outside her building, she said, "This is me."

"Is your roommate home?"

"Probably."

"Are you all right? You seem cold."

"I'm okay."

"I don't like leaving you here."

"It's where I live," she said lightly.

"Can I see you tomorrow?"

She gave some vague answer and escaped up the stairs and into the empty room, where she dropped her bag and lay down. She thought of meditation classes with her mother and tried to breathe evenly, but thinking of her mother didn't help. Some of the girls on her hallway talked about how horrified their mothers would be to know they were having sex. Abby thought her problem was the opposite: her mother would understand sex, especially wrong-headed sex, because it was exactly what Clarissa would do.

When she knew she could stand up safely, she started to move around the room packing up her clothes and books. She couldn't look too closely at the decision, but she had already made it. She called her academic adviser, knowing she would get the machine, and explained that she was needed at home. There was a problem with her father's estate, and solving it would help her gain closure. She thought the word *closure* would help, with the adviser. In the morning she left a note for Miranda and started the long drive home.

21

MARGOT'S YOUNGER SON, Danny, had been working in El Salvador with a Jesuit volunteer group. Neither of her sons was devout—they were boys of their generation—but Danny wanted to travel and help people, so he had been digging latrines *ad majorem Dei gloriam*. Owen was meeting him at the airport, and Margot had just put the sheets on Danny's bed and was washing the breakfast dishes when her mother called.

"I'm worried about Jamie," Yvette said.

Margot squeezed out the sponge in the sink. "What is it now?"

"He just seems so lost. I think we didn't pay him enough attention when he was little. Or I didn't."

"You paid him all your attention. Everyone did. He was the darling."

"But he's had so much trouble getting started," Yvette said.

Margot put a glass in the sink. "That's because he's used to being the darling," she said. "When the world didn't adore him as much as we did, he got confused."

"Do you really think that's it?"

"Yes," Margot said. She wiped down the kitchen counter with a sponge. Owen had left the tiny white grains from an English muffin scattered around the toaster. Some of the grains caught in the grout between the smooth tiles. Sometimes, in dark moments, Margot thought: *This is what my life amounts to. I wipe up English muffin debris from tile grout, I sort laundry, I tidy before the housekeeper comes. I cook dinner, raise funds, host parties. I reassure my mother on the phone.*

"I think about it all the time, about how he seems to have lost his way," Yvette said. "It makes me so sad."

Margot rinsed the sponge and watched the grains fall into the sink, and wrestled with the usual feelings of guilt and impatience she felt about Jamie. "He'll find his way," she said. "He has an indestructible ego, and that will help."

"He does?"

"We gave it to him," she said. "He had three adoring females instead of one."

"I guess." Her mother sounded unconvinced.

"You can't blame yourself, Mom. Why not take credit for the good things? He's fun. People like him. He grew up with teenagers so he was a teenager early, and now he's a teenager late. That's his character. It's not the end of the world."

"I blame myself for Clarissa," her mother said sadly.

Margot felt another stab of guilt. She hadn't tried to draw attention from her sister—she had been good because there was pleasure in being approved of. But maybe she had, unconsciously, wanted all the approval for herself. She put the clean glasses away in the cupboard. "Clarissa got a little lost in the middle," she said.

"I wish she'd found a man like Owen."

Margot laughed. "She would have lasted two minutes with Owen."

"Clarissa loves him."

"She loves him as a brother-in-law and an idea," Margot said. "You know she could never have married him. I'm surprised she lasted so long with Henry."

"So what kind of man did she need?"

Margot paused. "Maybe no man," she said finally.

"Oh, that," Yvette said. "You don't think that's just a reaction to Henry?"

"Well," Margot said carefully, "I think we have to take her at her word."

Yvette said, "I guess so. I still haven't told your father. I find it so hard to believe. If you met that Del—"

But the door had opened, and Owen walked in with a shaggy young man.

"Danny's here, Mom," Margot said. "He has a beard!"

Danny stroked his face, self-conscious. "It's hard to shave where I'm living."

"It's your grandma Yvette," she said. "Say hello."

He did, and then they said good-bye, and Margot kissed her son, feeling the strange roughness of the beard against her cheek. She felt a rush of gratitude that she was secure in the family she had made, and not beholden to the one she had come from.

"I'll shave it off," Danny said.

"I don't care!"

She felt instantly, in her son's presence, that her life did have importance. She was glad she had never been tempted away by something wilder. She would sort laundry and cook meals for the rest of her life, to keep these boys clothed and fed, to keep feeling this overpowering love for the adults they had become.

22

ABBY HAD BEEN IN her father's house a week, without doing anything about his estate except spend it on eight-dollar sandwiches, when she came in to the phone ringing. She answered because it could be Peter, but it was Jamie.

"Where *are* you?" she asked. It was dark in the kitchen, and she turned on the light and checked the lock on the door.

"I guessed you might be there," Jamie said. "I wasn't going to call."

"I hear you've taken up with Holly Golightly."

"It's a long story."

"Is it true?"

"Just talk to me a little," Jamie said. "Say nice things."

"What's wrong?"

"Nothing."

"You can talk about this girl," she said. "I won't be jealous."

"Why aren't you in school?"

"I don't know."

"Are you writing?"

"Sort of."

"What are you wearing?"

Abby laughed. "Don't start that."

"I'm sort of kidding."

"You sound so sad," she said. "What has she done to you?"

"I don't know," he said. "That's the problem, I'm not sure. It might be fine. I don't know."

"It doesn't sound fine."

"I know," he said. "I'll find out, and then I'll know."

23

JAMIE WOKE UP in the blue room from a dream he had already forgotten. It was dark and he was alone. Saffron and Martin had been playing War, and the cards were still on the rug. It was four a.m. in the blue light on his watch, and he got up from the couch and made his way to the stairs. He climbed to the second floor quietly, avoiding the creaking step at the top, and went down the hall to Martin's room. The door was closed, and he stood outside, listening. He didn't hear anything, but they might be asleep by now. He couldn't explain himself if he opened the door and woke Martin alone, so he moved down the hall to the room he shared with Saffron. That door was closed, too, and he stood outside it, thinking through the possibilities:

If he opened it and found Saffron alone, he would be happy. It wouldn't mean nothing had happened, but it *might* mean nothing had happened.

If he opened it and found no one, it would mean they were together in Martin's room, and he would have to go open that door.

If he opened it and found Saffron and Martin together— But at the thought, a door in his brain slammed shut before he could see what they might look like. What would he do? Stab them in their sleep? Demand that Saffron take off the ring that was already hers? Stand there and fume and sputter like the humiliated fool he was?

He put his hand on the knob, but he couldn't bring himself to turn it. He went back down the hall, past Martin's silent door, stepped over the creaking stair, and returned to the couch where he had made the mistake of falling asleep early. He lay there listening to the house, and fell asleep again sometime before morning.

He woke up to Saffron putting a coffee cup on the side table. Her hair had been piled up on her head in the way she kept it out of the shower. The loose hairs at the back of her neck were damp, and she smelled like soap.

"Good morning," she said. "Did you sleep well?"

"You were going to wake me up," he said.

"You looked so comfortable."

"Why," he asked, "when I fall asleep before you, do you take a shower in the morning?"

She looked puzzled. "I do?"

"Twice now."

"Sometimes I take a shower and sometimes I don't."

"You never used to take a shower. You're going to swim later anyway."

"What is it you think?"

"What do you think I think?"

"You say it."

But Martin Russell came downstairs then. He wore a blue bathrobe and didn't look like he'd been in the shower.

"You look disgustingly rested," he said to Jamie. "I need to start sacking out early, too."

He passed by the couch, and Jamie breathed in, to see if he could smell Saffron on him, but all he could smell was the coffee she had left for him on the side table.

That night on the porch, after dinner, Saffron sat on the wide arm of Jamie's Adirondack chair, her feet tucked up and her back against his shoulder. Martin yawned and stretched. "I'm beat," he said. "Good night, you two. Be good."

Jamie had felt like he had the upper hand, with Saffron sitting so close to him. But Martin's elaborate show of going to bed made the use of Saffron seem like a gift, something Martin could easily afford. The light was starting to fade, and the blue twilight made Jamie feel thwarted and old.

"Why are you so sulky?" Saffron asked, still perched on his chair.

"I'm not," he said.

"You are, too," she said. "You've been pouting all day, for no reason. It's *très mal élevé*."

"When I fall asleep—" he said.

She waited, watching him.

"When you stay up," he said.

"Yes?"

"What do you do?"

Saffron said nothing for a minute. "Do you really want to know?" she asked.

"Yes," he said.

"Would it bother you if I were doing this?" She leaned over to kiss him, her hair brushing his chest.

"Yes," he said hoarsely.

"Why do you care, as long as I'm here now?"

"I care," he said, and he slid a hand up under her dress. "Do you let him touch you like this?"

"Maybe."

"*Do* you?"

"Yes," she said.

He picked her up, clumsily, and carried her inside to the couch in the blue room. Ten minutes passed in which she was his alone, and then something about the expert way she helped his cock inside her filled him with jealousy again.

"Does he fuck you like this?" he whispered.

"Yes."

"Does he fuck your mouth?"

"Yes."

"Does he fuck your ass?"

"Yes."

"He *does*?"

"No!" she said. "Jesus. I'm just saying that. Don't stop."

When they finished, they said nothing for a while.

"Are you going to tell me the real answers?" he finally asked.

She sighed.

"You're engaged to me," he said. "You're supposed to become my wife. Do you want that?"

"I think so," she said. "But I never know what I want until it comes up."

"That could be a problem."

She didn't say anything.

"Are you really fucking him?" he asked. "Because I swear I'll kill him."

"Then *no*," she said. "I'm really not."

"Okay, I didn't mean that. Just tell me the truth."

She propped herself on an elbow and studied him. "I'm not," she said. "I thought you wanted me to say those things. I thought it was a game. You kept asking."

She could have passed a lie detector test; her eyes and her breathing were that steady. He almost believed her.

"There's no one else," she said. "I swear. I'm yours alone."

24

IN THE MORNING, when Saffron woke up on the blue room couch, Jamie wasn't there. She made coffee and took it upstairs to him, but he wasn't in bed.

She went to the bathroom, and his razor and toothbrush were missing. His duffel bag and clothes weren't in the closet. Downstairs, she sat at the kitchen counter where she had done some of the things with Martin that she had been foolish enough to tell Jamie about, and drank Jamie's coffee.

"Morning, sweetheart," Martin said, when he came into the kitchen. He poured himself a cup. "Jamie up?"

Saffron shook her head.

"Fancy a little morning entertainment?"

She shook her head again. "Jamie's gone."

The morning light through the kitchen windows lit up the left side of Martin's hair. "Oh, Saffron, you didn't tell him," he said.

"Not really," she said. "Well, sort of."

Martin shook his head. "You silly girl. You had everything you wanted."

"It wasn't fair to him."

"Nothing's ever fair, you know that."

"Maybe some things should be."

Martin looked at her. "You mean if he came back, you would be faithful?"

"Sure."

"No, you wouldn't. Poor wanton Saffron."

"Don't talk to me like that. I'm an adult."

Martin finished his coffee in a contemplative way and rinsed the cup in the sink.

"I have to leave today, too," he said.

A feeling of panic rose up in her, which she associated with her parents' suitcases suddenly in the hall, and the nanny having no explanations. "Are you afraid you'll get stuck here with me?"

Martin laughed. "I just have to go to New York."

"Are you coming back?"

"I don't think you'll stay in this house alone," he said. "So there won't be anything for me to come back to."

"What will I do?" she asked, and her voice sounded small to her.

"This is the question we all wake up one day and have to answer," he said. "You just put it off awhile. It will be interesting, to see what you do. I hope it's something good."

"Can I go with you to New York?"

"Absolutely not," he said. "That doesn't count as doing something."

"I could do something in New York."

"Yes, I know," he said. "You could carry on with one of my friends, and keep me as your new primary shareholder and cuckold."

"I wouldn't do that," she said, though she guessed he was right.

"I know all your tricks."

"I could design clothes."

"I hear there's a dire need for that," he said. "More coffee?"

She shook her head, and he poured out the pot in the sink and turned off the coffeemaker.

"Now I'm going to get packed," he said.

By lunchtime Martin, too, was gone.

Saffron was sitting alone on the porch feeling sorry for herself when the housekeeper brought a letter on her mother's stationery, with the Argentina address engraved across the envelope flap. It was the first letter she'd had from her mother in months, and it was a measure of her misery that she was almost happy to get it.

25

ADOPTING THE ROMANIAN child had seemed like a good idea to Josephine, especially when the newspapers were full of the fall of Ceausescu and the plight of the orphans. And she had been lonely, on her estancia in the unfashionable direction from Buenos Aires.

It wouldn't have been unfashionable if Josephine had kept her social power, but life had conspired against her, and she hadn't been able to draw the best people. Some of her investments failed, and she had overspent, and no longer had the money for grand parties. She had a fight with a woman who had loyal friends, and it was in the gossip columns. Even Taki picked it up. The woman had an old name, and some of her friends stopped coming to Josephine's.

So the idea of a child to love her, the way her own daughter did not, seemed a beautiful consolation in her old age. The child would be grateful for its rescue from violence and poverty. Josephine would be putting to virtuous use the beautiful empty rooms— empty because houseguests came rarely now, one or two at a time, and left after a day or two. They might have stayed longer if Josephine hadn't resented them so much. She had to think about menus when there were guests, and her confusion sent her running to the kitchen to intrude on the servants' privacy, only to find that she had already discussed dinner with Gautier that morning.

If she wasn't made frantic by visitors, she was alone with a nervous stomach, and Gautier's talents were wasted on unsalted oatmeal and consommé. He had begun to chafe, she knew, and to look at her with open disdain.

Gautier was French, so archness and superiority were expected, but the new Argentine maid had begun to imitate him. Josephine scolded herself for choosing the pretty one. It was always a mistake to choose the pretty one. The guests were partial to Magdalena, and the girl surely hoped that one might fall in love with her heart-shaped face and marry her. Or that someone might take her to work in a fashionable house where she would meet all of society, and *there* a man might marry her. But it would never happen. Josephine wanted to shake the girl and tell her it would *never happen*.

And then there were the guests themselves: a terribly fat man, someone's vulgar brother, had sat on the Marie Antoinette chair and broken the leg off, sending Josephine into a rage. Another smoked in bed and burned a hole right through the new sheets. Josephine couldn't control her anger. She shouted at Magdalena, and sometimes even shouted at the guests. Then she took to her bed out of shame, watched telenovelas on TV, and sent word downstairs that the wind was aggravating the stiffness in her neck.

The only person who didn't enrage her was her business manager, Fauchet, who arrived in a helicopter every month like a gift from the gods. He could smoke his little cigars and tease her all he wanted, because at night he held her in his arms and let her weep about her lost memory and the chaos of her thoughts.

It had just begun, this slippage she could feel but not control, when the baby came from Romania. The reality of the child was shocking to Josephine. It arrived red-faced and screaming from the helicopter, with a full diaper. She had almost forgotten it was coming. What did she know about children? Her mind had been fine when Saffron was young, and still her daughter despised her. What made her think she could care for this child now?

But she could, of course: she had resources, she had help. Those wretched people in Romania had nothing. The child was better off here, no matter what Josephine's memory might do. She named the boy Tomas Josef, with the vague idea that those might be Romanian names, and he became a favorite of Magdalena, who treated him as a small prince, as her own.

As Tomas learned to talk and walk, he grew round and happy and tyrannical, beloved of such a kind, pretty girl. He lived and slept in the servants' rooms, and days went by when Josephine didn't see him. Sometimes she requested his presence at lunch on the patio, but he smeared his food across his face and threw it to the floor. The sight annoyed and disgusted Josephine, and the boy seemed to be growing unattractively fat. So back to the servants he would go, with instructions not to give him bread or pasta for a while.

One morning when the boy was four and a half, Josephine had a particularly bad episode with her mind. She was confused about time again, and consumed with jealousy and suspicion, and she had a scene with Magdalena that sent the maid crying from the room.

When the maid was gone, Josephine called Fauchet in France. She had a dated note she had written to herself, although she didn't remember writing it. It said that Fauchet had promised to discuss her will. Josephine told herself she was calling for that reason, but mostly she wanted comfort. It was a Saturday, so she called him at home. His wife answered, and Josephine asked for the husband.

There was a meaningful pause, and then the wife said her husband was not home. It was a second wife, Josephine remembered, and there were children of some kind. Josephine asked politely when Fauchet would return, and the wife said she didn't know. Then Josephine heard a man's voice in the background, asking who it was.

"*C'est ta vieille,*" the wife said, not bothering to cover the mouthpiece: *It's your old woman.*

"*Quelle vieille?*" she heard Fauchet ask in the background.

"*La Flynn,*" the wife said. "*La folle.*"

Fauchet asked for the phone, and his wife told him that there wouldn't be any money from this crazy woman, that he was wasting his time. Fauchet said he was a business manager, this was his job. The wife said that fucking the clients was not included.

Except for the expletives, they spoke elegant French, and Josephine listened for a while with a curious detachment, and then she hung up the phone. It was an ivory-colored phone with a dial on its squat base, and she watched it, wondering if Fauchet would call her back when he finished his fight. The phone remained still and quiet, crouching there on the desk.

Her daughter was her next resource, but she couldn't risk a phone call in which Saffron, too, refused to speak to her, so she took out a piece of writing paper. "My darling," she wrote.

> *I know you don't think I have been the perfect mother to you, but I am writing to tell you that I do love you very much and I believe something is wrong with my mind. I lose track of my thoughts.*
>
> *This morning, for example, I thought you were still a child, and I was still married to your father. But darling I'm not crazy. I have moments like now, also, when I see perfectly clearly who and where I am, and I understand what happens to me in these small episodes when I am disoriented, or confused.* ~~*I believe*~~
>
> *The servants take good care of the boy, but he can't live with the servants forever, and they watch me, and see my confusion. You know that in Argentina,* <u>*only*</u> *the children may inherit, but I don't remember the details of the adoption and I fear the government may not recognize the boy. I am looking into my will, and I am inquiring with Fauchet, whose wife dislikes me. I believe the child speaks no English, a further problem.* ~~*You will*~~ *I realize you will say I should have thought of all this before, but that is the situation now.*
>
> *If you come to Buenos Aires I will arrange a car to the house. Please consider it.*
>
> > *All my love,*
> > *Your mother*

When she had finished writing the letter, she put down her pen and looked out at her lawn, and wondered if the gardener had been paid. The green grass stretched until it reached the trees of the windbreak. The windbreak marched diagonally toward the far field, the line obedient and orderly and strong.

Josephine tried to hold on to her moment of clarity, to her thoughts marching along as obedient and sequential as the trees, but she could already feel them start to weave and scatter. She tucked the letter into an envelope and hurried it downstairs so she wouldn't forget to put it in the mail.

26

A BBY STAYED IN HER father's house and made no plans to sell it. Now that she had come home, she felt his presence there, in every room. Once she left the house and let someone else move in, he would be gone.

She worked on the novel at the kitchen table, and took a job waiting tables in town. Her parents' friends and her friends' parents came into the restaurant. "I thought you were in college," they said.

"I was."

"Oh, well," one said. "You could have been anything, you know."

Peter had asked if he could visit, but she had dodged the question. There was nowhere for him to stay. She couldn't have him sleep in the house, with the way her father still felt precariously there. She couldn't put him in her mother's house, with Del. And if he got a hotel room, she would end up staying with him, and then she would regret it and fall apart. A week later he called again.

"I try not to feel like a stalker," he said. "It helps that you call me sometimes. But I have a question."

"Okay."

"A girl from the Scripps Institute gave me her phone number, and I didn't call her, and then I was lying awake thinking, Why *can't*

I get laid by a hot marine chemist? Why am I being faithful to someone who had such a violent physical reaction to me that she left *town*? But I liked what happened in that room, and I think you did, too, and I'd like to try again. I've probably said too much now, but I haven't said enough, before."

Abby heard herself say, "You should call the marine chemist."

There was a long silence. "You mean that?"

"Yes."

He waited, but she didn't change the answer. "Okay," he said finally, and hung up.

Abby lay on the couch in her father's living room, in the empty house, wishing her father hadn't left her alone. It had all started there, this fucking up and not knowing what to do. Peter was too smart for her. If he found out the truth about Jamie, he would be disgusted, and she would have trusted him and lost him. She had lost her father and she had lost Jamie, and that was enough.

Mornings were the best time, when she worked on the novel and didn't think about anything else. The shifts at the restaurant were a blur. A boy from her high school had seen her there and took her out for an awkward dinner. A man her father's age left huge tips and finally asked if she would see a production of *As You Like It* with him, but she said no. If she was careful not to make eye contact, most men left her alone.

Her father still got junk mail, which she threw away. A few things came for her—a letter from the university about registration, though her class had already graduated. Celebrity gossip from Miranda, who had an internship at *InStyle* magazine. And a letter from Gianni in England, from a life she barely remembered. It said:

Carissima,

I am getting married, I want to tell you, I think you will be happy for me.

She is english and very sexy and voluttuosa and <u>materna</u>, like a good mother. I think this is ruin for Italian men. Blonde. And she is very rich and wears the most ridiculos shoes. I dont know what she will *do in my little town, in my streets, in these shoes. But its all very erotic for me, and my father is very happy.*

I think you know I can't invite you to this wedding without alot of trouble, but I send you big kisses and hope you will wish me lucky. I think of you.

Gianni xxxx

She put the letter on the refrigerator with a magnet shaped like the state of California and wished him lucky when she went for the milk.

Then a postcard came from Peter, saying, "Marine chemist total failure. I will be in the lobby of the Catalina Hotel in S.R. this Wednesday at five p.m." On the front of the postcard was the blocky spaceship library with the basement room.

While she worked, she left the card on the kitchen table, where she could pick it up every few minutes when she lost her concentration. She wished that Wednesday would arrive and be over with, so that she could move on. The Catalina was a pretty Spanish hotel downtown; she had been to a wedding there. She tried calling Peter to tell him not to come, but he wasn't answering the phone.

On Wednesday, she put on Miranda's pink skirt, which she had kept because there wasn't time to wash it before she left school. Then she took off the skirt and put on jeans. Then she took the jeans off and put the skirt back on. She still had forty minutes before she had to be there. It wasn't fair of him to put her on the spot like this. She couldn't have sex with him when just a postcard had thrown her off for days. But she couldn't not go. She was brushing her hair when the doorbell rang, and she thought sadly that Peter had made a mistake. She would have met him at the hotel, but he shouldn't have come to the house.

She opened the door, and Jamie was on the step.

"Is it safe for you to just open the door?" he asked. "What if it wasn't me?"

"What are you *doing* here?" she asked.

"Visiting my favorite niece."

"I'm your only niece," she said, out of habit.

"You look nice."

"I have a job interview," she said, sure he would see she was lying.

"What job?"

"Waitressing," she said. "Just a better restaurant. Better tips."

He had already stepped through the door and walked into the kitchen, with its crowded table set up as a desk. "Hey, you *are* writing," he said. "But there aren't other rooms? You can't spread out a little?"

"I like the kitchen." She slid Peter's postcard under her computer when Jamie wasn't looking.

"Are you selling the house?"

"I don't know."

"Why aren't you in school?"

"Too lazy."

"You're the opposite of lazy."

He wandered out into the living room, and she followed him, trying to keep him from disturbing what was left of her father in the house. He dropped himself down on the couch, and she flinched.

"I'm not doing so well," he said.

"Why not?"

"It's a long story. I want you to go on a trip with me."

Abby laughed with surprise.

"Why are you laughing?"

Her eyes filled up with tears. "Jamie."

"What?"

"I'm just getting myself together again, barely, and you come back all wild-eyed and want to go on a *trip*?"

"Look," he said. "I know we shouldn't have done what we did."

"Okay."

"And I really need your help."

He seemed to be trying for a calm and reasonable tone. He told her he had gotten engaged to a woman named Saffron, but there had been problems, and he had tried to leave.

"Did you tell her about me?" Abby asked.

"That I have a lovely niece?"

"That you fucked your niece?"

"No," he said. "I didn't say that."

"Good," Abby said. "I don't want to be part of your pillow talk. I don't want her looking at me funny when you're married and have six kids."

"I don't think that's likely."

"Don't tell her anyway."

"I won't."

His fiancée's mother had adopted a Romanian baby, but she was in her sixties, and had some kind of dementia, and couldn't take care of the little boy.

"We've had some problems," he said. "I left, but then Saffron got this letter from Argentina, and she needs me, and—I don't know. She can't deal with her mother alone and needs a buffer. She says that spending fifteen minutes with her mother leaves her rocking like a rhesus monkey."

"So go."

"I want you to come, too."

"Are you crazy?"

"You speak Spanish," he said. "The kid's been raised by her mother's Argentine servants, that's all he speaks. I don't speak it. Saffron doesn't really. The mother does, but she's sort of nuts."

Abby studied Jamie, sitting on her father's couch. "You're planning some weird threesome."

"No," he said. "I want you there because then I'll know how I feel about her. I want that thing you get when you take someone home to your family: you see that person more objectively. Or anyway you can see if it makes sense."

"So take her home to Yvette and Teddy."

"I'm not ready for that."

"Have you asked Yvette if Margot's your mother?"

"God, no."

Abby checked her father's watch. She had twenty minutes to get to the hotel. "Look," she said. "I understand I can't be your girl-friend, but I really can't be your chaperone."

"I think it will work."

"I can't afford it."

"Saffron will get you a ticket."

"That's totally weird."

"She's rich. She's making the plans now. Just consider coming with me, okay?"

To get him to leave, she said, "I'll think about it."

"Thank you," he said.

She waited for his car to round the end of the block and then left for the hotel.

27

THE LOBBY OF THE Catalina was quiet. An older couple was checking in at the desk, and a bellboy walked through with a long stride. Peter waited in the sitting area behind a row of potted palms. He was nervous and didn't want to go back discouraged. His father liked to quote Isaiah Berlin, who said that teaching undergraduates was like striking matches on soap. Peter had started to think courting them was the same. Then Abby came in, and he stood up, and realized he didn't have any choice in the matter.

"Hi," he said.

"Hi."

She was wearing the pink skirt she had worn in the library, which he thought must be a signal to him, and he said, "This is a nice town," to cover how he felt about that.

She sat down in the chair opposite him, and he wondered why he hadn't kissed her hello. But she hadn't kissed him, either. He sat down, too.

"I'm sorry about the marine chemist," she said, though she didn't sound unhappy. "How's Poe?"

"Fine," he said. "What do you do up here?"

"I'm still waiting tables."

There was a pause.

"And trying to write a novel."

"Really?" He hadn't imagined that.

"But it's terrible," she said. "I don't know what I'm doing."

"Do you want me to read it?"

"No," she said. "You'll see how stupid I am."

"I've already made my decision about that."

"You'll see you were wrong."

"Try me."

A girl in a hotel uniform came into the sitting area. "Did you two need anything?" she asked.

Abby shook her head, and Peter thanked the girl, and she went away.

"I have a room upstairs," he said. The fact hung in the air between them.

"This town—" Abby finally said. "People talk here. They would come into the restaurant grinning at me if I went up there. That girl went to my high school."

"We could go up separately."

"I can't."

"I really tried to be interested in the marine chemist," he said, "but I kept thinking about you. You're wearing your roommate's skirt."

She blushed.

"I've thought a lot about that skirt," he said.

There was another heavy silence. He was afraid she might run away. The skirt had given him encouragement, and he didn't want to go home without *something* to take with him.

"Put your foot up on that ottoman, just for a minute," he said.

Abby, in the chair across from him, seemed to consider the proposition. He could see she wasn't wearing stockings. She looked back over her shoulder through the potted palms. No one was paying any attention. She put her foot on the edge of the ottoman, which raised her knee, and the hem of the skirt started to slide toward her lap. She stopped it with her hand, but he could see the pale hourglass between her bare thighs.

"Oh my God," he said.

Something dropped on the tile floor by the front desk, and Abby put her foot quickly back on the floor.

"It's just the bellboy," Peter said. "He's far away."

"Someone's going to see us."

"We can always go upstairs."

She shook her head.

The bellboy's cart rolled across the lobby floor, the wheels rhythmically hitting the seams in the tile. Abby laughed nervously, and it made Peter brave.

"It's not really because people would talk, is it, that you won't go upstairs?"

"No."

"And it's not really because of me that you left."

She hesitated.

"What is it then?"

She shook her head.

"Come upstairs," he said. "Please come upstairs."

28

ABBY WOKE UP when the sun came into the small, pretty room on the third floor of the hotel. In the bathroom she pulled her hair into a ponytail, distractedly considering her naked body in the mirror. There was no dizziness yet, which made her feel happy, but she guessed it was because she knew she had a way out; she was going to Argentina. She was going to a different continent, a different hemisphere. She went back out, and Peter was awake.

"Can I order room service," he asked, "or will some high school friend of yours deliver it?"

"I'll go in the bathroom when they come."

"Look at you," he said.

She climbed under the white sheets. "My uncle showed up, right before I left the house yesterday," she said.

"Have you told me about an uncle?"

"I don't think so."

"Is he an old, decrepit uncle or a young, handsome one?"

Abby wondered if everyone saw through her, or only Peter. "Young," she said. "He has a fiancée. He wants me to go to Argentina with them, so I can talk to her senile mother's adopted Romanian orphan."

"That would have been my second guess."

Abby smiled.

"You speak Romanian?"

"The kid speaks Spanish."

"So will you go?"

She hesitated. "I said I'd think about it."

"When would you leave?"

"Soon."

"It sounds weird enough to be something to do," he said. "What are the downsides?"

She smoothed the wrinkled sheet with one hand. "I'm not really sure."

"I feel like I'm missing something here," he said. "Is there more to the story?"

"No," she said.

"Really?"

"No," she said again. If she could say it with enough conviction, it might be true.

He waited, and she said nothing, and finally he said, "Then you should go."

PART TWO

29

ABBY HAD HER LAPTOP set up on the tiny antique writing desk in her room at the estancia, and she read over what she had written:

What Jamie didn't know was who was his father? He asked his sister about the dance teacher, though he didn't tell her what he suspected.

"He came to school on Thursday afternoons with Miss Adair," Clarissa said. "They taught dancing lessons—you know, waltz and fox-trot. All the girls had crushes on him."

"What did he look like?"

"He wasn't tall, I guess, but he was handsome. Dark hair. And Miss Adair was beautiful, with her hair in a French twist and perfect makeup. I wonder if she was sleeping with him."

"Probably."

His sister gave a little gasp of astonishment. "Oh, my God," she said. "That never occurred to me before now."

[Why should all this matter to anyone but Jamie?]

She stared at the question in brackets, which suddenly seemed like the whole question. And she would have to change the names, soon; she couldn't call them Jamie and Clarissa. There was a knock at the door, and she closed the computer and put a book on top.

The knock came again, a little louder, and Abby crossed the cold tile floor and the soft rug in her bare feet, and opened the door. Saffron stood outside. She was wearing a blue pireo tied around her narrow hips, and a white bikini top that showed off her lean torso and long brown arms. She was startlingly beautiful and completely disconnected from reality.

"Hi," Saffron said. "I wanted to make sure you were coming to lunch."

"Sure," Abby said.

"My mother wants to bring T.J. out and show him off." Saffron had made clear her annoyance at the idea that Tomas and Josef might be Romanian names, and she called the boy T.J. instead.

"Okay," Abby said.

"It would be great if you were there—so there's someone besides my mother who can talk to the kid. He already speaks Spanish too fast for her."

At dinner the night before, Josephine had told the same story twice between the soup and the chocolate mousse. Abby thought she must have seen the frozen smiles on her listeners' faces and guessed that something ungraspable was wrong.

"We're out by the pool," Saffron said. "What are you doing in there?"

"Reading."

Saffron looked over Abby's shoulder, as if for evidence. "Well, come out and read by the pool if you want." She gave a little wave and walked barefoot away.

Abby lay back on the bed and looked up at the ceiling, which had patterns in it, in relief in the plaster. The house had been a drafty, barnlike Spanish building for raising a giant family and sheep, but Josephine had made it grand and comfortable, with deep couches and red pillows and hammered silver. The idea that they needed Abby to talk to the kid was crazy. He was happy and smart, and if Saffron wanted to talk to him, she should just start speaking

English. He would learn. But maybe Saffron didn't want to talk to the boy any more than her mother did.

When Abby got to lunch on the covered patio, no one was there. The table was set for five, with blue and white linens and plates, and a vase of blue flowers. There were birds on the grass, with long legs and white striped wings. They marched purposefully across the vast lawn, hunting something.

Then Josephine swept onto the patio, in a green dress with a blue sash. "Darling," she said to Abby. "Where is everyone?" She rang the little bell on the table, and Hector the butler came outside. "Where is the child?" she asked. "Go find him."

Hector disappeared.

"Where is my daughter?" Josephine asked Abby.

"I think she and Jamie were at the pool."

"Run and get them, darling," Josephine said, but just then they saw Saffron and Jamie coming across the lawn from the pool house, Saffron still in the bikini top and the pireo. Jamie wore a wrinkled button-down shirt over his swim trunks. Jamie wasn't sleeping in Saffron's room, on some kind of principle, but they lay next to each other all day at the pool.

"Ah, there they are," Josephine said.

While they waited, Josephine put her hand on the carved stone statue of a squat bird on a small pedestal beside her. "Do you know what this animal is?" she asked Abby.

"A dodo," Abby said.

Josephine looked startled, and she stared at Abby in wonder. "Well," she said finally. "You're *erudite*."

When T.J. came outside with Magdalena, wearing a dress shirt and pressed pants, the pretty maid helped him climb into a chair. He had huge, dark eyes and fine, pale, almost colorless hair.

"Not that chair," Josephine snapped. "This one, by me."

Magdalena moved the boy, who stared up at Josephine as if she were a creature from outer space.

"You sit on the other side of him, darling," Josephine said, pointing, and Abby sat down, convinced that Josephine had forgotten her name. "That leaves . . . those two together. But oh, well."

Saffron and Jamie took the two remaining seats. Abby wondered if Josephine knew anyone's name—it seemed she remembered that couples shouldn't be seated together, but she couldn't remember what she'd called her own daughter.

Josephine smiled triumphantly, having successfully assembled a small luncheon, and rang the little bell. Hector came back, took the clean top plates away, and brought smaller ones with blue figs and prosciutto on them, the skin of the figs peeled back in sections so they looked like tropical flowers resting their petals on the plate.

The little boy, on Abby's right, bounced his heels against his chair and considered this production.

"*Son higos,*" Abby told him, producing the word from childhood. "*Y jamón. ¿Te gustan?*"

He looked unsure if he liked figs and ham or not. She cut a piece of fig and offered it to him, and he ate it, watching her. She did the same with a piece of ham, and then handed him his fork. He held it in his small, fat fist, close to his chest, still chewing on the ham.

"He's a very healthy boy," Josephine said. "He came to me when he was just a baby."

"Gautier feeds him well," Saffron said.

"*I* feed him well," her mother said.

"He lives with the staff, Mother," Saffron said. "Admit it. He's happy there."

"He lives with *me.*"

"Do you know anything about his parents?" Jamie asked.

Josephine widened her eyes. "The situation in Romania is terrible," she said. "There is murder, there is rape—total chaos. The children are left behind."

"She means she doesn't know," Saffron said.

"He might be a child of rape," her mother said.

"Mother, if you say that in front of him again, I will never speak to you again. I don't care what language he speaks."

Josephine ignored her. "My friend the princess knew this child must be saved, and she sent him here."

"Oh, Mother," Saffron said. "Don't act like you're on Amnesty's list of safe houses. You asked for a child and you got one. Everyone wants a white baby, and you pulled strings."

There was a long silence while Josephine stared at her daughter. Abby cut the boy some more fig. Then Josephine said, in a hurt voice, "I was pregnant with a boy once, myself, but I had malaria, a terrible fever. I had a very good doctor, a Jew, but I lost my son."

Saffron glared at her mother. "And if only you'd had the boy, things would be better now."

"To lose a child is a great strain on a marriage," her mother said. "You don't know. And it's very helpful to have a son."

Saffron clanked her knife and fork down on her plate and glared out at the lawn.

The fig plates were taken away, and plates of roast beef arrived. T.J. had a purple fig seed on his chin. Abby cut his meat into small pieces, then showed him the fork. "Fork," she said. He didn't say anything. "Knife," she said, pointing. "Napkin. Plate."

"Plate," he said.

"Beef."

"*Rosbif,*" he said, more confident, shaping the word with his small, fat lips.

"Yes. Roast beef. Water."

"*Agua.*"

"Yes, *agua*. Water."

"Teach him 'Mama,'" Josephine said suddenly, her eyes full of need.

Abby hesitated. "What does he usually call you?"

"I don't know," Josephine said. "I've asked Magdalena to teach him 'Mama,' and she says she will, but she doesn't."

"*¿Quién es ella?*" Abby asked the boy, pointing at Josephine.

"*La señora,*" he said.

"Mother, it's very weird to teach him 'Mama' at this point," Saffron said. "He's almost five."

The older woman's eyes filled with tears. "I wanted him to call me Mama," she said, in a plaintive voice, and Abby wondered how she hadn't accomplished such a simple thing.

"*I'll* call you Mama," Saffron said. "We'll all call you Mama. Don't do this to him. It's so weird."

"But if I'm not his mama, then he doesn't have one."

"Well, that's his tragedy," Saffron said. "It's still better than Romania."

The lunch plates were taken away, and small dessert bowls came in their place, and there was another silence while they consoled themselves with caramel ice cream. The boy got it all over his face.

After lunch, when the boy's hands and face had been wiped down, Abby took him for a walk, thinking she couldn't sit through another lunch like that. She said the English words for *stairs, flowers, fountain, garden, grass*. Two bounding yellow Labs appeared and leaped into the fountain, splashing water everywhere.

"*Perros!*" the boy cried happily.

"Dogs," Abby said.

That night, in her room, Abby was trying to come up with new names for her characters that were as good as the real ones—none were as good as the real ones—when the phone rang: Josephine calling from her own part of the house.

"Please come to my room," Josephine said. "Saffron isn't answering her phone."

Abby went out in her pajamas, past the open bedroom door where she could see Saffron lying on the bed in a baby-doll nightgown, reading a magazine. Her phone hadn't been ringing. Saffron's door seemed to be open to tempt Jamie, and the phone unplugged to deflect her mother.

Abby went downstairs in the guest wing, and across the big living room, and up the staircase to a little mezzanine with a piano and a backgammon table, outside Josephine's suite. She listened outside the door for a second, then knocked.

"Who is it?" Josephine asked. She must have been waiting just inside the door, because her voice was close.

"It's Abby. You asked me to come."

The door opened, and Josephine, completely naked, stood inside.

"Oh, thank you," she said, and she stepped back to let Abby in. "I'm frantic. I don't know if my business manager is coming for luncheon tomorrow."

Abby was trying not to look at Josephine's body, but there it was. Her breasts were small and still had most of their shape, and she was tan and surprisingly fit. It wasn't the body of a woman who forgot everything.

"I asked Magdalena and the laundress," Josephine said, "but they don't know. It's very hard to get good staff."

"Would you have written it down?" Abby asked.

"Written what down?"

"The date your business manager is coming."

Josephine looked around the room helplessly. It was all white, with a vast white canopy bed at the center, in the glow of a bedside lamp. "I don't know," she said.

Together they found a leather-bound calendar on a vanity under the window. Scrawled on the square for the next day was "Fauchet. 10 a.m. heli." Josephine beamed with amazement, as if Abby had produced the reminder out of a hat. "I can tell the chef!" she said.

"Good."

"Will you meet the helicopter in the morning? Fauchet is my good friend."

"Okay."

"We'll be five for lunch, not including the boy," Josephine said, writing it on a piece of paper, the tanned skin of her stomach folding as she bent over the desk. She seemed to draw strength from having facts at hand—a sudden clarity. "I wish we had a man for you. I don't think we'll have the boy at lunch, not tomorrow."

"All right," Abby said.

"Slip this under Gautier's door when you go down. He has the room next to the kitchen."

Abby took the piece of paper.

"I'm sorry to treat you like a little daughter," Josephine said. "I used to have a secretary to do these things, but she left. She was unhappy, and she wanted to marry. Good night, darling." Still naked, she saw Abby out and closed the door.

Abby went downstairs to slip the note under the chef's door, then back through the length of the dark house to the guest wing, and upstairs again. On the stairs she ran into Jamie coming down.

"Come for a walk with me," he whispered. "I can't stand this anymore."

"I don't have any shoes."

"Just out on the lawn, it's okay."

They went out a heavy wooden door to the dark patio where they had eaten lunch, and Abby rolled up the legs of her pajamas, but the grass wasn't wet, only a little cool and damp under her feet. The striped birds were gone, at night, and the trees at the far edges of the lawn made a dark border for the sky. There had once been trees all the way to the house, Saffron said, but a tornado had taken down a hundred and fifty of them, clearing space for the lawn, as if the tornado had been specially ordered by Josephine to open up the view.

When they were well clear of the house, Jamie said, "What do you think?"

"Of Saffron?"

"Of everything."

Abby thought about it. "It's not really your scene, is it?"

"I guess not," Jamie said. "But the people aren't the scene."

"Really?" Abby said.

"Okay, maybe they are."

They walked in silence until they reached the trees at the edge of the lawn, and then they started back toward the house, along the edge of the vast circle of grass. A light was on upstairs, in Josephine's room, and two lights were visible in the guest wing.

"Are you still engaged to Saffron?" Abby asked.

"I don't know," he said.

"You aren't even sleeping with her, right? There's some kind of moratorium?"

"I think I'm obsessed," he said. "I get so jealous. I know she's unfaithful and I don't want to get involved again, but I can't stop thinking about it."

"That seems like a good reason to get out."

"But I can't," he said. "I know I should, but I can't."

"What do you think about?"

Jamie said nothing. Josephine's light had gone out in the main house, and one of the lights was gone in the guest wing: Saffron's. "Her with other men," he said finally.

"Like Martin?"

"I can't even say his name—it makes me crazy. I can't get it out of my mind."

As if ashamed at having said too much, he said nothing as they crossed the last of the lawn, and then they were in the house, where they quietly climbed the stairs. He stopped outside her room and whispered, "I guess I can't come in?"

"No," she said.

He nodded as if he hadn't expected anything different, and went into his own room.

Abby sat down at the little desk to change the names. She was acutely embarrassed that she hadn't changed them yet. It had seemed pointless to stew over names when she might have to throw the whole thing away. But now it seemed important to change them, to keep the book and its invented but controllable plot distinct from the real and chaotic world.

30

CLARISSA FOUND IT impossible to break up with Del, and she thought this was the real problem with lesbianism. With a man, you might be friends eventually, but when you stopped sleeping together, there was a break. With a woman, how could it end? You were friends, you were best friends—you had confidences and other friends in common. Even if you stopped sleeping together, it could go on forever like that.

In the grocery store, in the dairy aisle, she got half-and-half for her own coffee, and two-percent for Del. Rounding the corner toward the produce, she found herself facing a handsome man with graying black hair. He stared at her.

"Clarissa Santerre?" he said.

She frowned.

"I'm Greg Haines, I was friends with Jimmy Vaughan. At Hermosa High. You went to Sacred Heart."

"Hi," Clarissa said. She didn't remember a Greg. And he looked so old.

He said, "You look exactly like you did then."

She laughed, a little bitterly, but pleased.

"I remember you so well," he said. "I was really jealous of Jimmy.

I wasn't very popular, at Hermosa, and no girl like you ever talked to me there."

"We didn't have any boys, at Sacred Heart," Clarissa reminded him. "We were happy to meet anyone."

"No, but it was just *in* you," he said. "To be warm and good."

"You were friends with Jimmy Vaughan?"

"It's okay if you don't remember me."

"I'm sorry," she said.

"What are you up to?"

"Oh," Clarissa said. "A lot of different things."

Greg picked up a tomato, weighed it in his hand. "Look, this is weird," he said, "but do you want to have dinner?"

"I can't. I have plans." The last thing she wanted to do was have dinner with a past she didn't remember.

"Take my card," he said. "I just moved here on a job. Call if you feel like it. It's okay if you don't."

"Thank you," she said, and she took the card. She couldn't get over how old he looked. She was desperate to see a mirror, even the polished chrome around the dairy case, to see if she looked that old, too.

That night—having studied her face for a while in the bathroom, inspecting the crow's-feet around her eyes—she had a shockingly explicit dream about having sex with Greg Haines in a Chinese restaurant. She didn't even like Chinese food. She woke up from the dream in a sweat, and was surprised to see Del sleeping beside her.

31

ABBY WENT TO THE helipad at Josephine's estancia to meet Fauchet when he arrived in the afternoon. He was a tall Frenchman with graying hair and a dark tan, who ducked as the helicopter rose again in a rush of air. He had two small bags. He shook Abby's hand, and they walked along the path toward the house.

"Horrible machines," he said. "I take a little pill." He spoke English as if he had learned it in London in a hurry. "A marvelous invention, this pill."

"You could take the car instead," Abby said.

"I need two pills for that." He eyed her. "Why are you in this crazy house?"

"My uncle is engaged to Saffron."

He seemed thrown. "Is she *here*?"

"They're both here."

"Well," Fauchet said. "Your uncle is a fool. But she's lovely to look at, yes?"

Abby shrugged.

"Women will never say it, to a man," he said, "but they understand a charming girl better than men do. They know how to analyze all the points."

"Maybe," Abby said. "She's in a bad mood. Josephine is forgetting a lot."

"I see," he said and seemed distracted. "I have thought about the man Saffron would marry," he said. "He must be a Rubirosa, your uncle—a talented lover?"

"I don't know how I would know that."

"Of course not," he said.

They were nearing the house, by the back, where the kennel was, and the two blond Labs barked happily at them. Abby lifted the latch and let the dogs come leaping out. The little boy, on the back patio with Magdalena, squealed when he saw them.

"Dogs!" he cried.

"Yes," Abby said. "Dogs."

"He learns English," Fauchet said. "Splendid."

"I don't know why he can't stay here and speak Spanish."

"No one should stay in this country," he said. "All the gifts in the world, the most beautiful land, owned by murderers and thieves. Argentina is like a beautiful woman who becomes a fascist's whore." He kissed the maid hello and said to the boy, *"Viens, mon petit."*

The boy held up his arms, and the graying Frenchman scooped him up. Magdalena went inside with the bags.

"Bonjour," the Frenchman said to the child. *"Comment vas-tu?"*

"Très bien," the little boy said.

"Tu as une nouvelle amie americaine?" Fauchet asked.

"Oui," the little boy said.

Abby said, "No one told me he spoke French."

"Mais tu parles très bien, n'est-ce pas, mon cher?" Fauchet asked the boy.

The boy nodded shyly.

"We've been naming things," Abby said. "He never once gave the French word for something."

"He's very intelligent. He knows what to speak to whom."

"What do you call him? Everyone here calls him something different."

"I call him *le petit*. It saves trouble."

Magdalena came back to say that Monsieur Fauchet's room was ready, and she led the new visitor away.

At dinner, with Fauchet beside her, Josephine seemed buoyant and happy. She wore more makeup than usual, and a narrow white ribbon in her hair. Saffron had kissed Fauchet on both cheeks, but he didn't pay her too much attention in front of her mother. The table was set in green and white, and there was cold cucumber soup, but Josephine barely noticed the food. She seemed to ring the little bell by her plate whenever she felt like it; the soup bowls stayed a long time while she talked about the terrible situation in Romania, and the meat course was taken away before anyone was half finished. Hector the butler seemed unsettled.

When Josephine's monologue flagged, Monsieur Fauchet said, in the silence, "Miss Collins was surprised to learn that *le petit* speaks French."

Saffron said, "He does?"

Josephine stared at Fauchet as if she were thinking very hard about the question, but it had startled her for a moment.

"Yes, of course," Fauchet said. "I speak with him. He does very well."

"Mother, why didn't you tell me?" Saffron asked. "I speak French."

"I forgot," Josephine said, flustered.

"That he speaks French?"

"No!" her mother said. "I forgot that *you* speak French. So you see, I didn't think it would matter."

"But you speak it, too," Saffron said. "You could talk to him."

"We speak Spanish together," Josephine snapped. "My Spanish is just fine."

"But French is your first language."

"Shut *up*, Saffron!" her mother said, in a shrill, high voice. It was the first time Abby had heard her say anyone's first name. They fell silent as Hector brought orange soufflés.

"O-kay," Saffron said softly, when he left.

"I knew he spoke French," her mother insisted. "I just—forget, sometimes."

There was a long pause, and then Fauchet said, "What a beautiful soufflé. You have the most brilliant chef, Josephine."

"I discovered him when he was only a *rôtisseur*," Josephine said, out of habit. She had said it at every meal so far. "I taught him how to cook."

Saffron said, "Don't you dare touch that bell before we're finished."

"I *never* ring it to finish," Josephine said. Then she sat chastened at the head of the table, looking diminished and sad. Even the white bow in her hair looked wilted. She had let her bright, defensive expression go and looked ten years older.

After they all left the table, Fauchet walked Josephine up to her room. Saffron and Jamie went to play backgammon in the guest wing, and Abby sat outside, to avoid being drawn into the game. Fauchet stayed in Josephine's room for a long time, and then he came out onto the dark patio.

"Ah, hello," he said. "I was coming to smoke. Should I go somewhere else?"

Abby shook her head, and he sat in a wrought-iron chair, a little distance away, and lit a narrow cigar.

"Where do you come from?" he asked.

"California." The smoke drifting over smelled sweet.

"I love California," he said. "I was there as a boy, during the war. My mother knew some Americans in the movies, and she took me to Los Angeles, to get out of France." He smiled, a little sadly. "I fell in love with Rita Hayworth, and I wouldn't eat for weeks. I was so enraged at being only fourteen, and meeting such a woman."

"I'm sorry."

He shrugged. "It got better. It's strange now, Los Angeles. You live there?"

"My grandparents do. I grew up north of San Francisco."

"You're very close to this uncle, James."

"Why do you say that?"

"Please, my dear. I have lived a long time."

"Yes," Abby said. "I am."

"He is not the match for Saffron, you know."

Abby said nothing.

"She was an immensely spoiled and beautiful little girl. With the adored father who is never there. So there is never enough for her, and she has learned to get more. This charm has the desired effect. Men go to her, but one thinks—this will be a problem."

"I think Jamie knows it's a problem."

"But he is engaged still?"

"I guess."

Fauchet smoked his cigar and looked out at the dark lawn. "I knew Josephine when she was twenty-three in St. Jean," he said. "You should have seen her then. More beautiful than her daughter. She was charming and happy, great fun. I used to take her up in a plane. Everyone wanted to take her up in a plane. There was a whole family of Brazilian playboy brothers, they were all in love with her, they would wait in line to take her up in the air."

"Where does the money come from?"

He laughed. "The great question. The father was in the shipping. He was not principled, I think, but very rich."

"Was Josephine the only child?"

Fauchet nodded. "Little Magdalena the maid is a good friend of mine. She says you write in your room."

Abby flushed.

"Is it a book?"

"I don't know."

"You have things here for it," he said. "Already you have the Brazilian playboys and the swindler's daughter."

"Thank you."

"This is not the kind of book you're writing?"

"I don't think so."

"You can keep the playboys," he said. "For the next one. Also the boy starving himself for Rita Hayworth."

"Okay."

"*Bon,*" he said, putting out his little cigar. "I will think of more."

32

Every time Saffron forgot where she'd hung her swimsuit, or transposed a French word for an English one, she had a shock of fear that she, too, was losing her mind. The fear made her irrational and anxious, which convinced her even further that she was becoming her mother.

The fact that Jamie wouldn't sleep with her made it worse. He was just trying to prove he could resist, but it made Saffron feel at once old and ugly, and that her youth and beauty were being wasted. That morning, Fauchet had caught her alone and said this was a nice young man, amusing, but not the one for her. He said the affair of the heart is like tennis. You should not play with someone so far below your ability; it will frustrate you both and make your game worse. Saffron had laughed. But she couldn't stand sleeping alone.

She went to Jamie's room and said, "I want to have a baby."

Jamie looked up at her. He was lying across his bed reading her mother's copy of *W*. "You're kidding me," he said.

"Why are you reading that?"

"To see if you were in the gossip pages."

"For what? Going to visit my crazy mother? They announced

my going to Stanford and then they lost interest. I was sleeping with boys without titles."

"Nasty habit."

"Hard to kick."

He closed the magazine. "What do you mean you want to have a kid?"

"I do," she said, and she sat on his bed. "I could start losing my memory soon. I'm twenty-eight. If I got pregnant now, I'd be forty-nine when the kid was twenty. I think my mother's problems started when she was younger than that. I don't want to go crazy when my kids are still in college."

"That's a lot of hypotheticals," Jamie said. "*If* you had a kid, *if* you lost your memory, *if* your kids could get into college . . ."

"This isn't funny."

"You already have a kid," Jamie said. "Someone will have to take T.J. eventually."

Saffron made a face. "I don't want *that* kid."

"Yours will be better?"

"It'll be mine. Why don't you want to sleep with me?"

Jamie stared at her, and then he started to laugh. "Is that what this kid thing is about?"

She thought about that. Did she really want a baby, or did she just want Jamie to stop acting like she was unfuckable?

"I don't know," she said.

"Are you still taking pills?"

"Yes."

"Come here."

He pushed the magazine off the bed, and she lay facing him. He pushed her hair from her face, and she tilted her cheek into his hand.

"Sweetheart," he said. "I'm afraid of you."

"Don't be."

His hands were cool on her skin. "If I do this," he said, "you'll start cheating again. You can't be with one person."

"That's not true."

"It is," he said. He untied the knot in the pireo at her hip and unwrapped a layer of it. She lifted her hip to let him pull the cloth free. "You need two men paying attention to you, so you can play them off each other. It must have to do with your parents."

"That isn't sexy," she said. "And it isn't true."

"Yes, it is."

"Even if it were," she said, impatiently, "there's no one here to cheat with. There's Fauchet and the gardener."

"And the chef."

"He's gay."

"I've seen him look at you."

Saffron got to her knees on the bed and unhooked the clasp of her bikini top, and she knew she had him. Jamie's face slackened with lust, and she felt whole again, and wanted.

When they were finished, she lay with his arm across her and thought about the ludicrous idea of her mother's old lover, or the gardener or the fey chef. None of them was a danger.

Then she remembered that Martin Russell would be stopping in Buenos Aires in a week. She thought, as she fell asleep, that she would wait a few days to tell Jamie that.

33

ONE MORNING IN Argentina, when Abby's days had started to run together, Josephine didn't come down to breakfast.

Magdalena took a tray up to her room and came back looking bloodless and inscrutable. She knelt by M. Fauchet's chair.

"*La señora se murió,*" she whispered to him.

"Oh, dear," he said. To Saffron, he said, "*Elle est morte.*"

But Saffron was already running up the stairs; it sounded like she was taking them three at a time.

At the table, they sat in silence, and then Jamie said, "Do you think I should go up?"

"In a minute," Fauchet said.

Magdalena said that Josephine had been in her bed, as if asleep. She didn't wake when the maid, noticing a strange smell in the room, set the breakfast tray by the bed, or opened the curtains, or even touched the señora's hand and felt for her pulse.

"*Pauvre* Josephine," Fauchet said. "She was such a lively girl, when she was a girl. You can go upstairs now, James."

Jamie went. Magdalena slipped away.

"Well, my dear," Fauchet said to Abby. "There are going to be some surprises now. All the money goes to the boy."

Abby heard a cry from upstairs—Saffron. But she couldn't have heard Fauchet; it must have been actual grief. Abby thought of her father's death, how it had taken her down for months and still exerted a dark pull.

"I expected Josephine would change her mind," Fauchet said. "I didn't expect she would die."

"Maybe she wanted Saffron to adopt him," Abby said.

"This may be a problem, too. We have a visitor today. Excuse me, please, I have to see some papers."

He stood with an apologetic nod, and Abby was left alone, feeling freshly robbed of her father among the abandoned coffee cups and jam jars and plates.

Josephine's doctor came from Buenos Aires in a helicopter, pronounced her officially dead, and called for a mortician's van to come and collect the body. The doctor had a wide mustache and a wrinkled gray suit. He asked for a drink, to calm his fear of helicopters and heights, and over a tumbler of scotch he warned Abby that the morticians were notoriously late. There was nothing you could do. Then he left.

Saffron and Jamie were upstairs in Josephine's room, M. Fauchet was holed up in her office, and Magdalena was on the back lawn playing with T.J., who didn't seem to understand what had happened. When a car pulled up on the white gravel driveway, too soon to be the mortician, Abby went outside to meet the visitor.

A girl in cheap sunglasses, with dark blond hair pulled back in a ponytail, stepped out. She was very slight, no more than five feet tall, and it was hard to tell how old she was, with the sunglasses covering her eyes. Her nose and chin were sharp and delicate. She wore a man's button-down shirt and jeans.

"I am so tired," the woman said, tilting her head to her shoulder. This last word had two syllables, "ti-red," and Abby couldn't identify her accent. "I am Katya," she said.

"Are you a friend of Fauchet's?"

Katya frowned. "Sometimes."

The driver took a black backpack out of the car and set it down. Without waiting for a tip, he pulled down the drive and disappeared. Abby reached for the backpack, but Katya snatched it away.

"I don't know which room you're in," Abby said, embarrassed. "We can ask Magdalena. Were you a friend of Josephine's?"

"No," Katya said sharply.

Abby realized the woman didn't know Josephine had died. In the dimness inside, still hugging the backpack, she took off her sunglasses, and she looked younger than Abby had guessed. Maybe twenty-five, maybe thirty. Her eyes were pale. Through the glass doors to the back lawn, they could see Magdalena throwing a small inflatable beach ball to T.J., and Katya seemed to stop breathing.

"This is the boy?" she whispered.

Fauchet came into the foyer, his heels sounding on the tiles, and said, "My dear Katarina. Welcome."

She turned on him. "This is the boy?"

"He is charming, no? See how happy he is." They heard laughter through the glass as he chased the ball.

"He is mine," she said.

"Miss Collins, I present Katya," Fauchet said. "She is a dear friend and a promising blackmailer."

"I am *no* blackmailer," Katya said. "He is my son. That woman knows?"

"She knew," Fauchet said. "Then she forgot. Now she is dead. You must be hungry. Come."

Katya followed Fauchet with the obedience of a child.

At the table, she ate as if expecting the food to be taken from her at any moment. She took small, guarded bites, and then glanced around looking for danger. She asked for milk and eyed Hector as he moved in and out of the room.

"Abby," Fauchet said, "perhaps Katya will like the bedroom near to yours. Will you take her there? I have many things to do."

Katya seemed about to protest, but she let Fauchet go.

Abby said, "Do you want to see your room?"

"You live here?" Katya wiped the milk from her upper lip with a green linen napkin, then folded the napkin to hide the damp mark.

"I'm just visiting." She wanted to ask about Romania, but didn't.

"How is she dead?"

"In her sleep," Abby said.

Katya looked thoughtful. "So the boy is free."

"Sort of."

"Is he rich?"

Abby hesitated. "He might be."

"Why *might*?" the woman asked, suddenly suspicious.

"I don't know," Abby said, wishing Fauchet hadn't left her.

The woman searched Abby's face, as if for signs of deception, and then sighed wearily. "Okay," she said. "I will see this room."

34

Katya lay in the deep enamel tub, in warm, sudsy water, and felt her body relax. She had not known what to expect from these people, so far from the places she understood. They could have killed her easily for causing them trouble, and driven her body out into the great empty plains she had seen from the airplane. But instead they gave her good food and a vast bed, and this bathroom that was only hers, like in a hotel. The American girl had helped her fill the bath and found a pink liquid that made bubbles. There was a thick white towel. She had taken a little pill to feel better.

In the back of her mind, through the haze of bath and pill, she was still waiting for the trick. She thought about the rats she had watched from the back stoop when she was living with the Russians. There were sometimes rats and sometimes mice, and they were both happy in the garbage, but if you hit the can with your hand, the mice would run out in a panic, not knowing where they should go.

But if it was a rat in the garbage, he went like lightning, straight back to the hole he came out of. No confusion. Rats were smart. They remembered—they were always ready, and thinking. She lay like this in her bath, ready to bolt if a hand came to pound on the door, wanting her out.

But half an hour went by, and the knock didn't come. She washed her hair, slowly. No one shook the doorknob, or banged on the door, or shouted. The water grew cool. It occurred to her that she could run more hot water into the tub, but they might hear it in the pipes and be angry at her greediness. She turned the hot water on, just a trickle, and listened for the sound in the walls. But this wasn't a hotel, and it was better to be careful. She turned it back off and climbed out into the enormous towel that swallowed her up. There was nothing extra to her body; it was small and lean, the breasts just enough to have them. She didn't look in the mirror as she dried herself; she knew it well enough.

She dried her hair with the towel and combed it through with her fingers, then unlocked the bathroom door, cautiously. No one was waiting for her in the bedroom, but her backpack had been opened and her clothes hung in the closet. She felt a rush of rage. The old aspirin bottle with her pills had been with her in the bathroom, but her underclothes were neatly folded on a little shelf. The dirty clothes were missing.

It was her own fault; she hadn't heard anyone come in, and she reproached herself for that. The doors were heavier than she had thought. A dark blue fig and a bunch of purple grapes had been left on a small plate on the desk, with a linen napkin and a bottle of mineral water.

There had been mineral water in the limousine, too, and the driver had shown her with signs that it was for her. He had been kind. She had almost fallen asleep, moving over the rough road in the big quiet purring machine, thinking about the East German cars in her childhood in Hungary, cars like cardboard boxes, with engines so simple that people fixed them with pieces of string.

She ate four of the grapes quickly, spitting the seeds on the plate, while she inspected her things. They had taken only the laundry.

Then she remembered the child. It was she who wanted something from them. The bath and the pill had made her a little dopey. She was not in her own territory anymore, not playing a game she was used to. The child wasn't the tiny baby but a running, laughing boy she didn't know. And then the solitude in her room was so unexpectedly sweet that she couldn't think of doing anything to interrupt it. After locking the bedroom door, she took off the towel and climbed naked into the bed. She lay back against the piles of pillows, sliding against the soft cotton, and watched the warm afternoon light through the window turn slowly to blue.

35

THE MORTICIAN IN THE van finally arrived with two assistants in dark suits, with solemn apologies to Saffron for his lateness and some talk about God. She found herself hovering near them as they collected her mother, then following them to the van. She thought she might climb in and ride with her mother over the bad roads to Buenos Aires. She was shocked at the force of her own grief. Finally she let the assistants close the heavy doors and watched the van roll down the gravel driveway.

She knew that another guest had arrived and thought it was just like Josephine to invite people without telling anyone. But as soon as she felt the old irritation, she was overcome with guilt because her mother was dead. Standing in the foyer, weak and exhausted, she heard Fauchet asking if she wanted some food. He said it had been many hours since she had eaten.

"Don't you have to read the will now?" she asked him.

"I've sent for the lawyer."

"What's in it?"

"I think we all should recover from this terrible shock."

Saffron considered him. He had known her all her life. He had bought her presents, told her secrets. At about ten, disillusioned by her father, she had thought Fauchet was the kind of man a girl ought to marry. Lately, though, he had seemed preoccupied and firmly in her mother's camp, for which she couldn't forgive him.

"She cut me out of it, didn't she?" she asked.

"I think we should wait to have this discussion," Fauchet said.

"Did you *help* her do it?"

"Of course not," he said.

"Why didn't you stop it?"

"I had no idea."

Saffron wanted to slap the old man's face. Instead she climbed the stairs, in a fury, to her mother's room. She couldn't believe her mother would actually disinherit her. When she was a little girl she had played with her mother's jeweled rings, and her mother had told her that someday they would be hers. There were also five or six crucifixes on chains, which Saffron coveted: a turquoise one, a silver one, one with diamonds, one with multicolored stones. When Saffron, at twelve, decided not to have a First Communion, her mother had made a point of telling her she couldn't have the crucifixes.

"When I die, they'll go to your cousin Nell," her mother had said.

"Why to her?" Her cousin was a dull, freckled girl with mouse-colored hair.

"You aren't Catholic," her mother had said. "What would you do with them?"

But Josephine wasn't religious. Catholicism was only one of her pretentious habits. She believed in earthly punishments and earthly rewards.

Now Saffron looked around her mother's empty bedroom. The whiteness of it had always annoyed her, as a symptom of her mother's insistence on innocence and purity. She pulled open the drawer in the center of the delicate white desk. Inside was a stack of her mother's ivory stationery, engraved with Josephine's initials. Each page had a letter begun on it.

"Esteemed Gautier," the first one opened, to the chef, in French.

Magdalena has delusions of grandeurs, she is stealing my earrings. This must stop. She wishes to take my place in the house. How can you help me.

Then the letter ended, unfinished.

"My dearest," the next one began, and Saffron wondered if it was to her, then realized that "my dearest" was Fauchet.

I have had to let the butler go, he tried to stab the chef with a fruit knife. They are both gays you know. I have found a new man named Hector, I believe he is a cousin of your favorite Magdalena, who is too pretty for her own good and can sometimes be quite a little bitch. But I cannot get by alone. This Hector is handsome, like his pretty cousin. When are you coming again? I miss you so.

"*Querida Magdalena,*" another began.

Creo que Gautier trata que envenenarme. Favor de observarlo con mucho cuidado. No quiero morir. Dependo totalmente de te.

Saffron wasn't sure what *envenenar* meant, but she guessed poison. "I believe Gautier is trying to poison me." There were more, all abandoned after half a page or a few lines, all dated within the last year. Saffron shuffled through them until she found her own name.

My dear Saffron,

Last night the bandits killed one of my cows at the western frontier of the estancia, took the best meat, and left the body to rot. The poor need to eat, I know this, but I begin to be afraid, living here alone.

I believe the servants may conspire against me. They have let the bandits come. They have told them I am a defenceless woman. I'm afraid to write this, so afraid they may find this letter and know that I know. I worry so much.

Saffron tapped the letters until the stack was straight. She could use them to show her mother's incompetence at the time of the will. She needed to think, before the boy got all the money. They didn't trust her to take care of him, so they'd given him everything. She didn't believe that Fauchet wasn't in on it.

She tucked the letters into the back of her skirt, but her shirt didn't cover them. So she went to her mother's vast closet, which was as big as the bedroom itself. The dressing-table drawers were full of costume jewelry and scarves, and some photographs of a young Josephine lounging by swimming pools with handsome Italian counts. Saffron looked around the closet at the rows of gowns, dresses, coats, blouses, trousers, suits.

When she went downstairs in Josephine's pink housecoat, Fauchet was sitting in a chair by the window, tapping a small, unlit cigar against the chair's arm. She guessed he was waiting for her, and she felt the stiff paper of the letters against her skin. He didn't ask what she had been doing.

"I was looking at my mother's clothes," she said. She could feel her heart pound.

"The cook left something for you, in the kitchen."

"I'm not hungry."

"I knew your mother since a very long time," he said. "I care about you like a daughter."

She stood glaring at him. If he had cared, he wouldn't have let this happen. He would have watched out for her. No one had watched out for her in any real way.

"Will you sit?" he asked. "Shall we talk?"

"I don't feel like talking," she said.

"I think it's important."

"Leave me alone," she said, and she kept walking to the guest wing and up the stairs to her room.

36

Fauchet watched Saffron go—she looked a great deal like her mother once had, in the half-light, especially in the old-fashioned housecoat—and then he lit his cigar. Of other people Josephine said it was a filthy habit, the habit of pigs, but to him she gave permission.

When they both were young, the air had always been a haze of smoke. She was so lovely then. She could arrive in a city and be sleeping with the most powerful man in it within a week. With women she was not so popular, but that was never her goal.

And then she had, out of sheer perversity, married a strong-minded Irish banker who was unfaithful but would brook no infidelity from her. Bets had been taken on how long the marriage might last. The winner, many years later, had been a little Spanish diplomat who loved her dearly. He had chosen thirteen years and six months, years longer than anyone else, in bitter hope that he would be wrong. He was right almost to the day. The money was collected, and a ceremony was made of delivering the bundle to the disappointed lover. The Spaniard was married by then, to a sensible woman, the father of two sturdy, intelligent children. He took the money with a rueful smile.

And then came Saffron. Fate, with its sense of humor, had given Josephine a daughter: a son she might have charmed, a daughter never.

Fauchet had, since that time, had two wives, who had become great friends with each other. They had much in common. The first became the godmother to the children of the second. This shocked only Americans; it was a reasonable arrangement. After he married, he had fewer affairs, because it was too difficult to maintain secrecy and discretion—the effort itself was diverting, but you began to have diminishing returns.

In the recent period, when there had been so few women that he could give each one his full attention, Katya, his little Magyar, had come along. She intrigued him because she was unbroken by her life: she had a will of light, flexible steel. She came from the plains of central Hungary, where her grandfather had been shot by the Germans, and her father jailed by the Communists. Her mother had died of pneumonia when Katya was a child. The little girl wound up with a sickly aunt, then with some Russians who used her for profit. The Russians had eventually brought her to Paris.

Fauchet had known other whores: the brusque, businesslike ones and the childlike, drugged, love-hungry ones who vibrated with need and couldn't be trusted. In both, something seemed to have snapped: some connection severed between the brain and the body. There were other kinds, too—the occasional bitter, witty girl—but none he had met was like Katya. She seemed to have retreated into herself and kept the connections intact, so that she might, when times were better, come out again. She had a quick mind and the sly, gypsy look of her people.

She had been the lover of his friend Gilbert, who found her in a Paris brothel and paid some money for her release. At the time, Fauchet thought his friend had lost his mind. Gilbert put the girl in a cheap hotel he paid for by the month, where she grew restless and bored. She walked the city alone, and Gilbert suffered untold agonies, thinking of what she might do.

Then Gilbert's wife discovered the girl. She must have sensed his level of attachment, because she threatened to take the children and everything he had. Gilbert wept, telling a dry-eyed Katya the choice he had to make. She didn't want to go back to the brothel, so she appealed to Fauchet, who had met her when Gilbert was showing her off.

Fauchet said she could stay a few weeks in the apartment in the septième that he kept from his bachelor days. There was a café on the corner, and he brought her pastries, which she ate as if someone might steal the crumbs away. They became friends. When they became lovers, she confessed that she carried a baby from Gilbert. Fauchet had noticed the tiny belly but thought she was only growing fat on the croissants and napoleons. He wondered where his old shrewdness had gone.

She would not have an abortion—an earlier one had led to septicemia, and a doctor had warned her there might be damage already from the others. And she didn't want to tell Gilbert. The question of Fauchet caring for the baby was absurd: an unasked question that he did not have to answer. So the belly grew, and Katya talked to it and sang to it, and moved around the little apartment like a diligent housewife, cleaning and arranging and airing, and waiting for Fauchet to come. She was so cheerful, and so sweet and warm in his old bachelor's bed, that for a while he didn't worry.

But gradually, as the months passed and her tiny body grew, it became clear that what she wanted was to keep on as they were, a little family in Fauchet's spare apartment. He knew this would not work, not with a crying baby; they would be found out. His wife sometimes put guests in the apartment; it was incredible that they had been able to use it so long.

When he finally told Katya that they could not go on as they were, she seemed to collapse, as if all the strain masked by months of cheerfulness came over her at once. She was nearly eight months pregnant, and she became ill, and lay in the bed with a fever and chills. She begged him to take the baby if she died, and then she begged him to take the baby either way. She wasn't fit to be a mother, she said; the baby would be better off without her. It was hard to tell what was delirium from fever and what was hysterical unhappiness. She refused to go to the hospital, and he was afraid to force her, afraid she would scream and lose her mind. She was sure she would die in the way she had watched her mother die, and she did not want to leave a child alone.

A few nights later, when the fever was gone, they talked seriously of the possibilities. Fauchet could give her some money. Gilbert might give her some, if he were told, but he already had trouble from his wife. Katya could put the baby up for adoption, but she had seen babies taken and sold, and sold again. Fauchet tried to tell her that it was different in France, but she held firm: no adoption unless they knew where the child was going.

At about that time Josephine Flynn in Argentina had decided she wanted a Romanian orphan, and she began hounding Fauchet to help her track down a princess she had met once at a charity ball. The princess was an abbess now, busy with causes and difficult to reach. The idea that there were government agencies that regulated adoption had never entered Josephine's mind.

It was not, he told himself, such a foolish decision as it later seemed. Josephine wasn't young, but she wasn't so ancient. She could afford a staff to take care of the child. He had an unwanted baby, and he knew a woman who wanted one: he had been a businessman his whole life, and here he had a supply and a demand.

He put the solution to Katya, telling her that Josephine had a big house with a vast lawn, and horses and dogs, and kind and faithful people to help her. He had a friend at the Argentine embassy who could finesse the paperwork.

Katya spent a few days thinking about it, and one morning— recovered from her illness, eating an almond croissant he had brought from the café—she agreed.

She gave birth to the baby in a busy hospital and nursed him for three months. He was the image of Gilbert, there was no question. The idea was to wait until he was old enough to travel, and to be sure she didn't want him, but things became more difficult. Katya was tired, and ill-equipped to take care of a child. They fought constantly.

She would ask Fauchet to stay the night, and he would remind her that he was married with children of his own. She would cry, and he would tell her to take it up with Gilbert. She would refuse; he would say there was always the Bureau des Adoptions—many Parisian couples who would never sell a child waited eagerly in nice apartments. Then Katya would swear in every language she knew. She did not want her child raised by those Parisian snobs, who looked down on her. She did not want the chance of meeting her son in the street, and having him look at her with open scorn.

The baby would wake, and Katya would comfort him in a distracted way, and then she would ask Fauchet to tell her again about the lawn and the horses and the dogs and his trustworthy friend, far away, and she would beg him to take the baby there.

His friend at the Argentine embassy told him it was very complicated. He could be prosecuted for baby trafficking if he was discovered.

"But it will be better for everyone, this way," Fauchet said. "For the child, who will have the best life. And for the father, who will not be exposed. And for his family, his children."

The man gave in and drew up an immigration visa for an orphaned Romanian child, out of old friendship. "I know nothing," he said, finalizing the papers. "You understand? I know nothing of your plans. Send me no gifts, no wine, no cigars, tell me nothing more."

Then Fauchet gave Katya another chance, asking if this was really what she wanted. She was dry-eyed and said yes. So he took the baby to Argentina, under the smiles of pretty stewardesses, and presented it to Josephine. He was apprehensive about the consequences but could see no better way, now that he was so far in. He interviewed Magdalena, the new maid, about her experience with infants. He tried to be thorough.

Four years went by, while Fauchet lived with a pocket of dread in the back of his mind, reading with mild nausea any newspaper story about illegal adoptions, and reassuring himself that these were rings, profiteers, traffickers who did not have his good intentions.

Trouble finally came not from the police but from Katya, who reappeared wanting the boy back. She could not sleep from the grief; she had made a terrible mistake. Fauchet tried to talk her down, but she was inconsolable, unstoppable—she came to his office, waited outside his club, called his house although he told her to stop. She had been working in a café, making the coffees and sweeping the floor, and she had saved a little money. A sentimental man had moved to the south and given her the use of a small apartment. She was on her feet and straight now, and she wanted the baby back.

Fauchet explained that the boy was not a baby anymore. It was not possible just to change your mind and remove a child from the home where he had grown up.

"We tell them it was not legal," Katya said. "We tell them the Romanian stole the child."

"But she didn't!" Fauchet said. "There's no Romanian. You gave the child away."

"What does he look like?" she asked, holding his wrist. She asked him this question every time. "I just want to see him."

"Just to see him, and then you will be satisfied? Oh, Katya, you know this is not true."

But again, maybe this was a case of supply and demand: in the past four years, Josephine's mind had deteriorated rapidly. There was a question now of who would take the child. Magdalena was good to him, but she wanted to marry and have children of her own. Saffron was a self-involved, delinquent debutante, threatened by the existence of the child and no more suited to motherhood than the little retired prostitute. Katya had rehabilitated herself, through great effort, he could see that. In a reckless moment, under threats from his wife about the constant phone calls—in some of the calls Katya alluded to Russian *friends* who would help her if he didn't— Fauchet thought it might not hurt to have Katya lay claim to the child. Josephine might even be relieved to have a place for the boy to go. He set off to Argentina to facilitate another transfer, if he could.

But when he got to the estancia, Saffron was there with the Americans, who would never understand, and Josephine had forgotten that he had found a good home for the boy. She announced proudly, when Fauchet arrived in her bedroom the first afternoon, that she was leaving the child everything, and that Saffron would be his guardian. She had seen some Argentine lawyer, who had done up the papers. Before Fauchet could straighten out the situation, she was dead. It was no longer a simple transaction, to return the boy to Katya. It was a horrible legal difficulty. Saffron would uncover everything, and there was no knowing what she might do. He felt he had boarded a very fast train, the wrong train, and now it was impossible to climb off.

Fauchet put out his cigar and eased himself out of his chair at the base of the stairs. He went to his room and undressed, concentrating on the buttons and laces so that his mind wouldn't spin on the question of the child. Naked, he climbed under the thick, soft sheets. He had kept his leanness without the foolish exercise people did now, and had no great trouble with his joints. All this running and jumping, and drinking too much water to flood the kidneys—eventually these people would collapse in a heap.

In bed, supported by the good mattress, he felt that his body had not fully betrayed him. He could almost imagine it to be the body of his youth. He ran a hand over his belly, distracting himself with solipsistic thoughts. The skin was looser, that was true. He remembered the first time, as a young man, that he had slept with an older woman, and noticed that her skin was different, looser and thinner than his. And he remembered the day, many years later, when he realized that he had undergone the same transformation. Suddenly he had the skin of an older man.

There was a knock at the door, and he thought it might be Josephine, before he remembered that she was dead.

Then he thought it could be Saffron, coming to have the conversation he had proposed.

Then he thought it was more likely to be Katya, venting her anguish at seeing her child as a stranger speaking a strange language—wanting to cry and pound his chest about what they had done.

The door opened before he had a chance to react to any of these possibilities, and pretty Magdalena slipped inside, her white night-gown dimly glowing and her black hair invisible in the dark. He felt himself breathe with relief. Sweet Magdalena.

"*¿Puedo entrar?*" she asked.

"*Sí,*" he said.

She closed the door and stepped lightly, barefoot, to the bed, where she pulled the nightgown off over her head. He could just see the shadows outlining her round breasts, the dark nipples, the black triangle. She folded her nightgown expertly, unable to break the habit of folding things, and climbed into the bed beside him. Her skin was warm and taut and young.

"Sweet girl," he said.

Her breathing was quick, which he mistook for arousal. She said, "I am thinking about what will happen," and he realized why she had come.

He waited.

"Everyone will go?" she said. "The house, too?"

"Yes," he said. "But there's money for everyone."

She shook her head. "You will protect the boy?"

"I can try," he said.

"Saffron will never love him."

"I know."

"I understand he has to go, but not to her," she said.

"I'll do my best."

"You have to."

"I will."

She sighed with relief, and wriggled close to him in the warm bed.

37

THE ARGENTINE LAWYER who had drawn up Josephine's will was coming to the house, and Jamie had promised Saffron he would go to the meeting about it at breakfast. He asked Abby to come, so he would have someone to talk to afterward.

"Talk to Saffron," Abby said.

"She's not in any shape to be objective."

"Have you told her that Katya's the mother?"

"Do I look that stupid? She'll go nuts."

"Why should she?" Abby asked. "She doesn't care about the kid."

"She will when she finds out he gets her inheritance."

The lawyer was sitting at the breakfast table in a black suit with a briefcase on his lap, looking uncomfortable. He was thin with a wide, high forehead, and he spoke only Spanish. Fauchet had a copy of the will in front of him. Everyone drifted in, or was sent for. Saffron was there in a bathrobe, wild-eyed and sleepless. Magdalena sat at the table, looking uncomfortable to be among the guests, with T.J. on her lap. Hector the butler stood against the wall, and Gautier was there in his apron, looking like he had more important things to attend to, like poached eggs. Then Katya came in, looking jet-lagged and uncomfortable with the idea of morning. There were dark circles under her eyes, and her face looked more drawn than it had the day before.

"Wait, why is she here?" Saffron asked. "This is private business. Who *are* you?"

"I am Katya," the girl said defiantly.

Saffron looked to Fauchet for help.

"I tried to talk to you," Fauchet said.

"About what?"

"About Katya."

"So talk."

Fauchet sighed and looked at the two women, and then at the will on the table. He said nothing.

"I am the mother to this boy," Katya told Saffron.

"Bullshit," Saffron said.

"I am," Katya said simply.

"He doesn't look anything like you. He's a Romanian orphan."

"He is not Romanian," Katya said, indignantly. "What proof he is Romanian?"

"That's where he came from!"

"He came from *me*," Katya said. "I was in Paris, very sick, I could not care for him. But I did not want to give him."

"There was the princess."

"There is no princess."

Saffron looked to Fauchet. "What do you know about this?"

He shrugged. "I tried to tell you."

Saffron turned on Katya again. "So are you going to describe his strange birthmarks?"

"He has no birthmarks," Katya said proudly.

Saffron looked to Magdalena, who nodded that this was true.

"Oh, my God," Saffron said, sitting back in her chair. "Why am I surprised? This is so like my mother. So what do you want?" she asked Katya. "Money? You can't just show up and take him. An adoption is an adoption."

Katya flushed with anger, and Jamie noticed how beautiful she was, with the color suddenly in her face. The lawyer from Buenos

Aires looked like he wished he were somewhere else. Fauchet asked if he could start explaining the will. Everyone settled into an uneasy silence. Jamie was glad the boy couldn't follow English enough to understand.

Fauchet started with the servants, who would all receive pensions. Gautier would get a little more. When his part was finished, he disappeared back to the kitchen. Hector slipped out and followed him, and Magdalena, trapped with T.J. on her lap, watched them go longingly.

The house, Fauchet said, was Saffron's to live in if she wanted, while the child was still a minor, but if it was sold—

Saffron laughed bitterly and said, "To what sucker?"

—Saffron would split the money from the sale with *le petit*.

"Jesus," she said.

The house, Fauchet explained, was the one thing Josephine hadn't been able to wrest from beneath Argentine inheritance law. It would go to the surviving children equally. Everything else that mattered she had moved to Swiss bank accounts, and she had left it all in trust to the adopted boy. Saffron had been appointed as his guardian, but was given no control over the money.

Saffron stared at Fauchet. "You're kidding me."

"I wish it were so," he said.

"My mother told me the adoption wasn't legal," she said. "She was worried that the kid would get screwed under Argentine law, and that I had to make sure he was taken care of. And all the time she had *this*?"

"This will is very recent."

"She *lied* to me."

"Or she was confused," Fauchet said. "She may have forgotten."

"My son receives this house?" Katya asked.

"*Half* this house, on the assumption that he's *not* your son, he was *Josephine's* son," Saffron said nastily. "If he's *your* son, then under Argentine law he gets *your* house when *you* die."

"Saffron, my dear," the old Frenchman said. "This is ugly."

"But it's true, right? Let's let her have him, and then he doesn't have rights to anything."

"Saffron."

"Stop saying that!"

"This is a difficult time," Fauchet explained to Katya.

Katya looked around at the group at Josephine's table. Then she said, "This woman is old, yes? She dies in comfortable bed."

"She was my *mother*!" Saffron said. "And she wasn't that old!"

Katya gazed calmly at Saffron. "My mother is dead when I am eight years, of a terrible sickness," she said. "My father is dead, too. I live with many people until one bad family sells me to some Russians, and *this* is difficult time. Three babies they were giving me the bad abortion. In Paris the doctor says maybe I cannot have more. So this time, I consider to keep him, and then I am sick and so confused, and cannot."

The table was silent.

"*This* is difficult time," Katya said.

"Oh, Jesus," Saffron said, and she put her face in her hands.

Katya said, "I consider he is mine."

38

YOU COULD WRITE a murder mystery," Jamie said.

"That's what Katya's story made you think?"

"That's what the whole thing made me think."

He was lying across Abby's bed, and she was sitting in the little desk chair. The breakfast meeting had ended unfinished. Saffron was talking to Fauchet in his room.

"Rich woman dies mysteriously in remote house full of potential heirs," Jamie said. "They all have to figure out who did it without getting killed for knowing."

"That's been written a thousand times."

"But not set in Argentina," he said. "And yours will have sex in it, and people speaking different languages, and the weird adoption plot."

"Poor Katya," Abby said. "To survive the Russians and then have to face off with Saffron."

"She can take Saffron," Jamie said. "She won the breakfast round. She was good, wasn't she?"

"Do you think she's the mother?"

"Sure," he said. "Here's a question for your mystery. Could Katya have done it even though she didn't arrive until after the murder?"

"I'm not writing a mystery."

"Her late arrival could be an alibi. Maybe she's been hiding in the pampas with an evil gaucho. Can my character solve the mystery?"

Abby shook her head.

"Can I be the romantic hero?"

"You're not being very serious."

"I was serious all yesterday, and all this morning," he said. "I'm tired of seriousness. What *are* you writing? Can I read it?"

"No."

"What's the point of writing if people can't read it?"

"You can't read it *yet*."

"You'll say that until you're ninety. If it were me writing something, I'd knock on your door every five minutes to make you read it. Tell me at least, am I in it?"

"Ja*mie*," she said.

"I am," he said. "I know I am."

After he had left, Abby thought that sleeping together was strange, but at least it was straightforward. Having done it in the past was unsettling and unstable, like walking a tightrope. At one end was the knowledge that it never should have happened, at the other the possibility it might happen again. They were balanced somewhere in the middle, feeling tremors run through the wire.

She read what was on the computer screen. The page she was on seemed plausible, but she wasn't sure about what came before, and there wasn't anything yet that came after. The niece character had slept with her uncle, and was pregnant. She didn't want Jamie reading that. She didn't want anyone reading it.

She figured the time difference to make sure Peter would be awake and called him in San Diego.

"I was wondering when you'd call," he said. "How is it?"

"The woman we're staying with, Saffron's mother, died yesterday."

"You're kidding."

"There are problems with the will. I shouldn't stay on long, but I have a favor to ask. I want to make a will, in case I get hit by a bus.

I'm going to leave my computer to you, and I want you to erase the hard drive."

There was a long pause.

"Are you okay?" he asked.

"I'm fine. It's just in case. I don't want my family reading something I haven't finished. I was going to ask Jamie, but I can't trust him. I don't think he could deal with the idea."

There was another silence.

"Maybe this is laying my cards too much on the table," Peter said, "but I don't know if I could deal with it either. I would be really—sad, if you died, and I don't think I could destroy what you'd written. I think I would want it."

"Really?"

"Really."

"I promise, it's not any good."

"I don't care," he said. "I don't want to be part of any scenario where you get hit by a bus. I want you to look both ways crossing the street."

"I will."

"If you don't, I'll publish the book as it is. I'll add a lot of bad sentences first. With bad punctuation."

"Peter, I'm serious."

"So am I," he said. There was something new in his voice.

"I'm on their phone, I should go."

"Give me the number and I'll call you back."

She read it off the phone. "Give me five minutes."

She hung up and sat thinking. The thing in his voice sounded like fear, and she wondered if he was really afraid she might die. She typed herself a note: "uncle has to deal w/ death of niece." She would give him some time to prepare—an illness, no buses. The niece in the book had a baby coming, but the baby shouldn't die. There could be a decision: to save the girl or the baby. The family gets involved. Her father would want her to live.

Henry had been on her mind all day, and she thought now about what her father would have thought of Peter: if he would have dismissed him like the others or approved. She thought he might have liked Peter's directness and his way of joking seriously, but she couldn't know for sure. The feeling of moving forward alone was strange and bracing and mixed with dread. Dr. Tirrett would say she was afraid of investing in people, if she were still seeing Dr. Tirrett.

Abby heard the door next to hers—Katya's door—slam shut, and she listened for a fight going on, but there were no more sounds. The bathwater started to run in Katya's bathroom, and then the phone on the little desk rang. Abby picked it up before anyone else could.

39

TEDDY'S EYESIGHT WAS worse, and he was even more depen-
dent on Yvette. He could still see, but he was relying on the memory of what things looked like to process what they looked like now.
He knew where his things were in the bathroom on bleary mornings:
the upright, red shape a toothbrush, the shorter, darker one a razor.

Since retiring, he had volunteered for the lay ministry at the
church: picking up the wafers from the priest and giving communion to people who couldn't get to church. But now Yvette had to
drive him on his visits. One of the old men was blind, and Teddy
thought soon he would be, too. He had seen plenty. He wanted no
extraordinary measures to keep him in this world, and eye surgery at
eighty-three was an extraordinary measure. And it was expensive;
the way he and Yvette were going, they would outlive their retire-
ment and be a burden on the children. He wasn't about to spend a
lot of money so someone could take a knife to his eyes.

"They have new ways of doing it now," Yvette said.

"So it's even more expensive."

"We have the money and we have insurance," Yvette said. "That
damn Depression was sixty years ago. I'm not letting you act like
we're still in it."

"I get around all right," he protested.

"You do not!" she said. "I have to drive you. I'm taking you to the surgeon, and if he says he can fix it, then that's it. I'm not your chauffeur anymore."

So Teddy found himself in an examination room, with a giant diagram of an eye on the wall. He knew it was an eye, he could see that. He wanted to go out to the waiting room and triumphantly say he could see things he wasn't used to seeing, just fine. But Yvette would point out that the eye on the wall was three feet tall.

The surgeon was disconcertingly young, as young as Teddy's children. He said Teddy's eyes were at just the right point, not too early and not too late, and it would be a simple procedure to remove the cataracts and give Teddy back his sight.

"Completely?" Teddy asked.

"I can't guarantee that, but I think so."

"How much does it cost?"

The young man named a figure, with no embarrassment.

"I'll have to talk to my wife," Teddy said.

"She already caught me at reception," the doctor said. "She told me not to let you balk at the price, because Medicare would cover most of it."

Teddy was indignant. "I'm not balking."

"I really think you'll be surprised at the results," the surgeon said. "Everyone is. My grandfather had it done. People don't realize how long their vision has been impaired, so having it restored is startling."

"You mean I'll see all my wife's wrinkles," Teddy said. He said it lightly, as a joke. He thought suddenly that maybe he *wanted* to see her clearly again.

The surgeon smiled. "I would guess so," he said.

The receptionist had a nice voice, and dark hair. Teddy made an appointment on a computer screen to have somebody's grandson put a sonic probe into his eyes and then suck out the lens and put in a folded-up new one, and he gave the pretty woman Yvette's e-mail address. He had begun life, he reflected, with the radio, the telegraph, and the Victrola, and had been perfectly happy with those.

He went out to the waiting room, and Yvette looked up from her magazine. He guessed that she was anxious. The doctor was right; he didn't know for how long he had been relying on an image in his head.

"Okay," he said. "You win."

40

IN THE LATE AFTERNOON, everyone from the estancia drove in two cars into Buenos Aires for the funeral. The mood was subdued, and Abby watched the ranchland go by outside the tinted window. Then they were on the freeway on the outskirts of town, with giant apartment complexes and dilapidated row houses hung with laundry, and then they were in the city, on a wide avenue canopied with trees. Outside the basilica and the cemetery there were milling tourists. Stalls sold leather bracelets and photographs of tango dancers.

Inside the church, they filed into a pew. Magdalena had been left at home; she hadn't seemed at all wistful about not driving on a bad road for the funeral of an employer who had never been particularly nice to her. The shrines on the walls of the church were ornate and gilded, and to Abby's right was a seated statue of Christ, looking gravely disappointed, with the crown of thorns on his head and his elbows on his knees in brooding thought.

A few gray-haired tourists passed through the church to visit the Franciscan cloisters, stopping to gape openly at the funeral. One of them, in snakeskin cowboy boots and a gray suit, with a turquoise ponytail holder in his white hair, slid into the pew next to Abby. "What'd I miss?" he asked, in an American accent.

"Nothing so far."

"Name's Freddie," he said, grinning to reveal two missing front teeth. "I'm Josephine's half brother. I guess from your face that they didn't tell you about me."

"No," Abby said, wondering if there would be more complications with the will. Saffron was at the other end of the pew.

"I knew Josephine on and off," Freddie said. "Our father wanted us to be friends. Saffron invited me, which surprised me a little. I'm a healer, so I can tell that my niece is very angry."

Abby nodded.

"If Saffron wasn't so resistant to me, I could heal her," he said. "I've healed people who weren't even in the same country as me, but it's easier up close." He paused, studying Abby. "Like if there was something wrong with you right now, it would be easy for me to heal you. You don't seem resistant."

"I think I'm all right."

Freddie shrugged. "Suit yourself."

"How are you the half brother?"

"Josephine's father had an affair," he said, "with my mother. I got my healing ability from her. But she was an actress and couldn't be known to have a baby out of wedlock. So I grew up with another family. But my real mother had *real* abilities, real sensitivities. I've read a lot about her. You've heard of Jean Harlow?"

"Yes," Abby said.

"No one knows this," he said. "They said she was on salary strike from MGM in 1934, but she was pregnant with me. It would have been a great scandal. I know she felt terrible about leaving me with that other family. But it wasn't her fault, she was trapped by her circumstances. She had kidney disease, you know, so having me was probably what killed her so young."

"I'm sorry," Abby said.

"You're not sure if I'm telling the truth," he said, watching her. "I did a lot of drugs in the sixties, that damaged my mind. I had to go into the hospital a few times. But I know a few things."

"Okay," Abby said.

"I'm much better now. My father helped me out when he was alive, and he told Josephine she had a brother. So when I had to ask Josephine for help a few times, she came through. A good deed in a naughty world. I don't know how I'll fare under Saffron. She's a tough one."

The choir had taken their places, and now they started to sing. Freddie stopped talking and watched the singers with interest.

From the other side of Katya, Fauchet tapped Abby's shoulder. He motioned her closer, behind Katya.

"Don't believe this story of Jean Harlow," Fauchet whispered, under the sound of the choir.

"Who is he?"

"The child of an ordinary mistress," Fauchet said. "He invents the rest."

The man was absorbed, by now, in the choir. Abby wondered if he looked like Jean Harlow but could remember only blondness.

T.J. was sitting on the kneeling pad at Fauchet's feet, drawing on a collection envelope with a stubby pencil. After Freddie's story, watching him filled Abby with surprising sorrow. The little boy would wonder for the rest of his life why he felt dislocated and unwanted. She wanted to write a letter to his future self that he could carry with him, sealed, until he needed it—a letter that would explain things. But it wouldn't work. So you had the explanation of the pain, so what? You still had the feelings, and the explanations didn't make them go away.

"Josefina," the priest was saying, *"era una madre buenisima, una católica muy devota, una amiga veramente leal."*

After the service, they went to see the tomb where Josephine would be, among the houselike monuments to the dead families of Argentina, outside in the blinding sun. Because there was no family tomb, Josephine had a slot in a long enclosure with rows of square tombs in one wall. Two men in dusty work clothes were sitting on a bench inside, eating lunch in the shade, and they watched as the sober little group came in. Some of the tombs were empty and the doors were open a crack; it made Abby feel queasy.

Freddie sidled close to Saffron, and either he really had healing powers or Saffron was too distressed to notice, because she let him put an arm around her.

"I can't *believe* she wanted to be here," she said.

Freddie steered her toward the door. "Let's go get lunch," he said, and the rest of them followed.

41

JAMIE WOKE AT THE estancia from a dream of a funeral Mass in which Martin Russell was dead in a coffin, killed by a pitchfork. It was morning, and Saffron wasn't in the bed. She had spent three days shut in her mother's office downstairs with the lawyers, coming out for sandwiches and sleep. Whatever winning meant, Saffron would win.

Martin Russell was arriving in the afternoon, stopping in Buenos Aires on someone's solid-gold yacht, and Saffron had made clear that she hoped Jamie could be civil. His head hurt. He went downstairs and found Katya in the big room with the fireplace, watching T.J. run a toy truck over the rug.

Jamie dropped down on the opposite couch. He saw himself in the kid—a certain absorption he had, as if he were screening out the rest of the world. It was how Jamie had felt rocking his head on his pillow at night to music in his head, and how he had felt learning to play the guitar. He hoped the kid wouldn't end up with people who wouldn't understand him, who would stop him disappearing into his own world.

Katya was wearing the bathrobe from her room, and it swallowed her up, but her legs were visible to the knee. Her feet were tucked beneath her. He had seen her only in big men's shirts and jeans.

"I was thinking he maybe understands my language," she said, as if it were a conversation they had been having. "But nothing."

To demonstrate, she said something incomprehensible. The boy went on playing with his truck.

"What did you say?" Jamie asked.

She blushed. "Only a stupid thing."

"Tell me."

"I said I wish to eat your heart."

"Yikes."

"It means how much I love him. But you see, this is very stupid."

He noticed again how different she looked when the color came into her face. "Do you?" he asked. "I mean, feel that way? You've just met him, right?"

"The feeling to be a mother is very strong," she said. "I cannot explain this."

Jamie thought of Margot and wondered about very strong feelings. "Teach me to say it," he said.

She repeated the words and laughed when he tried to say them. It began with *egdyem mega* and then became impossible. He wanted to ask about the Russians who bought her but was afraid of betraying how thrilling that suddenly seemed.

Then Saffron came in, wearing a tight gray sweater and a swinging skirt, a diamond crucifix between her lovely breasts. Her abject grief was gone, and she said good morning as she walked through, barely looking at Jamie, getting ready for Martin's arrival.

Jamie sat fuming on the couch and finally got up and stalked back to the guest wing. His own room depressed him, so he knocked on Abby's door. She had hardly come out in the past few days; she showed up at dinner, and swam in the pool at night. Now she opened the door, still in pajamas, and he invited himself in and sat on the bed.

"Do you think Katya's pretty?" he asked.

"Oh, no," she said, closing the door. "Jamie, not that."

"What?"

"Promise me you won't get involved with her."

"I'm not."

"You can't bullshit me, Jamie."

"Maybe I'm just looking for a distraction. I can't believe Saffron invited Martin here."

"It seems completely in character."

"You're supposed to be sympathetic."

"That's not true," she said. "I'm supposed to be objective and help you see Saffron clearly."

"And your objective opinion is?"

"That she can't possibly be worth it."

"I wish you knew her in private," he said. "She's so funny and sexy. She's different alone. I'm going crazy."

"She cheats, Jamie, and she'll always cheat. And you can't stand that—you want her to be yours. So you have a problem."

"Stop being so rational."

"Then get out of my room."

He looked at her, confused. "Are you jealous?"

"Oh, probably," she said. "Put yourself in my shoes. It's a very weird position I'm in."

"I thought you wanted to normalize things."

"This is not normal!" she said. "Would you like it if I came to you moping about the funny, sexy, cheating guy I was obsessed with?"

"No," he said. "But you wouldn't get yourself into such a mess."

"Just go away. Okay? That's what I want."

"Fine."

"Just go."

He reached for her shoulder. "Abby, babe."

"Don't touch me," she said, stepping backward and bumping into a chair. "You can't come to me when she rejects you."

"I'm not."

"Please go."

"Do you love me?"

"Jamie, I've always loved you, since I was seven. That's my problem."

"I'm sorry."

"Get out of my room," she said.

42

Dr. Tirrett was on call at the university counseling office, for walk-in support during exam time, but it was a slow morning and she forced herself to read through her divorce papers. She tried not to be enraged at her husband. She tried to understand the psychological process by which he had bankrupted his business and deceived his creditors, and to find in him the man she had married. When the receptionist said, "We've got one," she was glad for an excuse to put the papers away.

The walk-in didn't look like an undergrad, and she guessed he had come to lament his unwritten dissertation—to talk about the history of the electoral college or the double helix. She usually just let the grad students run on, hoping they would find their way to something she could address.

This one sat down easily on the couch—he'd done this before—and said, "This isn't academic, really." He had curly hair and seemed bright and agitated. She wondered idly if he was Jewish. He started talking about the university's ombudsman. Leila had worked with the ombudsman: he was tall and very black, and had the voice of an actor and wore three-piece suits. He made an impression.

"I keep thinking about the ombudsman," the young man said.

"Because he gave this talk when I first started teaching, and he said, 'I have one piece of advice for you, which should help you in your teaching and grading before it ever helps you with anything in *my* territory. That advice is, *Don't look for love in the classroom.*'"

Leila waited.

"But I got involved with a student, a former student now," the young man went on. "It's the first time I've done that. Those girls— I'm sure you know this, but they show up all wide-eyed and flirtatious at office hours. I know most of them don't really want to fuck their TA. They just want me to *want* them, and they want to please me. But it's a little overwhelming." He paused before going on.

"I think this was different. I'm sure everyone says that. But she never said anything in class or came to office hours. I didn't even notice her at first, she was so quiet. I called on her once out of curiosity, and she got so embarrassed I never did it again. But I sought her out, I made up an excuse. I said I needed her notes. And then I couldn't stop thinking about her."

Leila nodded, to show that she was listening.

"So the first time we had . . . a kind of sexual encounter," he said, "she left school. Her father died about a year ago, and she'd already left school once, and this time she went back to his house in Santa Rosa. I tried to keep things going, but she seemed sort of gun-shy. Finally I just went up there. She didn't want me in her dead father's house, so I got a hotel room and she stayed the night. And I thought—this is what I want. I *know* this is what I want. And then in the morning she told me her uncle had invited her to Argentina."

Leila was mostly following the story, and only a small part of her attention was on the divorce papers in the drawer of the desk. She would have to remember not to leave them behind where her colleagues could find them.

"She's been working on a novel," he said. "I know that sounds ridiculous. She's back at her father's house now, working on it, and she just sent me a draft. It isn't finished, parts of it are sketchy. But the point is, it's about a girl like Abby who has a one-night stand with her uncle."

Leila was suddenly alert and tracking. She had wondered when this would happen, working for the university. She had seen students who all complained about the same professor, and teachers in the same department with petty rivalries against each other. But the links had always been casual. She tried to remember Abby's last name, Abby of the dead father and the affair with the young uncle.

"I mean, the novel's about a lot of things," he said. "It's about a family, about being Catholic in America, which is not what I expected. It's sort of like me writing about being Jewish in America."

"Are you?"

"My father is, but—I didn't grow up with it. The novel needs some more Catholic stuff in the revision. But I haven't called to tell her that, because there's this thing with the uncle in it."

"And?" Leila said.

"I think that happened. I think she fucked her uncle. God, it's so weird to say out loud. My Abby."

Abby Collins. That was her name.

"Does this sound crazy?" he asked.

"I don't think so," she said carefully.

"I'm writing my dissertation about Poe," he said. "So maybe that's why this feels like a weird curse, that I would fall for this girl who's in thrall to this uncle who took her *out of my bed* and off to Argentina. So I came here to say that this is a damaged girl, right? And I should move on, and never sleep with a student who's screwed up enough to sleep with me."

"That sounds like a good rule."

"But this is the one I want," he said. "Do you think she slept with her uncle?"

Leila paused. "I don't know."

"Maybe she didn't," he said hopefully. "In the book it's only once."

"Whether she did or not," Leila said, "there will be things to work through. Some emotional inaccessibility on her part, from the sound of it. And the impact of her father's death. And possibly a history of incest."

He nodded.

"But it's hard for me, working for the university, to encourage you in this."

"I expected that," he said. "Do you see a lot of situations like this?"

"Not exactly like this."

"Does it ever turn out well—I mean with students?"

"What would 'well' be?"

"They don't end up together, do they?"

"Not usually."

"Do they come out unscathed?"

Leila studied his intent young face, and looked at the clock behind him, and thought about the divorce papers in the drawer, and how long and unpredictable life was.

"No," she said. "They don't. It's all how you look at the scathing."

43

WHEN KATYA CAME to Jamie's room in Argentina, she caught him at a vulnerable time, though he might always have been vulnerable to the kind of seduction she laid on. Abby had just kicked him out, and Saffron had thrown Martin in his face. And then there was Katya on her knees, sucking his cock with an amateur's enthusiasm and a professional's skill. He forgot about Martin, he forgot about everything. He stayed up at night playing songs for her on the guitar, singing "Love unrequited robs me of my rest," which wasn't technically true, and "I've Just Seen a Face," his own version:

> *Katya is a lovely lay*
> *She could have looked the other way*
> *But as it is she looked on me*
> *And now I only want to eat her heart*
> *Na na na na na na.*

Katya laughed at the *na na na*s even more than at the changed lyrics, but he made her sing them, too: that was the part that summed up the joy he felt.

He thought the whole thing over, sometimes with Katya sleeping next to him, sometimes alone in his room listing pros and cons. He explored the estancia with T.J., to confirm that they liked each other, and he talked to Magdalena about what she was going to do next. She had a marriage proposal and would be moving away; her fiancé ran a farm for a rich English family. She was wistful about leaving T.J., but she didn't seem to have any ideas about making her fiancé a stepfather.

Then Jamie went to Fauchet. He danced around the idea until he got the sense that Fauchet wasn't against it, and they started to work out the terms. He would marry Katya, and T.J. could be released to the responsible home of Mr. and Mrs. Jamie Santerre. They would go back to San Francisco, and Katya would get a green card, and T.J. would get an American father. Saffron would get her mother's money—which she was going to do anyway—but there would be a generous settlement to T.J.'s new guardians, and some money in trust until he grew up.

Jamie was determined about it; there was no other solution. There was something so abject about Katya, so utterly corrupted— he hadn't anticipated the effect of it. She wasn't like anyone. Even Saffron was always in control. So here he was escaping Saffron, and rescuing the orphan, all while fucking this odd little masterpiece of depravity, a girl raised from childhood to be his slave. He was in love.

When Abby found out about his plan, she was furious. She said they were using him. "Katya was raised by Russian pimps, Jamie," she said. "How much of a warning do you need?"

"She laughs at my songs."

"There are millions of girls who will laugh at your songs."

But there was no stopping him now. Jamie married Katya in Argentina, to facilitate the adoption. It upset his parents not to be there, but not as much as a City Hall wedding in San Francisco would have upset them. Abby refused to be a witness. It was thrilling to thwart his family for a noble cause. He was declaring his independence; he was finally growing up.

He flew to San Francisco alone and found an apartment, and

Katya and the boy followed. They both seemed exhausted by the trip, but Katya cheered up when she saw the apartment, which was neat and comfortable and bright on the bright day when they arrived.

He found a small private school with young, Madgalenaesque teachers, where T.J. learned English with amazing speed. The public schools were too scary, and anyway he had Josephine's money.

Katya was proud of her conquest: she had come for her child, and she had gotten him. There was novelty in living in America. And there was novelty in playing the loyal wife. She couldn't cook, and she didn't clean, but there were nights eating Thai food at the kitchen table, when Jamie made Katya and T.J. giggle helplessly, or when his lame attempts at pronouncing Hungarian words set them both off, and it felt like a family. Not a normal family, but Jamie had never expected that—it was the kind of crazy, invented family he had to have ended up with. It made perfect sense.

44

ABBY WENT BACK to her father's house, after Argentina. Jamie wanted her to come to San Francisco to approve of his marriage, Peter wanted her to come to San Diego to be with him, and her mother wanted her to stay in the new guest room—which was Abby's old room, repainted and refurnished—but Abby didn't want to see anyone.

She set up her computer again at the kitchen table, went through Peter's notes, and tried to fill in the parts he thought were missing. At night she read St. Augustine, and Abélard and Héloïse, and Saint Thérèse of Lisieux. She thought about Yvette and Teddy. It was part of every day: the dread of what would happen if she could actually finish the book, and someone would publish it.

Finally she called Jamie. "I think I might have a draft, of this novel."

"Hey, that's great."

"It has an uncle in it who has an affair with a niece."

"Oh, boy."

"They have a baby."

"Good God."

"Is that okay? You said it was, once."

"For them to have a baby?"

"For me to write a book. This book."

"Really? I say a lot of things."

"You seemed like you meant it."

"Are you sure?"

"Yes. If they ask, I'll say it's made up."

"Good plan. Can I read it?"

"Soon, I think. Are you angry?"

"I don't think so. But I haven't read it."

"I don't want to tell anyone else yet."

"Okay."

"It starts with a Catholic mother raising her daughter's baby as her own."

There was a silence on the line.

"Did you ever find out if that happened?" she asked.

"No."

"Do you think it did?"

"I don't know."

"Maybe we should find out," she said. "I hoped for a while that you were my cousin, but now I think I hope you're not. I'd like to know before I send this book anywhere."

"I can see that."

"That story line was your idea, too," she said, trying not to sound as defensive as she felt.

"Are you sure I really meant it?"

"I don't know," she said. "I thought you did. You should be careful what you tell people to do."

"Most people don't do *anything* I say."

"Well, you should be careful what you tell *me* to do."

"Now I know that."

"I don't think you'll be angry."

"Good," he said.

"So can we ask Yvette?"

45

YVETTE WAS WASHING the dishes when Abby and Jamie pulled into the driveway. She had been singing to herself, like she used to sing with her sister Adele while they washed the dishes at home, as girls. Their cousins in Montreal taught them French torch songs, and Yvette was singing one of those:

> *Comme la vie est un songe, et l'amour un mensonge*
> *Les plus beaux serments ne durent qu'un temps*
> *Quand la femme est jolie l'adorer c'est folie . . .*

Then, out the window, she saw the car.

Teddy was in the garage at his workbench, fixing a lamp, and Yvette wondered if he knew Jamie was coming and had forgotten to tell her. That would be just like him. She went to the door, drying her hands on a towel.

"What are you both doing here!"

"Hi, Ma."

"Hi, Grandma," Abby said and kissed her.

Yvette had just been talking to Clarissa about how Abby was

holed up in her father's house and hadn't gone back to school. "How are you, sweetheart?" she asked.

"I'm okay."

"I'll get Teddy," Yvette said.

"Wait a minute," Jamie said. "I want to ask you something first."

Yvette sat down on one of the chairs in the living room, and the kids sat on the couch like visitors. Then Jamie asked if Margot had been pregnant the year he was born.

Yvette was caught off guard. "What makes you ask that?"

"I was telling someone the story," Jamie said slowly, "how you went into the convent and Margot was in France, and then how you went to visit Margot and I was born there." He paused and looked to Abby, as if for encouragement. "And it sounded, to me and to this person, like maybe that wasn't the whole story. And maybe it is the whole story, but I just felt like I had to ask."

"I don't understand," Yvette said.

"Is Margot my mother?" he asked.

"*I'm* your mother," she said.

Jamie sighed, a little impatiently. "Did Margot have a baby in France?"

Yvette was so confused that she tried to remember if she could have forgotten a thing like that. *Comme la vie est un songe, et l'amour un mensonge.* "No!" she said finally. "She learned French, that's all. She lived with my cousins. They can tell you."

Jamie and Abby looked at each other. Teddy came in from the garage, looking pleased to see them.

"How about that!" he said. "Look who's here!"

"Hi, Dad," Jamie said. "Surprise visit."

Still baffled, Yvette said, "Isn't this wonderful, sweetheart?"

46

PETER READ ABBY'S NEXT draft and pronounced it a novel, and she locked up her father's house, drove to San Diego, and spent the night in his bed. He wondered if he would have lied about the novel to get to this place; he guessed he would have told her the truth and hoped she would come anyway.

The old Frenchman in Argentina had given her the number of a friend in New York who owned a literary agency, and Abby had sent the book there, and they had sold it. But given a contract and a check, she seemed overcome by guilt and fear that she was going to outrage her family. Peter hadn't asked her about the incest plot.

One night, sitting in his bed in her underwear and a UCSD T-shirt, she looked up from the manuscript. "How am I going to tell my grandparents?"

He was reading in the chair by the window and marked his page. "Don't you think they guess by now? They know you're writing something."

"They don't guess."

"So you're just going to let them find it in the bookstore?"

"No."

"It'll be okay," he said. "You've made so much up."

She looked sad and oppressed. "I'm not cut out for this."

"You have some other plans I don't know about?"

"I could be an academic."

"You're not an academic."

"How do you know?"

"I *know*."

"You liked my papers."

"But I didn't say you should be an academic."

She pushed the manuscript away, across the bed. "Tell me about getting kicked out of college."

"You know the story."

"Only in parts."

He thought about why she might want to hear it *now* and began deliberately. "I was drunk or stoned a lot," he said, "and failing my classes, and they asked me to take a year off. Told me to."

"Were your parents having trouble?"

"Some people manage to get depressed with married parents."

"But were they happy?"

"Happy enough," he said. "They live in the country of long marriages. They speak a different language."

"That's so strange."

"I was supposed to get a job," he said, "and show the disciplinary committee I could apply myself to something, but I spent the summer in New York and went to parties. Two of my friends had an apartment in the city and money for coke. I was always too broke to buy coke, which is lucky. I had a girlfriend who went to Stuyvesant, which felt very corrupt and exciting even though she was only two years younger."

"You were having sex?"

A startlingly vivid memory of his high school girl wearing only a baseball cap came back to him.

"Manhattan girls didn't mess around," he said. "It almost killed me when she dumped me. Then it was the end of the summer, and my friends were going back to school, but I couldn't. One of them had a lot of magazines he was throwing away. I was never a big porn guy, but there were all these pictures of beautiful girls—old-style, presilicone *Playboys*—and they were going to the garbage. So I said I'd take them, and I packed them into two old shopping bags."

"Oh—" Abby said.

"My friends left, and I took the train home to my parents' house in Philadelphia, where I was living in my old room. It was hot out, and humid. I remember sitting on the train by myself, with these two bags at my feet, with my friends going off without me. I had a Walkman, and I was listening to something classical, I don't remember what, but it was like a movie soundtrack in my head. It felt like the big music-swelling moment in a movie about failure, about a guy with no job, slumped and sweaty in a train, going back to his parents' house with two shopping bags full of porn."

Abby laughed. "I wish I'd known you then."

He shook his head. "You'd have run screaming," he said. "Anyway, you were ten. You know the rest. I got a job doing deliveries for a dry cleaner. I started reading books again and realized that was what I cared about. I finished college and applied to the graduate schools that were farthest away from where I'd been."

"I'm glad you ended up here," she said.

"I am, too. Now you have to tell me a story about shame."

Her eyes narrowed imperceptibly, and she shook her head.

"I told *you* one," he said.

"It wasn't supposed to be a trade."

"What were you seeing the shrink about?"

"My father's death."

"Is that all?"

"That isn't enough?"

"You're really different now from the girl who showed up in my section, who was absent and silent and kind of a wreck. And I wondered if you had done it all yourself, or if you did it by writing the novel, or if maybe going to see her helped."

"I was a wreck?"

"Weren't you? Your roommate said I was attracted to craziness."

"I don't really remember," she said, getting vague. He thought of Eurydice, how she vanished when Orpheus looked at her.

"Tell me about the uncle and niece in the novel," he said.

She pulled one of the pillows on his bed under her arm. The underwear she was wearing were made of mesh, transparent pink, with string sides: one of his favorites. "Are you going to come over here?" she asked.

"See, this makes me think you'd rather have sex with a teacher than answer a hard question. So you're sleeping with me only because I once called on you in class."

"That's not true."

"No?"

"No!"

"What did your Italian gold digger say," he asked, "who wanted you to make yourself come?"

"That I couldn't always have men do it for me."

"And you said, 'Why not?'"

"No, I didn't."

"But you thought it."

"Men do it better."

"I'll give you a choice. You can do it now, or you can answer my question about the incest plot."

"Is this Truth or Dare?"

"Yes," he said. "People in the English Department are always talking about *agency*. You should be able to do it yourself."

"It isn't about my *agency* if it's for you to watch."

"I'm just the facilitator."

"I'm too shy."

"Other people might buy that. Take off your underwear."

Abby sighed and rolled off the pillow. She lifted her hips off the bed and slipped the mesh underwear down, then shimmied them off her legs and kicked them off one ankle. He made himself stay where he was. The T-shirt had ridden up over her rib cage, and her stomach looked exposed and pale. She hesitated.

"What if I need help?"

"I'm standing by."

She tapped a thumb against her thigh, contemplatively, and then she drew her knees up, tugged her T-shirt down, and said, "I did."

"Did what?"

"With Jamie." She took a deep breath and ran the words together: "It wasn't at a reunion, like in the book, and it wasn't a one-night stand. It was more than once."

There was a moment of disappointment that she wasn't going to perform, and then he felt he had passed to the other side of something. He wasn't shocked, but he was surprised it had been more than once.

"How many times?"

"I think eight."

"Oh, my God."

"I can't really explain it, it was after my father died. It's not like Jamie was around all the time, when I was growing up, but he was very cool and funny, and he wasn't that much older. So he was sort of this romantic crush I'd always had, he was like a rock star. I know you're supposed to have those crushes and *not* have sex, but then he was there and I was twenty and I really wanted it. I think I started it." Her voice had faded so he could barely hear it.

"I can't hear you."

"It's so embarrassing."

"Don't be embarrassed. You should never be embarrassed."

Her breathing seemed uneven, too. "Are you going to come over here now? I answered the question, I told you the truth."

"Will you do the dare later?"

"Yes."

"I can't hear you."

"*Yes,*" she said, and by the time he had moved to the bed, he was shaking with desire. He hadn't been so overcome since he was seventeen.

"You're not disappointed with me?" she whispered, close to his face.

"No," he whispered back.

"I can't hear you," she said.

"No."

47

A<small>BBY SAT AT LUNCH</small> in New York with her editor, feeling like she was in a different world. Everyone in the restaurant wore a suit, and the hum of their voices was different from California voices. They looked polished and knowing. Abby felt scruffy and naïve, intimidated even by Diana's warmth.

Diana was in her fifties, tall and slim, with shiny dark hair, expensively cut. She had brought a description of the book for the catalog, and Abby skimmed it. The last sentence read:

> This remarkable family, undermined by their own secrets and by the changes of half a century in America, comes back together only after the tragic death of the matriarch in Rome.

Abby put the piece of paper aside. It made her feel sick.

"I'm not sure who wrote it," Diana said. "We can change it."

Abby nodded. They ordered a lunch she didn't want to eat.

"I love the dance teacher becoming a crazy healer," Diana said. "They're a very fertile family, aren't they? I mean, it takes one time with the dance teacher and one time with the uncle, to knock those girls up."

Abby blushed.

"I'm not saying you should change it," Diana said. "You know who I really like? I like the high school sweetheart the uncle finally ends up with, with his little boy. She's such a breath of fresh air—she's secular, she's sexual, she's candid, she likes her work, she's childless and okay with it. The book needed that, I have to tell you. I would have gotten impatient, without her."

Abby didn't know whether to thank her or apologize. "Do you have children?" she asked.

"No," Diana said. "I know—that's why I root for the happy childless woman. I get so tired of people insisting that kids are the *best* thing, the *only* thing. It's true for some people. But women will marry the guy standing next to them on their thirty-seventh birthday, just to get a baby." She smiled. "Listen to me yak. What are you working on now? Where are you living?"

"I'm not sure," Abby said. Her duffel bag was still in Peter's hallway, and when she washed her clothes she returned them folded to the bag.

"I was curious about you, I couldn't figure out where you were in the book. Can I ask—are you a lesbian?"

Abby felt herself blush. "No."

"Is your mother?"

Her face got hotter. "I don't know."

Diana nodded, studying her. "I'm sorry. I have to learn not to ask every question that comes into my head."

"It's okay."

"Have I upset you?"

She shook her head again.

"People will be interested because you're so young, but I don't think you want to be interviewed much, do you? You really turn an amazing shade of red."

"I'm sorry."

"Are you going to eat that salad?"

Abby shook her head.

"There's no hidden baby, is there? I mean, it didn't happen? There's no baby with an uncle?"

"Of course not," Abby said.

Diana folded her napkin and looked around the restaurant. "Oh, good."

48

THE FIRST TIME YVETTE and Teddy went to San Francisco to see Jamie's wife and child, the little family had seemed dazed but generally happy. The second time, Katya was snappish and sullen, and T.J. was having stomachaches at school. The third time, Yvette flew up alone. Teddy couldn't stand to go, but Yvette worried about T.J. He was a good boy, he was only having some trouble adjusting to a new country and a new language and new parents.

Jamie had made an appointment with a marriage counselor, and Yvette stayed home reading books with T.J. She read him Abby's old copy of *The Missing Piece,* in which a circle with a pie-shaped slice missing goes looking all over the world for it, rolling and singing as he goes. He finds missing pieces that are wrong, and don't fit, and when he finally finds the perfect one, and fits it in place, he discovers that his mouth is sealed by it; he can't sing. So he goes back to living happily incomplete and alone. Yvette thought about what Shel Silverstein meant by that. It seemed like an allegory of love, but a strange one, and it disturbed Yvette. She wondered if growing up with the book had made it hard for Abby to find a match.

T.J. had fallen asleep on the couch, and Yvette pulled a blanket over him. She put *The Missing Piece* away backward, so it was less likely to be spotted and pulled out.

Jamie's books were on the upper shelves, and Yvette scanned them, looking for one for herself. There was his old, dog-eared paperback copy of *Dune,* some John Le Carré, and a lot of nonfiction: *A Bridge Too Far, Seven Men at Daybreak, Cockleshell Heroes.* Then she came upon a narrow paperback with her granddaughter's name on the spine. She pulled it off the shelf. Abby Collins might be a common name, but on the back it said that the author was from Santa Rosa. The book had a glossy paper cover and said on the front, ADVANCE UNCORRECTED PROOF. NOT FOR SALE.

Yvette carried the book to the kitchen and sat down at the table. It began, "They were married during the war, after Mass one morning in a church looking over the sea." It was about a Canadian woman who moves to California to marry a pilot. Yvette felt her heart start to race. There was an incident with a photographer who was nothing like that man who had come to the house. There was a paragraph about the bride's father's jaundice—about *Yvette's* father's jaundice—that made her smart with pain because it was true. And then there were many things that simply weren't true at all, and she found herself saying, aloud at the kitchen table, "That didn't happen!"

She had read about forty pages when Jamie came in and said, "Oh, shit, Ma, what are you doing?"

She looked up at him. "You knew about this?"

Katya disappeared into the back bedroom.

"Abby wanted to tell you herself," Jamie said. "I begged for it early, and I promised I'd put it away. So I'm screwed if you tell her you read it here."

"Where did she get those stories? Why did you tell them to her?"

"I didn't tell them to her, Ma," he said. "*You* told her. You've told that bootlegging story a hundred times."

"Is this going to be in bookstores?"

"I think that's the idea."

Yvette stared at him, horrified. "Can we stop it?"

"Why would we?"

"Because it's private!"

"It's fiction."

"But why would anyone want to read it?"

"I thought it was great," he said. "It's all about me having adventures."

"It is?"

"You'll see," he said. "It's all made up. I'm Margot's kid in it, like I thought I might be."

"Oh, that crazy idea."

"You're not going to tell her you saw it here, right?"

"Why are you defending her?"

"Let me have the book back."

She gave it to him and sat at the kitchen table, thinking about her father. She didn't remember the Americans who had come to buy whiskey out of the basement, during Prohibition, and shot him in the liver. She remembered only the yellowness of his face afterward, and the way he would take an egg in his beer, to keep up his strength. That was in the book. It was so strange. What wasn't in the book was how he would pull her onto his lap and make her feel like the prettiest and smartest and most important girl in the world, even though they had moved to a tiny house where she had to share a dingy room with her sister, and where the nailheads popped up on the floorboards, and the kitchen smelled strange. On her father's lap, none of that mattered.

She had thought she could leave her attachment to him behind, when the war began and she moved to California. She was so young then, even younger than Abby. And then she had children and time passed so quickly and her father died of the old wound. She had missed so many years of his life, and he had missed so many of hers. It was *her* war injury, like the shrapnel that some men carried with them all their lives, and it had worked its way out a little, in her heart. If she sat very still, it might not do any more damage. She didn't even dare to breathe deeply but sat looking at her hands on the table, waiting for the sharp thing to settle back into place.

49

WHEN MARGOT HEARD that Abby had written a novel about a Catholic family keeping secrets from each other, she broke out in a sweat at the idea that Abby *knew*. Abby sent her a copy, and the back of the jacket said it was "carefully observed." Margot couldn't open it; the headache that had been coming on all morning split across her forehead like lightning and stayed all afternoon.

Abby had come to Louisiana during Clarissa's divorce, flying alone to Baton Rouge, and she had been a strange child, hanging back in corners. She made Margot feel she was being watched, which she guessed she was. Abby was trying, at seven, to learn all the things Clarissa hadn't taught her: to put her seat belt on in the car, put her napkin in her lap, ask who's calling when answering the phone, and pull a skirt *up* in a public rest room, not *down* so the hem hangs on the floor.

Or, Margot thought now, Abby might have been trying to understand all the things she had learned too soon.

She was distracted when the child arrived and resented the extra burden. Owen was working all the time then, at a new job with a different pharmaceutical company. Margot had dinner parties for his clients and colleagues, but they bored her, and she was restless.

There was a young man training to be a Jesuit brother, whose name was Dominick Jay. He wasn't a priest, though he would take a vow of celibacy when he officially joined the Society. He was a lawyer, doing work for the parish and living with a local order. The other Jesuits were older than Dominick, and Margot saw him one day, shopping for them at the grocery store. He compared the contents of their shopping carts—fresh greens and red potatoes and flank steak in hers, boxes of cereal and TV dinners in his—and begged her to come cook for them.

"You'd be like Wendy in *Peter Pan,*" he said. "We're like the Lost Boys over there."

She couldn't be their Wendy, so she invited him to dinner instead. Her mother had always had priests and nuns home to dinner in Hermosa Beach; it was a perfectly natural thing.

But she was nervous, the night he came: her pulse raced as she braised the meat and made the vinaigrette for the salad. She had gotten over her insecurity among the pharmaceutical executives and their debutante wives, but it was resurfacing, oddly, with this shy young man who had devoted his life and his income to the church.

Ben and Danny were on good behavior during dinner, chatting to Dominick about baseball and school, and Owen was vaguely friendly, his mind on something else. When they disappeared after dessert to watch a game on TV, Dominick came to help Margot with the dishes and hung his blue blazer over the back of a chair. He told her about a traveling exhibition of Whistler paintings, and they made plans to go.

An innocent social engagement: a cultural outing with a celibate man. So why, as she got ready to go out, was she being so careful with her makeup? Why had she chosen her simplest, most flattering dress?

Dominick was already at the museum when she arrived, waiting outside the main entrance. He looked so eager and childlike when he saw her walking up that she wondered briefly how old he was. Only a few years younger than she—but she felt old because her children grew so fast. He touched her back to lead her into the building, and she clutched her handbag to keep her hands steady.

The Whistler exhibition was deserted on a weekday morning. As they wandered through it, Margot felt her heart swell with the beauty of the paintings. Life was beautiful like that, it was *supposed* to be beautiful like that. It wasn't supposed to be all dirty Jockey shorts and rushed dinners after baseball practice, and reassuring her husband about corporate politics and the future of brand-name drugs. It was supposed to be clear sunlight and elegant lines and mysterious shadows, and that feeling of expansion she had when she looked at the beautiful women in the paintings.

Finally they sat on a leather bench in one of the galleries, facing a painting of a nude girl in a long blue robe, and Margot realized they were alone. The security guard was in the next room. Her heart started to pound, and she turned to see if she was alone in her panic, and Dominick kissed her. The kiss was so sweet, it was like looking at the paintings: she felt lifted up, and released.

Then he touched her face and said, "Sweet Margot," and looked unbearably sad, and she kissed him again to make the sad look go away.

So that was how it began. The glorious kissing—which they had done more of, furtively—made her feel free and unconstricted, and she craved it. But it was followed by the suffering of the damned. And then she had her sister's neglected child to deal with.

The boys were eight and ten, older than Abby, and she was shy about joining their games. They played progressive rummy on the living room floor, but one game was enough for all of them. Then the boys would go down the street to a friend's house, and Abby would wander into the kitchen and fix Margot with her big, uncertain eyes. If Margot was on the phone with Dominick, she would quickly end the call. If she was making a list of reasons she should stop the "affair" at once, she would put the list down the garbage disposal and listen to the blades grind it up.

One day Margot took Abby to the mall and left her in the children's section at Waldenbooks while she met Dominick in an empty restaurant and told him they should stop seeing each other. He was surprised and hurt. After half an hour of quiet arguing, she wiped her wet mascara off with a napkin, firmly said good-bye, and bought her niece two Black Stallion books and a translated Tintin.

Two painfully lonely days later, Dominick arrived at the house uninvited, and Margot had never been so happy to see anyone. Owen was at work, the boys were up the street, and Abby was reading on the porch swing in the backyard. Margot led her lover upstairs in the empty house, noticing from a distance that she was doing this unthinkable thing. It was the first time they had been truly alone together.

Dominick unbuttoned her blouse, slowly, and then they were both in a hurry. Margot managed to pull back the linen cover on the bed to keep it clean, but that was the last responsible thing she did before she had his long and slender erection in her hand.

When it was over, she was stricken by guilt again. She had just had her period and guessed she was safe, but all she could think about was taking a shower and stripping the bed and getting the sheets into the laundry. She asked Dominick to go, feeling shaky and miserable. The house was still empty, Abby still reading in the swing, but how did Margot know she hadn't come in for a drink of water and heard something? Or she might have seen him come in, or crept upstairs. Margot grew hot with shame thinking about it, and at the end of the week she told Dominick she could never see him again. He tried to change her mind, but this time she meant it. He withdrew from the Jesuits, wrapped up his work for the parish, and moved away.

It was only when Margot thought her headache couldn't get much worse that she worked up the nerve to flip through Abby's book, looking for mentions of the older sister's affair. It wasn't there—the older sister had a beautiful house and was married to a kind and prosperous man who couldn't make a salad, but those seemed to be the major likenesses. She was both faithful and childless.

Margot took courage and started reading from the beginning, and found herself sleeping with a dance instructor at fifteen and going to France to have a baby her mother raised as her own. It was a sad story, but it wasn't Margot's story, and she was so relieved that she didn't even mind that she got a bad rap in the book, for making life hard for the younger sister. Her headache faded and she started to wonder what had ever happened to Dominick Jay.

50

Wʜᴇɴ Aʙʙʏ ꜰɪɴᴀʟʟʏ sent her the book in the mail, Clarissa read it with growing horror. How would people be able to separate what was real from what wasn't? Wouldn't they assume everything was real? How did Abby remember all these things, most of which Clarissa didn't remember? And would people think she was such a bad mother? Would they think that she had a girlfriend who decorated cakes?

Abby had said in her note that it was fiction: that it wasn't about her, and it wasn't a letter to her. Clarissa understood that some of it might be fiction, but she couldn't focus on anything but the selfishness of her character. That was an indictment, no matter how you looked at it. She wished suddenly that she hadn't asked Del to move out. Del was always on Clarissa's side.

Then the book came out and her friends started to call to congratulate her. They said Clarissa had done a wonderful thing in raising Abby; the book was a tribute to her. Her friend Rae came by with a copy for Abby to sign.

"I just don't know how she could do that to us," Clarissa said, putting the kettle on in the kitchen. "My dad was in the Marines. And I had a Buddhist boyfriend."

"Did he meditate at the table with a water glass?" Rae asked.

"I can't remember."

Rae laughed happily. She had spiky gray hair and earrings all the way up her left ear. "Now you can," she said. "That's so great. Aren't you glad Abby recorded it? Everything noisily going on in this kitchen, like it always does in your house, and this guy meditating at the table, focusing on his arm lifting and his throat swallowing and his arm setting down? And if it didn't happen, it's just as great."

"I guess," Clarissa said, trying to remember him doing that. She remembered other things about him. He liked her to wear matching lacy underwear. "Do you think my father will think I'm gay?"

"Because of the book?"

"Yes."

"Well," Rae said, "do *you* think you are?"

"I don't think he'll read it," Clarissa said. "I told you I'm taking this film class, and I have to make a movie. I might make it about coming out to my parents."

Rae blinked and tugged on the ear with all the earrings. "I thought you were through with all that."

"Maybe I just want to *think* I am, because it's what my mother would want. The teacher wants us to make movies about things that terrify us."

"But do you have to *do* things that would terrify you? Just for this class?"

"Maybe it's an opportunity for me."

Rae said nothing and nodded. The kettle made rumbling noises. Then Rae smiled a wondering smile. "So do you think Abby had an affair with your little brother?"

Clarissa shook her head. "No."

"Where do you think that came from, then?"

"I don't know," Clarissa said. "They've always been close."

"Huh," Rae said.

"I just can't get over it. She made me seem so *selfish* in it."

"Clar," Rae said, squeezing her arm across the table, "try to let her have this, and be happy for her."

The kettle started to whistle, so Clarissa didn't have to say anything. She got up to take it off the stove.

51

PETER HAD SET UP a desk for Abby, a rectangular table pushed against the living room wall, and she was working on a new novel that wasn't going anywhere. When he went to the library to work on his dissertation, she wandered around his apartment, or around the tree-lined neighborhood. She hadn't heard from her family and dreaded what they were going to say. She rented out her father's house and hired Maricruz—who had hurt her back lifting other people's children—to take care of it and bring in people to fix things.

One afternoon, Peter came in flipping through the mail and handed over a postcard. "Love letter from Italy," he said.

"*Carissima,*" the postcard began.

How are you? I am here in my country and life is not what one expects. My wife finds it terrible here, she fights with my mother and sister, she is bored and delusa. She expects things to be grand, always, and this is a simple place in that way. She cannot understand the ways it is not simple.

I write this because you told me, we cannot choose in love this way. I will find what to do next. There is no baby yet, thanks God. I think of you.

Tanti baci—

xx

Gianni

"Are you going to be stolen away?" Peter asked.

"Only if you keep reading my mail."

He laughed. "I only skimmed. You have one from your mother, too."

Abby opened the envelope and read the letter aloud:

Thank you for the book. It has always been so interesting to watch you grow. I saw a talk in Berkeley once, about writing family memoirs, and someone said it was O.K. to do while people were alive if you did it out of love. Someone else asked, what if you don't love your family? I was fascinated by the talk, but I had no idea, then, what you were writing.

I really tried, Abby, to be the best mother I could, at the time.

I've been doing a lot of yoga again, so at first when I was very upset, I rested in savasana to the sound of Tibetan gongs, and that helped.

With love from,
Your Mom

Abby handed the letter to Peter, and he read it.

"She thinks it's a memoir?" he asked.

"Or a letter to her."

"At least she has the Tibetan gongs. I had the sense that you weren't that hard on her."

"No one in the book gets off easier than my mother, except maybe the Catholic Church."

"Wait till you get the letter from them."

"How can she think it's a *memoir*?"

"Well, it's not science fiction. Should you call her?"

"I can't until I hear from Yvette and know if I'm disowned."

"Do you want my advice?"

"Okay."

"Call Yvette right now and get it over with. I'll be in the other room."

He left the room, and she thought *he* must want to get it over with—he couldn't live with her like this anymore. Then she had dialed and there was nothing she could do to stop it.

MAILE MELOY

Yvette answered and said, "I got your book. It's very hard for me to read."

"I'm sorry," Abby said.

"My father's death was very hard for me. I know we laugh when Jamie tells that bootlegging story, but I loved my father, and it was hard."

"I know."

"And I know Jamie teases me about my relationship with my God, but it's the most important thing in my life. It's what lets me be a good person."

"I understand that."

"The book is very hard for me to read, because I keep thinking, *That didn't happen!*"

"I'm sorry," Abby said.

"I'm not that woman in the book," Yvette said. "I never would have done those things."

"I know."

"I know your parents' divorce was hard on you, and I've always worried about how it would affect you later. I wish I could have done something, then."

Abby waited.

"We try so hard, as parents, honey," Yvette said. "We try to do better than our own parents did. But we carry those hurts with us, you know?"

When she got off the phone, Abby went into the bedroom, where Peter was sitting in the chair by the window. He pulled her into his lap. "Did she forgive you?"

"I think so. I feel terrible. I feel sick."

Peter kept his arms around her waist and didn't say anything for a while. Then he said, "Czeslaw Milosz said that when a writer is born into a family, the family is finished."

"No, it isn't," she said. "They aren't going anywhere. They're still there."

52

Do you have a fantasy that the family *would* be finished?" Dr. Tirrett asked.

She had left the university for her own practice, so she could raise her rates and keep her house, and she had a new office in a high building with a view of Mission Bay.

Abby stared out the window rather than make eye contact. "Being disowned would be very restful," she finally said.

"It seems like they're responding better than you hoped."

Abby nodded.

"Have you talked to Jamie?"

Abby shook her head. "He's busy with Katya and the kid." She didn't say anything for a while, and then she made eye contact suddenly. "Did you like Peter, when you met him?" she asked.

Leila hesitated. "I don't want to influence you. But yes, I did. He's older than you are, isn't he?"

"He's younger than Jamie."

Leila smiled. "It's wonderful to have an affair with your uncle for comparison, isn't it?" she said. "The rest all come out pretty well."

"I loved Jamie. I still do."

"Of course you do," Leila said. "He's your favorite uncle. Tell me about Peter."

Abby looked down at the wadded Kleenex in her lap. "You know he was my TA. And he helped me with the book, he gave me notes on it. I couldn't have finished without him."

Leila said nothing.

"I know you don't approve," Abby said.

"It doesn't *matter* if I approve," Leila said impatiently. "And I didn't say I don't. Are you in love with him?"

Abby separated the two layers of a piece of Kleenex, then rolled them together.

"You don't know," Leila said. "Because no one ever modeled love for you."

Abby glared out the window, looking annoyed.

"We have to stop," Leila said, "but I want at some point to talk about where your anger is."

"I'm not angry at Jamie. I was part of what happened, too."

"Okay. Do you need more Kleenex?"

"No," Abby said, and she picked up her bag. "Thanks." Her eyes and nose were red, and she put on her sunglasses before going out.

Leila checked her voice mail to see if her daughter had called, or her patients. To her ex-husband she spoke only through the lawyers. The computer voice said there were no new messages. She had wanted a clean break from her husband, but it was like Abby's fantasy of being disowned: it was restful, but restful lasted only a few days and then it was desolate. She checked the messages again to be sure there were none, watching the blue surface of the water and the bright, flat San Diego day.

53

Mᴀʀɢᴏᴛ ʜᴀᴅ ᴀ ᴄᴏᴍᴘᴜᴛᴇʀ at home, and her son Bennett had shown her how to use Google to look things up: recipes, and the websites of museums, and lecture series.

She had not stopped thinking about Dominick Jay since reading Abby's book. He had probably married and had children; he was certainly not thinking of her. But she wanted to know. So she sat down at the computer one afternoon and typed "Dominick Jay" in the empty box. She hesitated a moment before clicking Search.

Six hundred and thirty-seven matches came up in 1.1 seconds. Some were about Ricky Jay, the card magician. Some were lists of names in genealogies. Some were entries about one person named Jay and another named Dominick.

She changed her search to "Dominick Jay, attorney," and got, along with the chaff, a law firm in Santa Barbara: Cassidy, Herrera, and Jay. She clicked a link to a newspaper article, and her computer slowly downloaded a photograph with the caption "Dominick Jay honored by Rotarians for community service." The story was dated three years before. Then the photo finished downloading, and there he was. His hairline had receded and started to go gray. His dark eyes were set back further in his head. But he was still the man who had kissed her in the Whistler exhibition and made her feel that all rules in the world had been suspended, and she was free.

She sat staring at the photograph for a minute, and then she shut down the computer and rose to make dinner. Her headache was starting again.

54

ABBY ENROLLED IN school in the fall, and Peter thought it was good: she was going through the motions of a normal life. It reminded him of a program he'd seen about an injured man relearning to walk on a treadmill in a tank of water, though he didn't tell Abby that. She would be offended by the analogy, because she didn't think she was injured.

And lately she didn't seem to be. She was taking an astronomy class for the breadth requirement, which seemed to diminish her feeling of having any effect on the universe, and she pretended to be jealous of Peter's girl students, which he found unconvincing but winning. He thought sometimes how glad he was that the ombudsman had been wrong.

One morning he left Abby in his apartment reading about black holes, and walked to campus to teach a section for an English lit survey class. As he walked, four boys in safety goggles were shooting each other with pellet guns, hiding behind cars and fences, and then jumping out and firing. They ran back and forth across the quiet street, in baggy clothes and big tennis shoes to look like gang-bangers. Professors' kids, who rode in station wagons with WORLD PEACE stickers on them but still wanted to shoot at each other.

The trailer he was teaching in was stuffy and warm, so he opened the windows. Students wandered in, and he marked them off his list.

"I loved that article we read," Debbie Serrano said. She always sat on his side of the room, six inches too close, and seemed embarrassed by the abundance of her breasts.

"You mean short story," he said.

"Short story," Debbie said. "Whatever. I loved it."

A tall girl named Robin Jennet came in, wearing jeans and a red leather jacket. He guessed she was over six feet, but she didn't slouch like a tall girl.

"Hey, was Abby Collins one of your students?" Robin asked.

He pretended to be absorbed by the attendance list. "Sure."

"Someone told me that," Robin said. "I read her novel this weekend."

"Oh?"

"I'm French Canadian, too. She's French Canadian, right?"

He shrugged, as if he didn't know.

"Did you read the book?" Robin asked.

"Yes."

"You know what I thought?" She slid the leather jacket off, with no embarrassment about her breasts, which were shaped like cocktail umbrellas. "I thought there should have been more sex."

Peter said nothing.

"And there should have been more about the husband's family, the pilot's," Robin said. "It was like he didn't even have a family. That was kind of weird."

"Doesn't he have a grandfather who dies?"

"Yeah, but nothing else," the girl said. "Hey, is Abby related to Jackie Collins?"

"I don't think so."

"Harper Collins?"

"I don't think so. It's a common name."

"How'd she get an agent?" the girl asked.

Peter saw where this was going. "Are you writing a novel?" he asked.

The girl shrugged. "Maybe."

You might want to learn how to use a comma first, Peter thought, but he said nothing. Tall Robin would write a runaway best seller, and an editor would put in the commas, and he didn't want to be the anecdote about how skeptical her teachers had been.

"Will you read it if I do?" Robin asked.

"Let's cross that bridge when we come to it," he said, realizing that he had already given her the interview anecdote: *My teachers never took me seriously, because I was young, and a woman. They wouldn't even read my novel, which went on to sell eight billion copies. So I had to trust my heart and find my own way as an artist.*

"Are you okay, Mr. Kerner?" Debbie asked.

"Fine."

55

CLARISSA BOUGHT A used video camera for her film class and spent two weekends putting together a loose outline of a script. She asked Del to come along and operate the camera when Clarissa needed to be the subject.

They drove in Del's truck, which had a camper top, down through Oakland, south through the desert, and over the mountains to Hermosa Beach. Del had never been to Los Angeles and seemed happy to be invited. They had burgers for lunch at the old diner in the bowling alley.

Outside St. Anne's, her first school, Clarissa unpacked the camera and then showed Del how to use it. A white vinyl banner hung out front that said, JOIN US AFTER SCHOOL! WINDSURFING SAILING SWIMMING HORSEBACK RIDING VOLLEYBALL.

"I was fascinated by the nuns," Clarissa told the camera, "and I wondered what was underneath their habits. I remember seeing the outline of some foundation garments—a girdle or garters—and being fixated on it. I was probably six."

Del lowered the camera. "Isn't that in Abby's book?"

"It happened to *me*."

"Okay," Del said.

Next they went to the public pool.

"This," Clarissa said, with the diving tank in the background, "is where I had swim practice. One of the nuns saw a bikini tan line on my back, and I was punished."

Del stopped the tape again. "That's in the book, too," she said. "What is this, a showcase of the real things from the novel?"

"No," Clarissa said.

"Because I don't want to be part of that."

"It isn't."

"I thought this was your own thing."

"It was *my* life, not hers!"

"Are we going to your parents' house?"

"Eventually."

"How are you going to introduce me?"

"As my friend," Clarissa said. "And producer."

Del looked out across the pool beyond the chain-link fence. Kids were run-walking across the concrete deck and jumping off the diving board, doing cannonballs that smacked the surface and sent water flying. "You know I always support you," she said. "But—I don't know."

"About what?"

"This whole project," Del said, and she laughed a hopeless laugh. "Coming out to your parents when you're not even in a relationship with a woman. It's hard for me to admit that you're not in a relationship with a woman, because I love you, but you aren't. So I'm not sure why we're here."

"I need them to accept me the way I am."

"Which is how, exactly?"

Clarissa looked at Del, her big ex-lover, who knew herself perfectly, and had known all her life.

"I don't know," Clarissa said. "I just want them to see me. If they *see* me, then maybe I'll know."

56

JAMIE HAD HIS OLD job at the guitar store—it wasn't a great job, but they had enough money from Josephine, and it was a place to go while T.J. was in school. The owner of the store was a real musician, and Jamie could talk to the kids who came in to gaze longingly at the electric guitars, and to the old guys with stories of life on the road with some forgotten band. When no one was in, Jamie could play the pretty new guitars before someone bought them and took them away.

Abby never called him anymore, and he wished he had remained the good uncle; he wished he hadn't fucked things up. He called from the guitar store and left a message on her machine. "You used to answer the phone *sometimes*, at least," he said. "Now you never pick up, and you never call. What's the deal? Where are you living? Is this a real phone or just a voice mail? Call me back, I'm at work."

He took three business calls on the phone behind the glass counter before it was Abby calling.

"Where are you?" he asked.

"At school."

"In the dorms?"

"An apartment."

He took a fresh-faced kid's dollar for a guitar pick. "Did you hear Saffron is marrying Martin Russell?"

"Are you the best man?" she asked.

"No," Jamie said. "Don't you think she'll cheat on him, too? Tell me you think she'll cheat on him, too."

"She'll cheat on him, too."

"Thank you."

"Is that why you called?"

"Also to talk. I read your book again, and I was thinking that in the second half you got timid. I mean it wasn't about us as much. And you killed yourself off."

She said nothing.

"And your dad lives."

"It's my novel," she said. "I can have him live if I want."

"I still liked it," he said. "Did anyone ask you if you slept with me?"

"No. Did they ask you?"

"They danced around it, was there anything I wanted to talk about. I stick to the plan. Mostly they talk about their own characters. Katya was reading it the other day. She hasn't said anything, but I don't know how well she reads English."

"How is she?"

"Oh, you know," he said, rubbing some adhesive off the glass counter. "She has this kid she never knew, and she's in a strange city in a strange country. It's a lot to process."

"I'm sorry."

"You should see T.J., though," he said. "Kids are amazing. When he's my age he'll have a nervous breakdown, but you should see how cool he is now. Sometimes I think we should go on the road in an Airstream, like in the book."

"With Katya, too?"

"Okay, maybe not." The idea of Katya in close quarters made him want to think about something else. "Can you *believe* Saffron's marrying that guy?" he asked.

"Yes."

"You can?"

"You knew he was her boyfriend."

"That's different," he said. "You can't take a boyfriend seriously. It's like someone saying, 'Hey, you know that mountain you want to climb? It sometimes has snow on it.' But what's a little snow to a mountain climber?"

Abby laughed. He liked making her laugh. He rang up some guitar strings for a bearded guy in a bandanna.

"So what about you?" Jamie asked. "Is there snow on your mountain?"

"I beg your pardon?"

"Are you in this apartment alone?"

"At the moment."

"And who are you expecting? Some lovely coeds for a pillow fight, or a mustached gent, doffing his hat?"

"Neither," she said.

"Come on, Ab, give me something."

"I should go."

"You could come up and see us."

"Sure."

"I love you, babe."

"Mm."

In the background Jamie heard a door close, and a man's voice saying something friendly. He imagined her in the long-lost summer sublet, near the bathroom with the rattling shower rings. Abby said a muffled "Hey," away from the phone, and Jamie felt suddenly cold.

"Is that him?" he asked.

"Bye," she said. "We'll talk soon."

"Abby, wait," he said.

"Bye."

PART THREE

57

ABBY SAT ON DR. TIRRETT'S couch, staring out the big window, the box of Kleenex resting against her thigh. "One of Peter's students said there wasn't enough of the patriarch's family in my novel," she said. "She thought that was missing from it."

Leila waited for her to go on. When she didn't, she asked, "Do you care what Peter's students say?"

"Well, they're readers."

"Aren't they the ones who call short stories 'articles'?"

"Yeah."

"So are they the best readers to listen to?"

"Maybe they're right."

"Do you think there should have been more about that character's family?"

"No," Abby said. "He had a brother once, but I cut the scene, the story didn't need it. His feeling about his wife was more important. I think I told what was necessary."

"So then you don't care what the students say."

"Yes, I do."

Leila said, "This wanting to please everyone—it isn't fair to give other people so much power. You tempt the greediest part of them."

Abby looked at her tiredly and then said, "Jamie sounded sort of desperate when he called. I don't think it's working out with Katya."

"And what if it doesn't?"

"It will be so hard for the kid. What if she takes him away? You think I'm damaged, but she's *really* damaged."

Leila hesitated. "You spend a lot of time talking about people you can't fix."

"I don't think I can be fixed, either. I think I'm hardwired this way, and kind of unhelpable."

"I don't think so."

"It's your *job* not to think so. But I know what it's like inside my head."

"Are you saying you want to stop coming here?"

Abby looked out the window. "No."

"Have you told your uncle about Peter?"

"No."

"Because he would be jealous."

"He's already jealous. But it's not his business. It's my private life."

"And it's taboo, like the relationship with Jamie," Leila said.

Abby gave an impatient little shake of her head. "Students are going to sleep with teachers. That taboo doesn't stand a chance."

"You never talk about it, so I just want to make sure you've thought about the similarities."

Abby paused. "I think I'm trying to protect Peter."

"From me?"

"Yes."

"I'm not against him."

"I know."

"The only thing that worries me," Leila said, "is that the moment you carved out some ground from your family's needs and wants—and stabilized yourself mentally after a relationship with one of them—you ceded that ground to another person."

Abby sighed. "I did *not*," she said. "He read the book, that's all."

"But the book was the thing you were using to claim your territory, make your stand."

"Everyone needs an editor."

"Not everyone sleeps with them."

Abby looked at her watch. "I think it's time to stop."

"How do you feel right now?"

"I don't know."

Leila waited.

Abby said, "If this is some transference game to get me to be angry at you, that's going to make me *really* annoyed."

"It isn't a game."

Abby rolled her Kleenex into a ball and looked at her hands. "I know I don't talk much about Peter," she said. "It's not that I'm not thinking about it. It's that I'm *happy,* when I'm with him. It's the first time in a long time that I've been actually *happy,* and it's hard to talk convincingly about it, because it sounds—ridiculous, and I'm afraid to talk about it because I'm afraid it will go away."

Leila was surprised. "Okay," she said.

"I hate being made to say it, because I know I sound defensive, but he's not some cliché about teachers and power."

"I believe you," Leila said.

Abby picked up her bag to leave.

Leila said, "Before you go—it isn't a game, but I do think it's good for you to argue with me. Maybe think this week about not doing what people want you to do. And not caring what Peter's students think."

"That's easy for you to say."

"Just try it," Leila said.

58

TEDDY HADN'T READ Abby's novel, but he knew there were some disturbing things in it. When Clarissa showed up unexpectedly with her mannish friend and a video camera, she told him more than once that he didn't have to read it.

He had seen, that day, what he thought was a news team out on the sidewalk in front of the house. It was still amazing to him how much he could see since the surgery, and he watched them through the window. The man had a camera on his shoulder and was filming what looked like a reporter, who had her back to the house. Then the reporter turned and gestured, and Teddy had a disorienting start, because the gesture was Yvette's. A second later, he recognized his daughter and went outside. When he had hugged Clarissa and realized her friend was a woman, he invited them in for a drink.

"So you raised an author," he said in the kitchen, filling glasses with ice.

"It isn't your kind of book, Dad," Clarissa said.

He guessed that was true. He liked adventure stories and historical novels, and books like one he'd just read about an Englishman who inherited some land after World War I and nurtured the land

and the people who lived and farmed around it. He kept the land from being subdivided, though they didn't call it subdividing then. He got to know the people. There were no crises in the book, and no negativism. There was enough of that on the evening news. When he read a novel—which wasn't often—he didn't want to feel like he was watching the news.

They took the drinks to the living room, and Clarissa asked if she could film him a little. She was taking a class.

"I don't have anything to say," he said.

"Sure you do, Dad," Clarissa said, setting the camera up on her shoulder. "Tell me about your first love."

Teddy felt his face heat up, remembering his pretty cousin Gabrielle, with her black braids. "That was your mother," he said.

"Oh, come on, Dad, really?" Clarissa said, behind the lens.

"Sure."

"Okay, tell me about your childhood."

He thought. "Well, my father had a lot of brothers," he said. "We used to go visiting on Sundays. You know, no one had any money then, and it was something to do. And it was important to my father, to see his brothers."

"You don't sound like you enjoyed it."

"Not much."

His uncles had lived in small frame houses and two-family flats in Detroit, kept scrubbed to varying degrees of spotlessness by their wives. The older uncles, adults when the family moved down from Canada, said "tree" for "three," and slapped him too hard on the back. They never hit him in anger, like his father did, but he was proud that his father sounded American. They all worked in the automobile plants. The youngest, Frankie, was still a bachelor and lived glamorously in a small room in a big Georgian house divided up for boarders.

And then there was Gabrielle—Teddy didn't tell Clarissa about her. Gabrielle's father was his father's least favorite brother, so their visits there were short and perfunctory, and for a long time Teddy couldn't say more than hello. But slowly he built up his courage, and there was an impossibly sweet time when he would meet her under the back windows, where no one could see them, and kiss her there, and finally touch her ironed Sunday blouse with the tiny breasts underneath.

He had never been caught with his cousin; there had been no traumatic end. Instead, he and Gabrielle had just grown up, and taken an interest in people outside their family, and maintained for each other an abashed kind of affection. When he first saw Yvette, years later, she had reminded him of black-haired Gabrielle and those Sundays behind the house.

The war was on in Europe by that time—this he told Clarissa—and people in Detroit were saying America would stay out of it. But Teddy's European history professor was a Prussian named Hecht who had been a German officer in the last war. He had a glass eye and a scar over the same eyebrow. When he heard Teddy was taking flying lessons—they were free to college men, great fun—he took him aside and explained that Roosevelt was training his pilots quietly, getting ready to enter the war.

"We didn't know, you see," Teddy told Clarissa. "It was just a thing to do, like the football team."

He went home to his parents' house—he couldn't afford a boardinghouse like Uncle Frank's—and thought it through. If America was going to the war, then Teddy wanted to be a pilot. He had spent too many hours in the air now to want to fight on the ground.

In the spring he finished his flight training and enlisted in the Marines. He hadn't known they would dilate his eyes, and he couldn't see to take his European history exam. The professor told him to come back when he could read again. So Teddy wrote the exam in Hecht's office the next day, his head full of dates and campaigns. When he finished, the old man kept him there. The glass eye was never quite straight, and it unnerved Teddy.

"You have a girl," the Prussian said.

"Yes, sir."

"She's beautiful? You love her?"

Teddy felt his face heat up. "Yes, sir."

"When you go," Hecht said, "if you want to keep her, you marry her. They don't wait so long, if they don't marry. And it won't be short, this war."

"I don't have the money to get married."

"No one has the money," Hecht said, waving his hand as if to brush the objection off his desk. "You made this decision to enlist. Now you make the decision about the girl. Or some other will come for her. This might be a relief to you."

The Marine Corps sent him to Corpus Christi for training, and there he came down with a terrible fever. He was in the infirmary when he received his orders to go to California, and he called Yvette. Half delirious, he put the question to her, and she said yes. He tried not to cry. Nineteen years old and barely out of Catholic school, she took the train by herself out to Santa Barbara to meet him, against her father's wishes. It took his breath away that she had done it, his beautiful, brave girl.

And California was worthy of her—he would never go back to the long winters and dirty snow of Detroit. Here were palm trees, and blue sea and clean sand, and it was always summer. And it was for everyone; you didn't have to be rich. The military put them in hotels on the beach, and there were tea dances and buffet dinners right there next to the waves. He knew he couldn't go home after the war and drive through the gray slush to work for the auto plants. He felt a physical revulsion at the thought of more Sunday visits to the uncles: his back being slapped, and sweet Gabrielle fatly pregnant with twins. When he finally went to sea, he had long hours to think on the carrier in the Pacific, to be sure in his mind that he would stay.

He was telling Clarissa's camera about sitting on that carrier, waiting and thinking, when Yvette came into the house from working in the garden.

"His mother was so worried about him," Yvette said, and Clarissa turned the camera on her.

Teddy felt robbed, for a second, of his daughter's attention, but then he sat back to watch Yvette talk. It was a perfectly natural thing to her, to perform: there was no flustered transition from pulling weeds.

"His brothers were all in the service," Yvette said, taking off her gardening gloves, "and his mother just worried herself sick. She called me a Pollyanna because I didn't worry. But I was just *sure* he would come back." She looked at Teddy. "And he did."

"Were *you* worried, Dad?" Clarissa asked, turning the camera back on him.

"Sometimes," he said.

"Like when?"

"Well, there was a moment," he said, trying to think of a good example. "We were laying mines across a harbor in the Solomon Islands. To keep the Japanese ships inside, you see. We dropped the mines on parachutes, and we had to fly very low and slow to do it." He showed with his hand how slow. "On the first night of the mission, the lights came on from below as we were flying over. Anti-aircraft fire hit the plane in front of me, and it went down. We lost a plane every night we flew that mission."

"How many men in a plane?" Clarissa asked.

"Three," he said. "A pilot, a gunner, and a radioman."

"Could they have survived?"

He shook his head. "They went down too fast. And the plane was usually on fire. Thirty-six men went out on each mission, in twelve planes, and every night thirty-three came back."

"Oh, Dad, I'm so sorry," Clarissa said. She looked at her camera. "I think that's the end of the tape."

"Are you staying?" Yvette asked her. "Are you two hungry?"

The girls went with Yvette to the kitchen, talking, and Teddy stayed in the living room, thinking about the pilots they had lost, men he played cards with in the wardroom lounge, who the next night were suddenly gone.

He had thought about Hecht sometimes, the man who had guided him into his life. When Margot and Clarissa were children, both in school, Teddy had thought about writing a letter—not to thank the old man, exactly, but to let him know how things had turned out. But when he wrote to the university for an address, they wrote back that Professor Hecht had died of a stroke the year before. Teddy had felt cut loose, then, as if his own father had died; the author of his life was gone.

59

JAMIE CAME BACK from putting T.J. to bed and sat down at the kitchen table, where Katya was drinking coffee and playing solitaire. She played all the time now, to keep (he assumed) from smoking, talking, drinking, thinking, practicing English, bonding with T.J., or getting a job. She was fast: she knew instantly whether she could use a new card and never looked for possibilities that didn't exist.

He didn't mention the Kit Kat wrapper he had found in the laundry, or the defensive way T.J. had said, "It appeared in my pocket." He sat down at the table and said awkwardly, "Katya, I know you're unhappy. I wondered if you might want to see someone."

"See who?"

"A therapist, maybe. Like the marriage counselor, but alone."

"I did not like that woman." She went back to the cards.

"You could see someone else. Or they have support groups." He wasn't sure what the support group would be for. Retired Hungarian prostitutes? Mothers who had recovered their adopted foreign-raised children? He knew she took some kind of European tranquilizer and had run out of it, so maybe Narcotics Anonymous. He allowed himself to think that her problem was just withdrawal. She hadn't asked for a new prescription. He wondered if she had tried to get the pills on the street.

"I cannot explain myself in English," she said. "It is so frustrated."

"Maybe we could find a Hungarian therapist," he said. "I worry about T.J., that's why I bring it up."

Katya said nothing.

"Have you thought about why you might be crying lately?" he asked.

Katya rolled her eyes. "You want to do this analysis?" she asked. "How do you know *lately*? Do you know how I cry before?"

"No," he admitted. "Did you cry a lot before?"

"Never," she said vehemently.

Jamie felt like she was walking circles around him with a rope, winding it tight around his chest. "Okay," he said. "So why now? Is it the pills?"

"*What* pills?" she said.

"Is it me?"

She glared at him, foxlike. "Do not give yourself this importance."

Jamie sat back in the kitchen chair. He suddenly wanted a cigarette, though it had been years since he had smoked. It wasn't like he was so happy, either. He would never do anything with his life, and they were ruining T.J.'s, and Katya cried at night and wouldn't touch him. He guessed that when she had discovered, with a mixture of scorn and relief, that she *could* refuse him, he was doomed. Why should she give herself to such an unforceful man? But he couldn't bring himself to force her, so he was stuck.

"Do you know how T.J. ended up with a Kit Kat wrapper?" he asked.

Katya paused and then said, "I buy this for him at the store."

"He told me it appeared in his pocket."

Katya placed a card and moved a stack. "Yes," she said. "I give it as a present."

"Okay," Jamie said. "But maybe he shouldn't have candy between meals."

"He is a little boy, he likes the chocolate, so what does this matter?"

Jamie gave up and went down the hallway toward their bedroom. He stopped outside T.J.'s room and opened the door slowly, without making any noise, and saw T.J.'s big eyes above the blanket.

"You awake, buddy?"

"Yes," T.J. said.

"What's up?"

"I'm thinking."

Jamie went in and sat on the bed. "About what?"

T.J. said nothing.

"About the candy?"

T.J. nodded.

"How did you get it again?"

"It appeared in my pocket."

"Did someone put it in your pocket?"

T.J. shook his head.

"Did you find it somewhere?"

T.J. nodded.

"Where did you find it?"

T.J. whispered, *"At Safeway."*

"Did anyone pay for it?"

T.J. shook his head.

"So did you steal the candy from Safeway?"

T.J. was silent.

"I'm not mad at you," Jamie said. "I just want to know what happened."

"What you said," T.J. whispered.

"Which thing that I said?"

"About Safeway."

"That you took it from Safeway and didn't pay for it?"

T.J. nodded.

"Was it your idea?"

T.J. shook his head.

Jamie sighed. Katya had been the mastermind; that was clear.

But he didn't want to make the kid snitch on her. He thought of his own delinquent youth, of the many things he had done that were worse than stealing a candy bar: getting stoned on the beach on stolen lawn chairs, getting kicked out of school, driving a hot-wired car into the ocean. But he felt an immense burden of responsibility about this boy. He wanted T.J. to get through life more smoothly than he had.

"Okay, Teej," he said. "That's called stealing. And all those people at Safeway, they work really hard, so if we steal, we aren't just taking things from the store, we're taking things from *them*. And they have to feed their families." He was laying it on a little thick, he knew.

T.J.'s eyes were huge. "I'm sorry," he whispered.

"I know," Jamie said. "Here's what we do. We go down to Safeway, and we tell the manager and apologize, and pay for the candy, and then it will all be behind us. Okay?"

T.J. looked mortified. "Okay."

Jamie checked his watch. It was eight-thirty. "We can go tonight, or we can go in the morning."

"Tonight!" The poor kid didn't want to sleep on the guilt Jamie had laid on.

So Jamie helped T.J. change back into his clothes, and they took his piggy bank. Katya was out on the balcony with the sliding door closed, and Jamie decided not to say anything to her. They went down to the car and headed for Safeway.

"What will the manager say?" T.J. asked.

"I don't know," Jamie said, honestly. "We'll just tell him and see."

"*Him?*" T.J. asked, horrified. "It's not a lady?"

"It might be a man, I don't know."

T.J. fell silent.

At Safeway they had to wait by the customer service desk, and T.J. squeezed Jamie's hand in a vise grip. Finally the manager showed up. He was just a kid, handsome and olive-skinned and clean-shaven, and he had dark tattoos on his arms, under the thin white cotton of his shirt, and a silver stud in his right eyebrow. He wore a red tie and a name badge that said "Samvat."

"Hi," Jamie said, feeling ridiculous. "We live in the neighborhood, and T.J. has something to tell you."

The tattooed manager looked down at T.J., who squeezed Jamie's hand harder.

"You tell him!" T.J. said.

"No, you have to."

Samvat was waiting, pierced eyebrows raised, so finally Jamie crouched down to whisper the cues: *"When I was in the store with my mom . . ."*

"When I was in the store with my mom . . . ," T.J. recited.

"I took some candy without paying for it . . ."

"I took some candy without paying for it . . ."

"And I'm really sorry."

"And I'm really sorry."

At this point T.J. produced the crumpled Kit Kat wrapper from his pocket and held it up as evidence of his crime.

The tattooed kid looked at Jamie like he was a freak. People stole things constantly, his look said, and Jamie was the first parent who had ever dragged his son in on a guilt trip like this. Jamie smiled back hopefully, counting on him to play his part.

"Okay!" Samvat said, in a hearty voice, and he clapped his hands together, looking like he needed whispered cues, too. "Um, stealing is really bad," he said. "It could get you in a lot of trouble. But it's real great that you apologized and everything. So I'll tell you what, you just keep that candy."

"Actually, we've brought the piggy bank," Jamie said, "and we'd like to pay."

Again Samvat looked at him like he'd lost his mind. "Okay . . . ," he said slowly. "Let's see, that's sixty cents, plus tax, so, what . . . I guess sixty-five cents."

Jamie helped T.J. count it out—his small hands were hot and damp—and the boy handed the money over. Dark flame tattoos licked out of Samvat's shirt cuff as he reached to take it.

"I'll ring that up at the front," Samvat said, pocketing the money. "Thank you for being so honest, T.J. We need more people like you."

"Thank you," T.J. said breathlessly.

Samvat gave Jamie a questioning look to see if that was what he had wanted, and Jamie shook his hand and thanked him, too.

When they got outside the store, the boy was dancing with relief. His whole body moved like he was shaking the thing off, and he was making happy little noises of having survived something horrible. He seemed so elated that Jamie worried he would be addicted now: the stealing felt bad, but the relief on confessing felt *so good*.

In the car, T.J. got reflective and said, "Do we have to tell about this?"

"No," Jamie said.

"Not even to Katya?"

"Not if you don't want to. I'll leave it up to you. You can tell who you want."

"Let's not tell anyone," T.J. said, as they turned up their street.

"Okay," Jamie said. "It's a deal."

60

MARGOT CALLED THE law firm in Santa Barbara from her kitchen in Baton Rouge, with her heart pounding, just to hear his name. The secretary answered brightly, "Cassidy and Herrera."

"What about Jay?" Margot asked. As soon as she said it, she had a sharp fear that something had happened to him.

There was a pause. "He left," the secretary said.

"Oh," Margot said. "Is he working somewhere else?"

"I think so," the secretary said. "I can give you his new information. Or what I have, anyway. I think he's still there."

Margot wrote down the new number and the address in Santa Barbara but didn't call.

She decided she would go visit her parents in Hermosa Beach. It was nothing more than that. She was a good daughter, and Teddy and Yvette weren't getting any younger, and Los Angeles happened to be close to Santa Barbara. That was all—she wasn't thinking any further ahead. She flew standby and rented a car at the airport, feeling a kind of dreamy ease because she wasn't really making a decision.

At home, she admired her mother's garden, and talked to her father about his improved vision, and was glad she had come. But by the second day, she got restless. Wandering around her parents' house while they were both out, she left a note by the phone:

Mom and Dad—
Such a beautiful day. Going to drive up the coast. Don't plan on me for dinner. Will call.

xxoo
Margot

She put the pen down and thought that if she were really a good daughter she would have gone with her parents on their errands, and then she wouldn't be doing this thing. She packed an overnight bag and went out to the rental car her mother had insisted she wouldn't need.

Santa Ana winds had blown all the smog out to sea, and the air was clear, the waves laced with silver. The mountains were sharp against the sky and dark green. Margot took the long coastal route north through Malibu and Oxnard, because that was what she had said she would do, but she was longing to be inland on the freeway, moving fast in a straight line. She didn't know what she would do once she got to Santa Barbara, but whatever happened would stop this agonizing, restless feeling in her stomach. She wished it would happen soon.

Finally she was in Montecito, then Santa Barbara, and then she was parked outside the address the secretary had given her. She sat and looked up at the white Spanish building, not knowing what to do. She got out of the car.

She surveyed herself mentally: she was wearing Capri pants and a fine-gauge silk cardigan, and she had kept her figure. She'd had her hair trimmed before leaving Baton Rouge, and the gray didn't really show up against the blond. Men still looked at her—not like they used to, but she wasn't invisible yet. She closed the car door, feeling exposed and on display, as if she were naked.

Then, because there wasn't anything else to do, she climbed the stairs to the front door of the law firm and went in.

61

JAMIE WAS VACUUMING the apartment the morning after the Kit Kat incident. Katya was out somewhere, smoking or plotting against him. T.J. was playing in his room with the door closed against the vacuum noise.

There were long hairs shed by Katya on her side of the bed, gold in the window light on the carpet, and he moved the little cabinet that was her nightstand to be able to vacuum straight through. The base of the cabinet dragged a pile of hidden twenty-dollar bills across the floor. Jamie stood with the vacuum cleaner running and considered the money. Then he turned the machine off. He sat on the bed and counted the bills: three hundred and sixty dollars. There weren't a lot of reasons he could think of that Katya would be hiding cash. He had heard a prostitute on a radio call-in show say she got eight hundred dollars an hour, even if it took ten minutes, but he didn't think Katya was getting that. He guessed he held multiple payments in his hands. He wondered if she had ever brought anyone to the apartment, while he was at work, but he couldn't think about that for long.

He left the twenties on the bed and checked the nightstand drawer, her clothes drawers, and a black purse he found in the closet.

No money. He checked the freezer—he'd seen it as a hiding place in a movie—and found no cash but a pack of Marlboros behind the ice trays. He was checking the back of the silverware drawer when Katya came in. He watched her hang her jacket on a chair and go down the hall. She made no sign that she had seen him in the kitchen, but she had. Say what you would about Katya, she didn't miss much. He heard the toilet flush, and then he guessed she was headed for the bedroom. A few seconds later, she stormed back into the kitchen.

"Why do you sneak in my things?" she demanded.

"I was vacuuming. Where'd you get the money?"

"I can have money! I am adult in America!"

"Sure," he said, feeling weirdly calm. "But I'm asking where you got it."

"I keep it for T.J., for later."

"You mean like the trust account, at the bank?"

"Yes."

"So why not put it there?"

She hesitated. "Maybe banks are not so safe."

"And where did it come from?"

"It is a gift for him."

"Katya, I'm not stupid."

"I am not stupid, also!" she said. "I was reading this book of Abby. I am slow to read English maybe, but I am not *stupid*."

"What does that have to do with anything?"

"You are not police here. I have some small money. The boy has this chocolate. And you are *no one* to say this is wrong."

"I don't want my kid stealing," Jamie said, "and I don't want my wife turning tricks. I think those are pretty basic requests."

"What do you know, *tricks*? You know nothing. But I know you fuck this niece."

"It's a novel!"

"This means what? Nothing is real? I know a little bit, Jamie. I was doing many things in my life, but nothing so *fucked* like this."

Jamie felt as if she had slapped him, and he tried to find words to defend himself, and then he saw T.J. standing against the wall in the hallway, watching them. He didn't know how long the boy had been there. He wished he could disappear, and sink down into the floor, and everything would be over.

Katya shoved past him, into the kitchen, while he stood there, and T.J. watched with those big eyes. She took down a box of cereal and pulled a stack of cash from between the plastic liner bag and the cardboard. She folded the money and put it in her jeans pocket. Then she pulled out the drawer under the oven, lifted the old cookie sheets the last owners had left behind, and produced another stack of bills, held together with a rubber band. She put that in the other pocket, went back to the bedroom, and closed the door.

62

FAUCHET WALKED HOME from lunch at his club in Paris one afternoon—a good lunch, but he had drunk too much wine. His doctor had forbidden wine at lunch, but at his club he thought he should be able to have this small pleasure without remorse. And it was not even really remorse he felt: it was a little pain in his chest. Not a heart attack, just a tightness, a reminder that he would die. Because he had—what, ten years left? Maybe not so many. Ten years, this was nothing, and the best years were gone.

There was a girls' school on his way home, where the students loitered outside in their fetching uniforms: the navy blue sweaters, the long socks, the short gray pleated skirts. Even old as he was, there were one or two who would deliberately catch his eye, bold little thirteen- and fourteen-year-olds. Each year there were new ones.

He'd had an affair once, with a woman who had come out of this school fifteen years earlier, and she told him how they had talked about the men who walked by in their long coats and Burberry scarves, with their furtive glances. She said the girls had a game, to see who was looked at the most. One couldn't try to bring attention, or it didn't count. It was meant to be entirely on merit, on innate desirability. There was a bold *jolie laide* who won the contest again and again, without seeming to do anything but lean sulkily against the brick wall, until she finally disappeared to a school in Switzerland. His lover was thrilled to discover that he had been one of those men. He thought it was her favorite thing about him, and kept her interested much longer than she might have been.

He had always seen a few of the girls smoking: sneaking cigarettes when they were out of sight of the building. Now they talked on tiny silver mobiles instead. They had a new way to look grown-up and sophisticated—a thing to do with their restless hands and mouths. Not one of them looked at him; they were all engrossed in telephone conversations about nothing: *"Qu'est-ce que tu fais? Moi non plus. Je suis à l'ecole."* They would all now get brain cancer from the little telephones instead of dying from the cigarettes.

His wife was gone for the day, and the house was empty when Fauchet let himself in. He thought he would put his feet up and close his eyes, and the pain in his chest would go. On the table in the hall was a little stack of invitations, opened by his wife and left for him. He flipped through the white cards: a dinner, a vernissage. He put them down. Next to the cards was a long white envelope for him. His wife always disappeared with the bills before he saw them, and many of his old friends were dead, so he rarely got mail at home. It was airmail from the United States, postmarked in San Francisco. He found the letter opener in the dish of change on the hall table.

"Hello, my old freind," the letter said.

I am practicing Englisch now more than French, so you will forgive me because I write in it, and I am so bad. But I onderstand the fast Englisch on the radio now. Once I thout I will never onderstand it.

I want to thank you for helping Jamie to adopt the boy. He is a good father, I think. You will be plesed. And the boy is good, and hapy.

I am not so happy, I will say it quickly. I think I am not rite for this life. The city is very interesting. Some pepole are very nice. The little boy is beutifull. There is plan to visit Jamies parent's for Thanks Giving. But I am not Thankfull. I am thinking all the time that I am going crazy. I am not for the good, safe life, and the rich stores, and the people

*who no nothing. I should be Thankfull, but I cannot change the way
I am.*

*I am so un happy everyday, and I make fights. Somtimes I have
reson and sometimes no. I want to go back to my contry, where I know
life is dificult. Or to Paris where are people from my contry. I have to
leve this place.*

*This is one small part of what I feel. There are so many things I
wish to say in my own languege. I can say none of them here. I seem so
stupid.*

*I write to you beaucose you have always helped me. Also I wish
Jamie to keep the boy, so he can grow up not so unhappy here like me. I
wish him to have the American things and the safetey, in hapiness.
With out me, they can be O.K. You have been my freind always, and I
think may be you can onderstand me.*

Your Katya.

(P.S. Did you read this book the neice was writing abuot Jamie?)

Fauchet folded the letter back up. He hadn't read the book,
though his agent friend had described it to him on the phone, and
sent him a copy when it was finished. He felt pleased to have noticed
the closeness between the girl and her young uncle; he still had the
eye. He guessed it had given Katya another reason for leaving.

He did not forgive himself for seizing the chance to pack the boy
off to America. It had solved so many of his problems at the time:
it pleased Katya, it helped Saffron, and it avoided a scandal. He had
reasoned that it was good to give the boy a father and mother, but
in truth he had been skeptical of Katya's ability to become, just like
this, an American wife. Jamie was an appealing young man, but he
was not the one to take Katya in hand.

He went into the library, as he had planned to do, and sat on his
old leather couch with his legs up. He pulled a small blanket over
himself, feeling chilled. Through the windows the yellow Paris
autumn light was beautiful but did nothing to warm him. He
thought about what he could do for Katya.

The key turned in the front door lock, and his wife's shoes clicked across the floor and onto the rug in the foyer. She stopped to look at the hall table—he could track her movements even though he could not see her—and then she went to hang up her coat. She must have seen that he had picked up the envelope. Heels off, she padded to the kitchen for a glass of something, then appeared at the library door. It was a glass of wine she had gone for, a small tumbler of red.

"*Ciao, bellissima,*" he said. "*Come stai?*" It was one of their ways around each other, to speak in Italian. It allowed them not to face each other head-on.

"Why do you have a blanket?" she asked him in French.

"I was cold."

"You opened the letter?" she asked.

He said he had.

She waited. She was his second wife, and she looked like a second wife, still very beautiful in a hard, Parisian way. The city did something to women, made them part stone: hard and lovely and less physically corruptible than the women of flesh who lived elsewhere in France. She wore a thin black sweater and diamond earrings. Her dark hair curved smoothly toward her chin.

"It's from my friend in America," he said.

"Which friend?"

"A lover of Gilbert's."

"Your lover, too?"

"No," he said. It was true now. And Gilbert was dead of a heart attack the winter before, in his sleep.

"Does she want money?"

"She has a little."

"What does she want?"

"Why are you so curious?"

"You rarely get letters here," she said. "And you're acting strange."

"I am acting perfectly normal."

She tilted her head, and the curve of hair sought its plumb. "No," she said. "You're not."

He sighed. "She has a child in the United States, and she wishes to leave him there and return to Europe," he said. "She is unhappy."

"Is it Gilbert's child?"

"I suppose. Now the boy is about six, but he was raised by others. Her American husband has adopted him."

"Is this the foreign girl who used to telephone?"

"Yes," he said.

"Is she a prostitute?"

"In the past."

"Is the American husband a homosexual?"

Fauchet shook his head. "No."

His wife took a sip of her wine, thinking the matter through. "Then the child is better in America than with this mother," she decided finally. "I wouldn't normally think so. But what kind of mother is this?"

"She's not a bad girl," he said. "A little bit damaged."

His wife frowned and studied him. "Will she come to Paris?"

"I don't know. Come sit with me."

She crossed the carpet in her stocking feet and set her glass on the low table, her wrist cocked at an elegant angle as if she could do nothing inelegantly. Then she lowered herself to the couch and tucked her ankles up sideways, all in one motion. She tugged an end of the blanket out from between them and pulled it over her.

"So?" she said. "I am here."

Under the blanket, he put an arm across her knees. "This is good," he said. "Like the kids in the park."

"Not much like that," she said.

"Exactly like that." He was about to tell her about the pain in his chest, but he couldn't. He told himself it wasn't an important pain.

"If this damaged girl comes to Paris," his wife said, "you won't sleep with her."

Fauchet put his head on her shoulder. "At seventy-one," he said, "you expect so much from me? You are a transparent little flatterer."

"I'm very serious," she said.

"My love," he said. "My little one. You are too kind."

63

WHEN MARGOT WALKED into Dominick Jay's small law office in Santa Barbara, the receptionist's desk was deserted, piled with papers and manila folders, so she went to the open door beyond the desk. Inside was another cluttered office, where Dominick stood looking out the window with his hands behind his back. She saw no wedding band, and she felt a flood of old desire. She knocked on the open door, and he turned and looked at her. There was a long moment before he spoke.

"Margot," he finally said.

She thought she saw pain in his eyes, or bafflement and irritation, but then he came out from behind the desk and grasped her shoulders and kissed her cheek.

"My God," he said. "Sit down."

There was a little couch, and she sat in one corner of it and he sat in the other. His legs were long and their knees were close. There were no pictures of a wife.

"Is this how you sit with all your clients?" Margot asked.

"No," he said. "Are you a client? Do you have a legal problem?"

She shook her head.

"So it's different," he said. "Tell me everything."

Margot took a deep breath. "My niece, Abby," she said, "you might have met her when she was little, wrote a book."

"Congratulations," he said.

She laughed. "Well," she said. "It's not that simple. I know this sounds crazy, but before I read it, I found out it was about a Catholic family keeping secrets from each other. So I got it into my head that Abby knew. About us. Because she was there that summer, the summer I knew you. I was sure our affair was what the book was about. It had me in a panic."

"Oh, Margot."

"But the book isn't about that at all," she said. "It's about crazy, made-up secrets. But then I couldn't stop thinking about you. I wondered where you'd gone, and what had happened to you, and if you'd married." Here she paused to let him interrupt, but he didn't, so she went on. "I looked you up on the Internet," she said. "I've never done that before. I'm a very moderate person. Now I've said too much."

He considered her. "So you came all the way here, from Louisiana?"

"I was visiting my parents in L.A., and I drove up."

"Do they know you're here?"

"No one does," she said, and she felt her heart start to race. When was the last time no one had known where she was? She couldn't remember.

"You're still married?"

She nodded. "Are you?"

"Divorced."

"I'm sorry," she said, but she felt a leap of joy.

"Never marry for the wrong reasons in a community property state," he said. His jaw tightened, and then he seemed to make himself relax and shrug.

She looked around the office. "Do you do family law?"

"No," he said. "The hymn to the prenup is just a little song and dance I do when I'm nervous. You can understand me being nervous."

"Where's your receptionist?"

"She found fault with the working conditions here and left."

"Do you have help?"

"I had a paralegal."

"And?"

"She's gone, too. I used to think about you walking through my office door," he said. "I wondered if you could find me, I wondered if you would. Then I stopped thinking about it. I thought: This is healthy. I'm moving on with my life, like a man. And then you walk in. Jesus. In my version you didn't still have a wedding ring on your finger."

Margot covered her hand, ashamed. "I'm sorry," she said. "I just had to see you, I was going crazy."

"Well, here I am," he said.

Margot nodded. "I didn't have any plans past getting here."

He was silent for a moment. Then he said, "I can tell you how my version went."

"Okay."

"First you agreed to sit on the couch with me," he said. "Then I told you about my tragic marriage—briefly. You told me about the breakup of yours. I was very sympathetic. We didn't spend much time on the disappearance of my legal staff. Then there was an awkward silence, and you leaned forward and kissed me."

Margot looked up at him, wondering what she had done, by coming here.

The moment passed, and he sighed. "Would you like to have dinner with me?"

She managed to nod.

"Good," he said. In the process of swinging his long body up, he leaned over and kissed her temple. "I'm glad you're here," he said.

Margot called her parents from the receptionist's desk to say she was too tired to drive back safely and was getting a motel room.

"Of course, honey," her mother said. "Do the safest thing."

Margot suffered a moment of aching guilt, then drove Dominick to a restaurant with a table by a big brick fireplace.

"This was in my version, too," he said, reading the wine list. "But it happened later. Other things happened first."

The wine was very good, and Dominick made her laugh over dinner. When he left the table to pay, Margot realized she was drunk, and her lips were a little bit numb. He was gone from the table a long time.

"Well, the third credit card worked," he said when he returned.

They went out to her car, and the cool sea air felt wonderful on her face—she had forgotten how wonderful the night air could be, after so many years in muggy, air-conditioned Louisiana. She followed his directions home, still pleasantly tipsy and thinking it seemed like a roundabout route, and finally she parked where he told her to stop. She felt faint when he kissed her. Then she must have agreed to go in, because they were walking together up some steps, and he was unlocking the door, and they were inside.

64

Jimmy Vaughan was in Santa Barbara, meeting with a lawyer named O'Brian, when he saw, sitting across the restaurant by the brick fireplace, his high school sweetheart's older sister, Margot Santerre. Jimmy hadn't seen Margot since her wedding, but he would have known her anywhere. No one sat up straighter. The way she leaned toward the man she was with, and touched his arm, made Jimmy say nothing. It wasn't the guy she had married, and Jimmy would have known from his mother if Margot had divorced. He read the menu and kept his face turned away from that side of the room.

When the waiter had gone, Jimmy asked the lawyer casually, "So who's here tonight? Anyone you know?"

O'Brian looked around the room. "Well, that's my dentist, there in the black dress," he said. "Is that what you mean?"

"Sure," Jimmy said. "This always feels like a small town. I just wondered."

"That's the owner of the restaurant, standing by the door, but that's obvious," O'Brian said, scanning. "Oh, here we go. Over by the fireplace, with the blonde, that's a lawyer we used to work with called Dominick Jay. Someone told me he used to be a Jebbie."

Jimmy glanced over and saw that Margot was laughing. There was something of Clarissa in the way she laughed, something more free and easy than he'd ever seen before in the older sister, and he felt a nostalgic pang.

O'Brian said, "I mean a Jesuit—sorry."

Jimmy said, "I liked Catholic girls, but I never really got the lingo." He thought of Clarissa coming to his house after Mass one Sunday, dropping to the sofa in disgust in her pleated skirt and saying he was *so lucky* to be a Protestant and already damned. It had gone well that day, on the sofa. Clarissa Santerre at seventeen—it hurt his heart that such things were no more.

O'Brian was studying the couple across the room. "There's been talk about Jay," he said. "He had a nasty divorce, and now—I guess I shouldn't spread rumors."

"Who do I know to tell?"

O'Brian laughed. "No chance to spread gossip when you live off the grid? I envy your life."

Jimmy lived alone on a leaky sailboat and was tired of denying the romance of it. He said, "But the rumors?"

"He's stopped practicing law," O'Brian said, "though he still has an office. His paralegal works for us now, and she seemed a little shell-shocked when she came."

"In what way?"

"No one's really sure, and the girl from his office isn't talking. It might be drugs. I can't tell if she was fucking him."

Jimmy waited.

"But it seems like more than that," O'Brian said. "Like maybe he was really a little nuts."

Jimmy pretended to be wholly engrossed in spreading green-flecked herb butter on his bread. "Anyone else here?"

"Oh, I don't know," O'Brian said. "No one of interest. You know, we could go say hello to Jay and check it out."

"I don't think so," Jimmy said, too quickly. He couldn't imagine catching Margot out on a date.

"You're right," O'Brian said. "He was a nice guy. I always wondered if straight guys joined the Jebbies, but he seemed like one." He laughed. "Maybe he's no worse than the rest of us—you never know."

65

CLARISSA HAD JUST come from the screening of the student films, where she stood and explained to the class that hers had become a movie about *not* coming out to her father. The teacher, who was raised Catholic, had talked afterward about the confessional and the documentary film camera—how sometimes telling things to a camera feels private when it's exactly the opposite.

At home, Clarissa had gone outside to think about the experience, taking the phone with her, and she was deadheading the last roses for the winter when Jimmy Vaughan called. She hadn't talked to him since Margot's wedding, when she was nineteen and already going with Henry, and it had been awkward and sad. She couldn't believe, now, that it was really Jimmy Vaughan.

"I just wanted to ask if Margot's okay," Jimmy said.

In Clarissa's fantasy of her first love from Hermosa High tracking her down, he had not asked about her sister first. "Margot's fine," she said, a little annoyed. "You know Margot. She's with my parents."

"I saw her in Santa Barbara the other night," he said.

"With my parents?" Clarissa thought if they had come even a little bit north, she should have been invited.

"No," he said.

"Who was she with?"

Jimmy paused. "I'm not sure."

"Did she say why she was there?"

"I didn't talk to her."

Clarissa was confused and impatient. "Why not?"

"She's probably fine," Jimmy said. "She looked good."

"I don't understand."

Finally Jimmy told her about the man Margot had been with, and it seemed to Clarissa that an alien must be masquerading as her sister.

"I got a bad feeling about this guy," Jimmy said, "and I thought you could keep the secret for her, if it turned out it was no big deal. But don't tell anyone. I'm sure she's fine."

"It's so strange to hear your voice. I met a friend of yours in the grocery store."

"That's how I knew where you lived."

Clarissa laughed. "This is what we get for staying in California. My poor sister can't even go on a date here."

"You know that if I hadn't heard things about this guy," Jimmy said, "I would never say anything."

"I know. It's just too bad that the first time in her whole life Margot does something wrong, she gets caught. God wants her to be good."

"It's God, is it?" he said. "Do you still go to Mass?"

"Oh, no," she said. "I've been doing a lot of tantric yoga." She meant it as a description of her spiritual state, but it sounded like a sexual come-on. She wondered if subconsciously it had been.

Jimmy said, "I was thinking about sailing up north for a few days. I have a little boat. That's where you are, right? You're near Bodega Bay?"

"Sort of."

"I remember you not getting seasick."

"I never get seasick."

"Would you want to come out on the boat, if there's wind?"

Clarissa stood in her garden with one glove off and the pruning shears still in her hand. It was a beautiful fall day, and she felt the light breeze through her clothes, against her body. "I'm not seventeen anymore," she said.

"Neither am I," he said. "I think we're still allowed to sail."

"Okay," she said. "If there's wind."

66

PETER SAT IN THE passenger seat while Abby drove them north to Teddy and Yvette's for Thanksgiving dinner. It was only midday, and the freeway traffic wasn't bad yet. Peter had the sense that everyone on the road was driving to meet the families of the people they were sleeping with. Abby's mother had gone sailing, but the rest of them would be there.

"Tell me what you're missing, at home," Abby said.

"Is this to keep *my* mind off seeing your family, or yours?"

"I just want to know."

"My mother has stuffy relatives and crazy ones," he said, "and she's chosen the crazy ones to be friends with. Her cousin Sylvia in New Hampshire teaches belly dancing and has a big studio lined with mirrors. Twenty-seven relatives go there for Thanksgiving—twenty-six this year without me—and with the mirrors it looks like there are fifty-four. Sylvia covers these long folding tables with clipped-down plastic tablecloths, and there's turkey with stuffing, and sweet potatoes with marshmallows, the whole deal. After dinner, the men and children and the misfit women play speed charades on one side of the studio—or some other game, sometimes it changes. They scream out words and grab at some kind of plastic timer. The rest of the women spread newspapers on the tables on the other side of the room, reading the sale announcements, because at dawn they go to the stores to get free prizes for getting there first."

"There are prizes at the stores?"

"You should come some year," he said. "The whole thing reminds you why Americans like America so much."

"Our dinner will be more subdued and French Canadian."

"Are your grandparents going to be bothered that you're living with me?"

"I don't think they know."

"Will they be bothered that I'm a Jewish Lutheran?"

"Maybe you shouldn't mention the Lutheranism."

"I'm actually serious."

"No," she said. "They're Vatican II Catholics."

"Jamie can't be happy about me."

"He's my uncle, he doesn't have any rights."

"He got rights when you slept with him."

"I didn't. That's just in the book."

"Abby," he said. "You're staying on message with *me*?"

They left the freeway and took surface streets into Hermosa Beach, and then they were in a neat residential neighborhood of small houses with trimmed lawns. The haze had burned off, and the day was sunny and blue. Abby parked the car.

"It was the hottest summer in years when I had the chicken pox here," she said. "God, I was miserable. Until Jamie came."

"Nothing happened then, did it?"

"No!" she said. "That's disgusting."

"Just asking."

She pointed out a yellow board-and-batten house. "That's where Cara Ferris lived. She could twirl a baton, and she was Miss Hermosa Beach Recreation. I would have given anything to be her."

They walked up to the house, Peter carrying the pumpkin pie. He hadn't been so nervous in a long time, and he felt himself sweating in the sun. Back in Pennsylvania it would be cold and crisp. Abby rang the doorbell.

"Sweetheart!" Yvette said when she opened the door. "I'm so glad you're here." She was a lot like Peter had expected: she wasn't trying to hide her age, but she must have been something when she was young. She kissed him and said, "Thank you for taking care of Abby. What a beautiful pie."

"Abby made it."

Abby said, "I left the other one with Peter's Punjabi neighbors."

Peter noticed that she didn't say *our* Punjabi neighbors, and he reminded himself to be consistent with that. In the living room, he was introduced to T.J., who was reading a comic book and seemed like a normal kid. The grandfather stood from a chair and shook Peter's hand. He was short, and Peter thought maybe it was good for pilots to be small. No one else was in the room, which was as neat and orderly as the neighborhood. He felt like he'd walked back into the fifties.

"You know Clarissa isn't coming," Yvette said. "And Margot was here, but—" She looked nervously at Teddy. "She's up in Santa Barbara. We don't really know why."

Teddy clapped Abby on the back. "How are sales of your book?"

"Fine, I guess. They're doing another printing."

Yvette laughed. "Oh, isn't that wild," she said. "I don't know why anyone would want to read that thing."

"It's a small printing," Abby said.

"Can we do something?" Peter asked. "Set the table?"

"It's all set, sweetheart," Yvette said. "Come sit down. Can I get you a drink? We've already started."

As soon as they sat down on the couch, Jamie came in hugging two bags of groceries. Peter stood to say hello, relieved that the uncle wasn't as good-looking as he had imagined, but Jamie said, "Come help me unload, Ab."

Abby gave Peter an apologetic look and followed her uncle to the kitchen, and Peter was left stupidly standing. He sat back down on the couch.

"They've always been close," Yvette said. "I'm sure they'll be back in a minute."

"That's all right." Peter turned to Teddy. "So what did you fly in the Pacific?"

They talked about fighter planes until Jamie and Abby came back. Abby must have said something to him, because Jamie came straight over to shake hands, looking Peter in the eye like someone in a training video about business introductions.

"It's good to have you here," he said. "Will you join us for batting practice?"

T.J. yelped with pleasure and scrambled up off the floor.

"Peter can catch," Jamie said.

Abby crossed the lawn to the outfield by the rosebushes. The neighbors across the street watched from deck chairs on their front patio. Jamie gave two little shakes of the head, then a nod, as if Peter were calling for pitches, and then tossed an easy underhand throw. T.J. swung and missed, and Peter caught the ball and threw it back to the uncle who had fucked Abby when she was twenty. Who was now a cheerful dad with a young son. Peter understood why he was likable without really liking him.

Jamie pitched, and T.J. hit the ball.

"Home run!" Jamie cried, letting it go past him. Abby got the ball out from under the bushes while T.J. tore around the lawn. Peter applauded, and so did the people across the street. T.J. rounded home grinning.

After two more strikes, T.J. hit the ball and ran again.

"He's Babe Ruth!" Jamie cried. "Look at him go!" It went on like that until Yvette called them in for dinner.

In the house, Peter followed Abby into the bathroom and shut the door.

"My grandparents are out there," she said.

"If you can be alone in the kitchen with Jamie, you can be in the bathroom with me." He helped her sit up on the counter, wondering what they had time for.

"He was telling me about Margot," Abby said, letting him stand between her knees and untuck her shirt but not paying any attention. "She thought my novel was about an affair she had once, and then she got obsessed with the guy and tracked him down in Santa Barbara. That's where she is."

He stopped with the shirt. "Oh, Abby," he said.

"Margot swore my mother to secrecy, but my mother told Jamie. It's funny that the novel is about a family keeping secrets."

"And you think Margot leaving is your fault."

"Things are causal," Abby said. "If I hadn't written the book, she wouldn't have left."

"Abby of the Universe," he said. "You're being psychotic."

"I'm being honest."

"What would Leila say?"

"I don't know. But we can't stay in here." She tucked in her shirt, pushed herself off the counter, and gave him a depressing kiss on the way out.

At the table, Teddy clasped his hands and said, "Lord, we thank You for this food and for our health and our total well-being, and for giving us Abby and Peter and Jamie and T.J. today. We wish Clarissa and Margot could be here with us, and we pray for them. Also for Owen and Bennett and Danny and Katya, and Your children everywhere. Amen."

Yvette and Jamie said "Amen," and then they started passing the food. Yvette held the green beans for Peter and said, "So what kinds of books do you teach?"

"Whatever they'll pay me for," he said. "The Americans when I can. My dissertation is on Poe."

"Oh, he's very dark, isn't he?" she said.

Peter took a bread roll from Jamie and said, "Yes."

"I like books with happy endings," Yvette said. "That's what I didn't like about Abby's book, when I finally got through it."

Abby was helping T.J. choose a piece of turkey and didn't look up.

"You know what my favorite poem is?" Yvette said. "*Evangeline.*"

"That's Longfellow?"

"Oh, it's such a beautiful story," she said. "'This is the forest primeval.' That's how it begins. They're in a French settlement in Nova Scotia—what's now Nova Scotia—and Evangeline is the beautiful and virtuous daughter of the seigneur. She's so good to the poor and everyone loves her, and then the English soldiers tell them they have to leave, because they don't want the French in Canada. But these people aren't political—all they want to do is farm, and have babies, and live their lives."

"In disputed territory," Jamie said. "Can I have the potatoes?"

"Oh, it's just this harmless little town on this island," Yvette said. "And the English load them all onto ships and send them away. It's so cruel, and they're all on different ships. And then France doesn't want them back, and some are lost at sea, or in the forest, and some go to Louisiana, and they become the Cajuns." She smoothed the tablecloth under her wineglass. "And in the dispersal, Evangeline loses her true love. She spends the rest of her life looking for him, all over the country, in the forests and in Louisiana. When she finally finds him, many years later, he's on his deathbed. Oh, that poem used to make me cry."

Peter couldn't help himself. "I thought you liked happy endings," he said.

"I do."

"But your favorite story is about territorial war on civilians, and dispersals of people, and lives that go unfulfilled, and people dying."

"Oh, well," she said. "It was so romantic."

Abby said, "It's because the girl was like you."

Yvette smiled and said, "Oh, no."

"Maybe," Peter said, "it's because it's the hard things that make people interesting, in stories—more interesting than if everything were happy."

Yvette looked at him as if deciding whether to accept the challenge or not. Her eyes, from wine or the hour, had lost some of the brightness they had before dinner. She said, "I don't know. I was younger then, I guess. Let's talk about something else." She looked around the table for a topic.

"Like Jamie's friend Saffron having a baby!" she said.

"Go ahead, Ma, turn the knife," Jamie said.

"It's a happy thing."

"For who? Not for the baby."

T.J. had been mostly silent to that point, but now he asked Abby, "Did you have a baby?"

Abby seemed surprised. "No," she said.

"Katya said it was in the book."

"That I had a baby?" Abby asked cautiously.

"Yes."

Abby paused and then said, "I can see how she might think that, but the book is about made-up people. I don't have any children."

"Are you in love with Jamie?"

"No," Abby said.

"Why not?" There was silence at the table, and Peter didn't know where to look.

"Because Jamie's my uncle," she said.

"So?"

"I do love him," Abby said, "like I love you and . . . Yvette."

"Can you marry him?"

"No."

T.J. seemed to think about that. "Can I go live with Magdalena again?"

"Come here," Abby said, and T.J. climbed down from his chair and into her lap. She put her arms around him. "Magdalena loves you so much that she wanted to be sure, before she started her own family, that you were taken care of, and went to a school you like, and made friends. You've done all that, right?"

T.J. nodded.

"Do you think, if you went back to Argentina, you would miss playing baseball with Jamie, and seeing Yvette?"

T.J. nodded again.

"It's confusing," Abby said. "It would be easier to have one place where all the people you love are. But you have so many people that you're going to miss some of them wherever you are."

Jamie and Yvette got up to clear dishes, and T.J. seemed to have

run himself out. He accepted a promise of pumpkin pie for breakfast, and Abby took him to brush his teeth and go to bed in her
mother's old room. The water was running in the kitchen, and Jamie
and Yvette were in low conversation there.

Peter was left with Teddy, who said, "Yvette liked that poem
because dying was just a romantic idea to her."

Peter nodded, but Teddy was looking at his own hands on the
table.

"I'm not afraid of death," he said. "Sometimes I feel how close
it is, and when there are troubles here, I think, Well, I can leave
soon. That might be a cowardly thing to say."

"I don't think so," Peter said.

"I know where the door is, you see. I'm close enough now."

Yvette came in, drying her hands on a checkered towel. "What
door?"

"The one that goes out." Teddy made a little motion of escape
with his hand.

Yvette eyed him. "Teddy."

"Yes?" He blinked innocently, teasing her.

Yvette turned to Peter. "I used to think when I was younger that
I couldn't live without a man," she said. "So if Teddy died, I was
going to have to find someone else. But I don't feel that way anymore. So he'd better live." She pointed her finger at him. "You'd
better live, honey."

"I know," he said. "That's the deal."

67

SAFFRON WAS PUT on bed rest, in danger of preterm labor, and had never been so miserable. What had she been thinking, wanting a baby? It had just been a weird hormonal surge, a temporary madness designed by evolution. Now she didn't want a baby at all. She nurtured a deep and bitter resentment toward Martin for getting her into this mess.

She was bad about bed rest. She kept getting up, and then she started bleeding, so they put her in the hospital. There she asked the doctors what would happen if she just went home. Secretly she thought she might lose the baby, which wouldn't be so bad. But the doctors told her she might bleed to death.

"Childbirth is still a dangerous business," the handsomest one, Dr. Davies, said.

"Are you just saying that to make me stay here?"

"No," he said.

Saffron couldn't stand that her relationship with the handsome doctor consisted of lying in a bed getting fat while he stood close to her, nonchalant and oblivious, flipping through charts. She had dreams about him. No one had ever told her that being pregnant made you have such intense sex dreams. Crazy dreams, with changing acts and participants, but mostly just a kind of pink haze that the dreams moved through, and a feeling that was like the moment before coming. She finally asked a nurse about it, and the nurse said there was a lot more blood concentrated down there, when you were pregnant, and blood was part of orgasm, just like it was for men.

"Gross," Saffron said.

"You asked."

Every month there had been something new. For the first three, she had thrown up. She had gone through a bulimic stage in high school and didn't think puking was so bad. But she had forgotten that when you weren't making yourself do it, there was actual nausea involved. The nausea didn't go away, and she was exhausted all the time. She had decided not to tell anyone about the baby yet, so she had no sympathetic attention—she had only the constitutionally unsympathetic Martin—and it was hard to pretend she wasn't feeling so vile.

In the fourth month, she started to feel like her bones were being pulled apart, like her hips were being pulled away from each other, each to one side. At night, when Martin was asleep, she wept silently into her pillow, not about the pain but about her prospects when it was over. She had liked her body and her life, and she had traded them for a child she didn't even know. There might be something horribly wrong with it, that they couldn't detect in any of the tests. Or it might just be an unpleasant human being: it might have her temperament, and Martin's detachment.

And then when was the payoff? There would be a year of sleep deprivation, even with a baby nurse, and then many years of killing boredom: conversations with a toddler, potty training, picture books, deadly birthday parties. Then maybe, if she was lucky, there would be a year of sweetness at nine or ten, just when she was starting to feel really *old*, and then the child would be a hateful adolescent who wanted nothing to do with her. Then it would be a college student joking about Saffron, and then a neurotic adult crying in a shrink's office. Even as the slim and glamorous and busy and popular (and also warm and nurturing) mother she intended to be, she might still be harboring a person who would feel about her *exactly* the way she had felt about Josephine.

Then, as if in punishment for her negative thoughts, there came the bed rest, and then she was in the hospital with the handsome Dr. Davies and the sex dreams and the boredom and frustration. Martin brought her magazines—*Vogue* and *W* and *InStyle*—but there were too many interruptions to read a book, unless it was a particularly gossipy book with very short chapters. She tried to keep herself from looking too much like a hospital patient, and she thought Dr. Davies must have taken a Hippocratic oath not to even *want* to fuck her. But then she would remember that she was six months pregnant with someone else's child.

Dr. Davies stopped by one day when Martin was visiting. He said a cheery hello to Martin, looked at her charts, and left whistling as Saffron blushed.

"Poor Saffron," Martin said thoughtfully from his chair by her bedside. "What an inconvenient time to be smitten."

"I'm not smitten," she said.

"I know what it looks like by now."

"No, you don't. He's my doctor."

"Yeah," Martin said. "So's the old gray-haired guy with the limp. I don't see you batting your lashes at him."

"Don't tease me."

"Have you made any progress?"

"No!" she wailed, and she burst into tears, surprising herself. "I'm so unattractive! I'll never be pretty again!"

He handed her a Kleenex. "The runny nose doesn't help."

Saffron blew her nose loudly and scowled at him.

"Everyone says you'll feel different when the baby's here," he said.

"You've said that before."

"I'm just reminding you."

"What if I don't feel different?" she said. "What if I have horrible postpartum depression and want to push the stroller into traffic?"

"Then we won't let you have the stroller."

"That happens, you know."

"I know."

"Anything could go wrong. What if it's really funny-looking?"

"We'll sell it to the circus and get rich."

"I'm serious."

"I think you're going to feel differently when it comes," he said.

She sniffed. "Dr. Davies told me the pediatricians have a code for the medical charts, when they don't know what's wrong with a child," she said. "They write, 'FLK,' for 'Funny-Looking Kid.' And if it turns out the parents are funny-looking, too, and it probably comes from them, they write, 'PS' for 'Parents Same.'"

Martin laughed. "So you're making some time with the doc after all," he said.

"I can't tell you how uninterested he is."

"Try," Martin said.

"He's so uninterested."

"How uninterested?"

"His erection goes down when he sees me."

"Really?"

"No," she said. "I mean, probably."

Martin took her hand in both of his. "Saff, you're pregnant, and in the hospital," he said. "This isn't the height of your glory. But your glory has had some heights, and will again."

"I'm hideous."

"No, you're just monogamous, for now," he said. "I could get used to this. I might keep you pregnant all the time."

"Just you try it," Saffron said.

68

OWEN HADN'T SLEPT WELL or eaten real food since Margot left. He had never known how to make vegetables edible: Margot was in charge of all that. She was supposed to visit her parents for only a few days, but then she decided to stay.

He wasn't alarmed right away; he was busy with work and assumed she would be home to plan Thanksgiving. He came home late the next night, poured himself a bowl of cereal, and played a phone message from Margot, saying she was with another man.

Owen, sitting over his cereal bowl, was startled into tears. His Margot. Everyone's standard for propriety, the woman who wrote thank-you notes for thank-you notes and hosted parties where even the drunks didn't get surly, simply because Margot was in charge. People who lived to offend wouldn't dream of offending her. He played the message again and tried not to have specific images come into his head. She hadn't left a number.

He wiped his face and tried to remember the last time he had cried. At Danny's birth, maybe. Sometimes the evening news or the illness of friends made him sad or angry, but not enough to cry. He felt like a man who has lain for years in bed and is suddenly forced to run a marathon. He wasn't in shape for this; he didn't have the right muscles or the training.

He wished he had faith. If there *were* a Catholic God, He surely wouldn't want Margot to leave. Owen had done no wrong and deserved to have his old life back. But a just God wouldn't waste His time plucking errant wives from Santa Barbara when there were earthquakes in Mexico, and wars in the Balkans, and starving children everywhere. A just God might even be reasonably annoyed at Owen, living alone now in a four-bedroom house with a stocked pantry, unable to make an omelet for dinner, feeling sorry for himself while people slept in the streets a mile away.

But again (Owen argued with himself at the kitchen counter), he was small potatoes compared to the real masters of greed. He was a charitable, taxpaying man, not a target for vengeance.

So clearly he was on his own here, God or no God. And to be honest, he leaned toward no God, not even the indifferent one.

He had stopped crying, and now he sat over his empty bowl looking at his reflection in the kitchen window. He looked sad and pathetic, with his shoulders slumped, and he didn't bother to square them. He wondered how Danny and Bennett would take it. The image came back of his wife's body, and then of a man on top of her, straining and sweating away, and Owen made himself stop. He stared down at the milky sheen in the bottom of the cereal bowl. He had never run a marathon, but he guessed he would need to start slowly, pace himself, focus on the steps he was actually taking, and not think about the distance.

He carried the dishes to the sink and washed them by hand, focusing on the spoon, the soap, the water, the sponge. He put them in the drying rack. One task done, and no thinking about Margot. But now what? He thought of reading, but couldn't imagine the book that would keep his thoughts on the page.

He remembered a model airplane he had started with the boys, who had abandoned it when baseball practice began, and he found the box in a closet full of old sports gear. He brought it to the kitchen table and carefully spread the day's newspaper to protect the wood finish. They had barely begun to assemble the plane, and all the old paints seemed to be usable. It was a Corsair, the kind Teddy had flown in both wars, which was why they had picked it out. Owen laid out all the pieces, and the tools, and the paints in a row, and set out for mile one.

69

FOR FIFTEEN YEARS, Dominick had considered his affair with Margot to be the pivotal event in his life, not counting his diabetic father's death when he was two. His mother, a parish secretary, had raised him alone, and he had grown up inside a church. But Margot's appearance and disappearance had changed his life completely. When she stopped seeing him he had prayed, because that was still his habit, and determined that the life of a Jesuit brother was not for him if he was lusting after married women.

But the Society of Jesus had dealt with illicit affairs before. His confessor, a gentle, white-haired old man named Father Gabriel, told him he should see the encounter as a gift, a challenge, a cause for meditation and reflection. They spent hours hashing it out. He understood that he craved the approval of his superiors because he lacked a father, but the understanding didn't diminish the craving. When he finally won the argument and left his training, it was with a heavy feeling of grief that he had missed his chance not to disappoint.

Dominick moved to Santa Barbara to avoid the temptation of showing up on Margot's doorstep: he would make a new life. He took a job at a law firm, where one day he was visited by a man from the local diocese, who seemed to know his history with the Jesuits. The man was an energetic Californian, persuasive and determined, and he talked about the interesting opportunities the Church could offer a smart young lawyer. He hoped Dominick would come to Mass on Sunday.

Dominick thanked him and then didn't go, and after that felt he was being watched. He met a pretty girl who wanted to be an actress, and they were married with his mother in tearful attendance. The marriage created a beautifully distracting noise in his life until his mother, back in Louisiana, died of a brain aneurysm. He went home to bury her next to his father, astonished by the grief he felt. He was alone. His wife, with two living parents and four grandparents, thought he was overreacting. One morning as he dressed for work, he caught her watching him from their bed and then feigning sleep so she wouldn't have to talk to him, and he realized she despised him. By the time they went to counseling, she was already sleeping with a director of television commercials, but Dominick didn't know that yet, and his wife didn't mention it while listing her griev-ances in the therapist's office.

The therapist asked to see them separately, and suggested to Dominick alone that he needed more help than just marriage coun-seling. He had obsessive thoughts of his dead mother and his kindly confessor. He had dreams of being attacked by someone from Opus Dei for betraying the Church. When his wife finally left him for the director (and a part in a Pepsi ad), he stayed in bed for a week and then filled the prescription the therapist gave him.

The years passed, and he worked and became a partner and tried to contribute to the community, but the nightmares continued, and he never felt right. Eventually he met a young woman named Laurel, who worked in a dress shop and went to bed with him in a casual, cynically promiscuous way, and then introduced him to heroin that was very pure and could be sniffed, no dangerous nee-dles. It was infinitely better than the pills. It took the nightmares away, and it felt *so good*: it was the obvious answer. He couldn't believe it had taken him so long to find. Laurel insisted you could live a perfectly normal life with the occasional high; her shop sold eighty-dollar T-shirts and eight-hundred-dollar handbags, and she said Coco Chanel used to shoot up right through her little black dress. But Dominick didn't have the fortitude of Coco Chanel, and his life quickly ceased to seem normal. There were some lost months, a lost year, nightclubs with kids half his age. A young resident who stitched up his hand one night told him he had chosen a good way to die and listed all the possible effects of heroin use. One was a diabeteslike inability to process glucose. Dominick wanted more details and told the resident that was what killed his father, but the irony was lost on the impatient young man.

In rehab, his roommate was an ex–pro surfer, Cordy Hays, who was three weeks ahead of him on the road to sobriety. Dominick, in withdrawal, had chills and cramps and diarrhea and wanted to die, but Cordy had a beatific way of talking about what would come next, and how it would get better, that made it seem possible to get through the hours. Finally the clinic sent Dominick back clean and HIV-tested to the world. His legal staff had moved on to more promising jobs, and his clients had moved on to more reliable lawyers. He set about getting one or two of the clients back and went to the gym to build up his strength. There was the little trouble of the rent and the fucking alimony, but he managed to keep the rent covered.

And then Margot showed up in his office, like a ghost, but she didn't look like a ghost, and she didn't feel like one when he managed to touch her. He couldn't believe she had come to find him. He was tremendously moved.

He didn't tell her the details of his troubles; he had an instinct to preserve the glamour for her. Adultery without glamour was going to sour quickly for a woman like Margot, who had thrived on her ordinary life for thirty years. The week she arrived, they saw a dance band setting up on the pier. Over Margot's protests, he bought her an insanely expensive and very beautiful dress at Laurel's old shop. Laurel had moved to New York, but the shop was still associated with temptation for him. At sunset they walked to the pier, which was strung with lights.

They had both grown up in the age of dance lessons, and the steps came back like a song from childhood. There were other couples their age, who danced covering their shyness with ironic smiles. And there were kids, twenty-year-olds in nineteen-fifties clothes. The girls wore poodle skirts, twisted-up hairstyles, and tattoos on their ankles and shoulders. They did the Lindy Hop, somersaulting through the air, their skirts flying. A skinny kid in a powder blue zoot suit turned the girls every direction, looking like he was thinking about something else.

Dominick didn't turn Margot upside down, but he spun her around and brought her back in tight. She was a good follower and paid attention to where his hands were and what he wanted. The band played "Oye Como Va," and "My Baby Just Cares for Me." He lifted Margot's hand above her head, and she smiled at him over her shoulder. The green skirt of her dress swung around her knees. The last years felt like nothing; time vanished. He hadn't thought he would do anything this wholesome ever again.

They found an empty picnic table, and the hanging lights were soft on Margot's face as she watched the dancers. The band was playing slow.

"It's so strange that I'm here," she said. "I don't know what to do."

"This," he said. "Do this."

"I've thought of myself all my life as good," she said. "A good daughter, a good student, a good wife, a good mother. I've lost everything, do you see? I've lost who I am."

"And now you can have a new life. Not everyone gets this chance. Not everyone takes it."

"They take it all the time," Margot said. "And they ruin their lives and alienate their children and end up alone."

"You'll never be alone."

She looked at him. In this light she looked like she had fifteen years before. "I'm afraid," she said. "My sons will never understand."

"They will," he said. "They're adult men."

She took his hand in both of hers and turned it over, studying it. It was the hand the resident had stitched up, and she ran a finger over the scar. "What happened here?" she asked.

He stretched his hand, moving the scar like a narrow worm between his finger and thumb. There had been glass, he thought. A window? A bottle? He remembered that when the resident asked him what happened, he'd said, "How the hell would I know?"

"If I tell you the story," he said, "you can't be disgusted and run away."

"Of course not," Margot said.

She was concerned now: her whole body was turned to him, in the green dress, with that womanly, motherly need to make everything all right. She pressed the injured hand between hers, and he wondered if it were true, if he had found a way to make her stay.

70

AFTER THANKSGIVING, Peter tried to convince Abby that he had not looked into her family and seen the heart of darkness. This was what families were like. He joked: he said he was writing about Poe and Southern Gothic, and it was useful for him to see California Gothic. But Abby was in a funk in which it was her fault that Margot had left Owen, that Jamie had married Katya, and that Katya had abandoned Jamie and T.J. She was preoccupied with her own guilt.

One night Jamie called while Peter was reading, and Abby spent a long time on the phone in the bedroom. Then she came out, sat at Peter's feet on the couch, and said T.J. had the flu and was home from school. Jamie wanted her help: he had to go back to work, and T.J. was comfortable with Abby. Katya hadn't been much of a mother, but she was still his mother, and the loss had been hard.

"I have to go up there," Abby said. "Just for a few days. I can't stand that he's sick and miserable and Katya left him."

"Who's 'he' in that sentence?" Peter asked. "Jamie or the kid?"

"The kid," she said.

"You have classes here."

"Astronomy doesn't need me," she said. "T.J. does."

But she didn't have the oppressed look of family responsibilities on her face; she seemed too energized for it to be about visiting a sick kid.

"I think you should finish this semester," he said. "You'll see them at Christmas."

"I have to go."

She got up from the couch and went to the bedroom, and Peter followed her. She was gathering dirty clothes.

"This is the old joint custody habit, isn't it?" he asked. "You pretend this is your life for a while, and then you go back there, knowing you can come back here. Everything can be temporary."

She laughed and moved past him with the laundry. "*What* would I do without you to explain me?"

"Oh, I don't know. Sleep with your uncle?"

She paused, looking astonished and hurt. But she didn't have an answer, or she wasn't going to deign to answer. She put the clothes in the little stacked washer-dryer in the kitchen. She was washing T-shirts and jeans and underwear to take with her.

"I have an assignment for you," he said, forming the idea as he said it. "You can go up there, but your assignment is to remember that I'm here."

She started the machine and it hissed, filling with water. "Of course," she said, without conviction.

"You can't pretend that I don't exist."

"Of course not." She poured soap into the machine.

"It's an imaginative exercise," he said. "You're going to tell me what happened, eventually, because that's in your nature. So just remember that I'm here."

She put the bottle back in the cupboard and turned her whole body to face him.

"Peter," she said. She seemed completely serious now, tired but focused and in the room with him. "How could I forget?"

71

SAFFRON WAS NUMB from the neck down but wide awake and staring at the little green curtain beyond which the doctors were making an incision she couldn't feel, well below the bikini line as agreed, and then she felt them lifting the baby—she felt the new lightness of her body—and suddenly she was shaking uncontrollably. They had told her that there was a hormonal shift at the moment of separation, but she hadn't expected anything this strong. Her whole body was shaking, she knew it without being able to feel it. She felt suddenly protective; she wanted to shout at the doctors not to take him out, to put him back. She started to sob. Then he was lifted high enough that she could see, through the blur of tears and drugs, his little ear. The side of his face, wet with blood, and his slick, dark hair. He took a breath, and she saw him do it—a little gasping fish—and she felt left behind. *She* had been doing his breathing, *she* had. Now he was doing it without her, and the sobbing came harder. She had been prepared to fake emotion—to simulate, for the doctors and for herself, feelings she would never have, and now she couldn't speak for the trembling and the tears that soaked her face and her gown.

"Martin," she said, and she searched for him in the blur of the room, blinking.

"I'm here," he said. He was wearing green scrubs and looked pale and traumatized.

"Oh, you didn't watch, did you?" she said.

"Couldn't help it," he said.

"Martin, the baby," she said, fighting the drugs to be coherent.

"They're just cleaning him off."

"Martin," she said.

"What?"

"He's *alive*."

72

DOMINICK WAS DRINKING coffee on his tiny balcony one morning when Margot came out in that damn kimono she hid herself in. It was a beautiful, clear blue morning, not hazy like the last few mornings had been, and Margot sat down in the other plastic chair, crossed her legs with the flowered kimono over them, and said, "I'm going to go home."

Dominick felt the shock but had expected it and kept very still, looking for his next move. It had been an enormous, a colossal mistake to tell her about his drug trouble. He had counted on her wanting to save him. "This is your home," he said.

"I mean with Bennett, with my son. To Louisiana."

He hated the idea of Bennett, who had been sent by the family to fetch her, but the kid was not the point. "You mean to your husband."

Margot said nothing.

"To go fuck your husband in your big expensive house," he said.

"Please," she said.

"You turn my life upside down *twice*," he said, "and now you want to go back to a life that bores you, and leave me here. How does it feel, to take people so lightly? Other people don't take things so lightly, you know? How do you know he'll take you back?"

"He will," she whispered.

"He says that now," he said, warming to the topic. "But I'll tell you something about men: he's going to think of me every *single* time he goes down on you, every *single* time he fucks you. You've wronged him, Margot, and you can't expect everything to go back the way it was. The bitterness will fester. Every day, he'll think of me."

Margot didn't move. "Are you finished?"

"No. I'm not finished. I'm not even started."

"Have you taken your pills?"

"I don't need the pills."

"You do."

"What I need," he said, "is for you to explain to me how you justify this. You abandon your husband and come halfway across the country to finally acknowledge, after fifteen years, that you love me—that we fit together in a way you never fit with anyone else. You make me finally feel that the one thing I always wanted is *mine*. And you string me along for a while under this delusion, and I feel safe enough to tell you I've made some mistakes. But this scares you, so you start to believe that you miss your good towels. Or your fancy refrigerator. Or the library committee. What is it you miss? The big Christmas at your parents' house? Is that the bait?"

"There's no bait."

"Or are you just revolted by me? Say it. You wrecked his life, and now you're wrecking mine *again*. I want to know how you justify it."

"You can't hold me responsible for your life," she said, but she didn't sound like she believed it.

"Is that what your son told you to say?"

"Everyone wrecks their own lives."

"Actually, they don't," he said. "Other people help, all the time. Your son is—what, twenty-six? He doesn't know *anything*, Margot. No one knows anything at twenty-six." He felt a throbbing in his left temple and blinked a few times to force it away.

"You're disturbed."

"You bet I am," he said. "But I've been better since you came." He took her hands in his. "I'm better because of you."

Margot didn't pull her hands away.

"Give me a little more time," he said. "Stay a little longer."

Margot took one hand back to wipe her eyes with it.

"You *love* me," he said. "You know you do."

Tears ran down her face, but she let him kiss away the salty trails. He kissed her cheeks, her eyes, her mouth, and then he stood her up and led her back inside.

73

MARGOT WOKE UP in Dominick's apartment not knowing where she was. She got up to go to the bathroom, but she was thinking of her own house, and she walked into a wall, bumping her forehead and cursing softly. Dominick's bathroom was on the other side of the bed. She turned and went the other direction.

The anxious, buzzing sensation that came and went, sometimes in her chest and sometimes at the base of her skull, was there this morning, just at the place where her hair was tied back, as she washed her face. She had lost weight and could see the ridges of her sternum marching down between her breasts. She put a hand flat over her chest, to cover it up. Then she remembered she was supposed to meet Bennett for breakfast. She had promised him she would make the break, and now what would she say?

Dominick was awake when she went back into the bedroom, so she took her clothes to the bathroom to dress. He thought it was the addiction that bothered her, but it wasn't, it was the amorphous darkness in him that she couldn't get her arms around. She pulled on the skirt she had bought in town, the cotton sweater.

"Where are you going?" Dominick asked when she went back out.

"I'm having breakfast with Bennett."

There was a silence.

"I'm coming with you," Dominick said, swinging his legs out from under the bedcovers.

"No, you're not."

"I am, it's my right," he said, and he stood, naked and handsome, with his thick black hair starting to gray on his chest and around his penis. He ran his fingers over his head, where the hair stuck straight up, and pulled on a pair of trousers lying over a chair. "What time are we meeting?" he asked.

"I'm going alone."

He buttoned and zipped. "It's time young Ben and I hashed a few things out."

Bennett was already waiting at a table in the coffee shop when they arrived. He looked startled to see Dominick, and Margot was shamed into silence, caught between the two of them. Bennett was the good older son the way Margot had been the good older daughter, so it was only natural that he had been sent to tell her Owen was languishing at home making model airplanes. She loved Danny, who was mischievous and wild, but Bennett understood her, and knew the burden and the pleasure of being reliable. He had arranged for time off from medical school, which seemed rash. She wondered if someday he would do something as entirely irresponsible as she had done, and give up all claim to being good.

"Benny!" Dominick said, and he clapped Bennett on the shoulder as he stood to meet them: the hearty lawyer act. "I'm Dominick. I'm glad we have a chance to talk."

"There's nothing to talk about," Bennett said, but he looked panicked.

"She's changed her mind," Dominick said.

"*Mom,*" Bennett said, looking at Margot. They were attracting attention.

"So it's okay, you can go home now," Dominick said.

"She's my mother."

"Exactly," Dominick said. "She's a separate person, with a life of her own."

"She has a life with us."

"Had," Dominick said. "You have to go have your adult life, and be a doctor, and she gets to have her adult life, with her kids grown up. And in that life she's staying with me."

"You said you were leaving him," Bennett said to Margot.

"I know," she said, confused.

"Dad really needs you."

She looked around the coffee shop, at the moms with strollers, and the girls with sunny hair and short skirts, and the brooding young men with laptops. Two of the girls were openly watching her. "Maybe we shouldn't talk about this here."

"It's all right," Dominick said. "You kiss your son now, and he goes back to school to learn how to cure diseases."

Bennett seemed to be in tears. *"Mom,"* he said.

In that moment, an odd feeling came over Margot, a warmth in her whole body and a very specific physical pull that was almost sexual, a kind of contraction, a memory of birth. She realized that Dominick had made a mistake in provoking this scene, because she couldn't leave her son for him. Her husband was a separate being, someone she could lose, but her sons were part of her. She would walk over Owen's body to protect and console them, and she realized now that she would walk over her lover's body, too. She moved to Bennett and pulled his head close to her; he was actually crying now.

"Sweetheart," she said. "It's all right. I'm coming home."

"Margot," Dominick said.

She turned to face him, protecting Bennett.

"I'm going home," she said. She had not yet ruined her life. They would take her back.

"This is home," Dominick said, obviously trying to keep his voice under control. "He doesn't need you anymore. *I* need you."

But she was sure of her obligations now, which were not to Dominick. They had always been to her sons, and the vengeful look in Dominick's eyes told her she was right. She had been right fifteen years ago. She had wasted so much time, and hurt so many people.

There was some confusion, then. A waitress approached them, and Dominick called her an insensitive cunt and tipped a chair clattering to the tile floor. A male manager asked him to leave, and Dominick did, and it was then that Margot lost her composure. She sank into the booth where Bennett had innocently waited for her to join him for breakfast, and she thought she would never stop crying and trembling. She held her hands tightly together to keep them still. It was like being caught in the circulating surf, unable to get air. It would never end. Bennett finally fell back on his training and drove her to the hospital, where they gave her a sedative and put her, weeping, to bed.

74

JAMIE WAS SITTING on the couch in his apartment, with only the kitchen light on, listening to Abby putting T.J. to bed. He couldn't hear their words, only the reassuring low voices. T.J. had gotten better since Abby arrived, and was happier, and Jamie felt a weight lifting off him. He was thinking how nice it would be to go to a bar with decent music and cold beer when Saffron called from the house in the wine country.

"Fauchet told me that Katya left," she said. "I'm so sorry."

"Thanks," he said, trying to decide how he felt about hearing her voice.

"How's T.J.?"

"Better some days than others," he said. "I haven't told him yet how Aunt Saffron stole his millions. One thing at a time."

"Oh, Jamie," Saffron said. There was a pause. "I'm calling about Christmas."

"What about it?"

"I'm going crazy up here, it's so lonely. My father's going to Scotland with a girlfriend. And Martin's family gives me hives."

Jamie waited to see where this was going.

"If you're going to your parents' house," she said, "I wondered if we could come, too."

"You're joking, right?" he said—though there was a small, secret thrill that she wanted to be with him.

"I want my baby to have a more normal childhood than I did," she said. "I want him to have Christmas in a house with wall-to-wall carpet and some nice people, and a TV on somewhere, with a football game. I don't think that's so much to ask."

"So find another house!" he said. "America is full of them! Don't you see how that might be uncomfortable for me?"

"Abby's novel made your family seem really appealing."

"It's a novel. It's not my family."

"Just think about it, okay? My uncle Freddie needs a place to go, too."

"The nutcase healer?"

"We don't need to stay at the house," she said. "It would mean a lot to me. I'll call tomorrow."

He hung up the phone. Abby came in from T.J.'s bedroom and sat at the other end of the couch. "Who was that?"

"Saffron, inviting herself to Christmas at my parents' house."

Abby laughed. "Not really."

"I think your novel made her curious."

"Did you tell her no?"

"Not really. I tried."

Abby stretched out on the couch, with her back against the armrest. "We don't have to go," she said. "It's such a coercive holiday. Maybe Jesus will come back for the millennium and say, Folks, this whole Christmas thing has gotten out of hand. It's a little embarrassing to me, all the fuss and the shopping and the suicides. And I wasn't even born in December. So let's just have Thanksgiving and leave it at that. And then he'll go back up to heaven."

Her socked feet were close enough that he could touch them if he wanted. He could pull her ankle into his lap and the rest of her might come, too; she might climb over, limber girl, and kiss him like she had before.

"What does Peter think of your being here?" he asked. He could hear the catch in his own voice.

Abby was silent for a moment. "He doesn't like it. But he trusts me."

"Should he?"

She hesitated. *Now* was the time to move to her side of the couch; he could feel it in every part of his body except his poor brain, which pulled back on the reins, trying to keep control. He waited.

"I think so," she said.

"So no backsliding."

There was a catch in her voice now, too. "No."

He put a hand on her foot, he couldn't help it, and slid it up to the bare skin of her ankle. She didn't pull back. He heard Katya saying, *Nothing so fucked like this,* but it seemed to come from very far away.

"No one would have to know," he said. "I'm not going to come over there, but you could come over here. No one would know."

Abby looked agonized.

"Just come over for a second."

"I would know," she whispered.

He waited. "Just for a second," he said. "Just come sit with me."

She glanced at T.J.'s bedroom door, open two inches and dark inside, and she sat up and moved toward him. He ached with longing, and with the idea that he was going to do this again. He hadn't changed. She nestled against him, still hesitant, with her back to his chest as if they were just going to watch the night sky out the window. He ran his hand over her breast, remembering the exact size and give of it through her shirt, a thing he had thought he would never do again. Then she turned her face up to his and kissed him urgently, all the hesitation gone. He let go of the reins and let the horses tumble toward the edge of the cliff.

75

Dominick found his old contacts, his friends, when Margot left. He found his roommate Cordy, the graying pro surfer, who wasn't preaching sobriety anymore, and getting high after so long was sweeter for the wait. He sat on the beach listening to Cordy talk, and had what he had always wanted, what he had sought in the Jesuits before he disappointed them by being lustful: he had an elite group of brethren. People who had risen above the everyday and knew exaltation.

He woke up alone and chilled on the sand, the air misty with morning fog. He brushed the sand off his jacket on his way to the bathrooms and stretched his aching legs.

"It's gonna be a good day," a sunburned woman with dirty hair and a roll of blankets said. "I got a hunch."

"You said it," Dominick said.

"Good vibes," the woman said. "I'm telling you."

He waved good-bye before she could ask him for cash. He wanted to remember the night's elation, but his head was starting to throb. The surfers and the Rollerbladers were coming out: a freckled girl tugging on her wetsuit, a muscular black man dancing in skates. All the healthy people. Where do they all come from?

He sat on the low concrete wall at the edge of the beach, noticing the pain that spread across his lower back. He shouldn't have fallen asleep on the beach, he was too old for that. A surfer in dairymaid braids was rinsing off in the shower, and something was wrong with the right side of her face. The skin was tighter, shinier, with a smeared texture. As his mind warmed up slowly, the two things seemed connected: there was something wrong with him, and there was something wrong with her.

He wished Cordy would come back and talk some more. Maybe teach him to surf. What had Cordy been saying on the beach? That life is like the ocean, it's huge and uncontrollable and dark, and you get your little place on the edge of it. You either sit on your board outside the breakers, and be afraid, or you paddle like hell and try to get up on the wave that might break your neck or drown you, and you get the rush and the view and the ride for as long as you can. The analogy had seemed convincing and bracing the night before.

If Margot had stayed, he could have managed. He would have been buoyed by her sensible presence, her ardent fucking, and her steadying love. He would have gone to work and come home to the smell of baking banana bread. She would claim there was something wrong with it, the bananas were too ripe or not ripe enough, but it would be perfect and sweet and nourishing and he would drop his briefcase right there to eat some. Her sons would vanish and her husband would die an unlamentable death, and everyone would whisper, *It's better, really, this way*. And life would be unendingly happy. He could have ridden that particular wave for a long time. He felt a black mood clouding the inside of his skull.

The girl with the damaged face had peeled off her wetsuit under the shower and wore a red bikini and a white nylon top. She shivered, goose bumps rising on her pretty thighs.

"What happened?" he asked, touching his own cheek.

She looked up, flipping a braid over her shoulder. Her eyes were wide and pale, and must have been trusting once, when she was just an attractive girl, when everyone smiled at her happily. Now she was suspicious. "I rescued a baby from a fire."

He had the feeling he always had, coming down from a high: that he had to struggle to register things at his usual speed. But he knew she was lying. "I didn't mean to offend you," he said. "Is surfing hard?"

"No." She picked up her board and swung it onto her hip. He was going to lose her, too.

"Is it like life?" he asked, to keep her there.

She looked over her shoulder at him, and he saw only the flawless left side of her face. "No," she said. "It's like surfing."

Then she was gone. The sun had come out and made him squint. He felt his hair to see if it looked like he had slept in the sand, and felt his pockets to see if he had any money. Not even a dollar for coffee. He was off to a bad start this morning.

"Good vibes," he told himself. They had to be out there somewhere.

76

By THE MIDDLE of December, Peter was faced with the question of what to do about Abby, who still hadn't come back from San Francisco. She said on the phone that T.J. was over his flu but he seemed so cheerful that she couldn't leave him yet. It was just as easy to stay until Christmas.

"And at Christmas?" he said.

"I have to go to Teddy and Yvette's," Abby said. "You should go see your family." It was the same way she had said *You should call the marine chemist*. He was back at square one.

"Is something going on with Jamie?"

"No," she said.

He didn't ask if something *had* gone on with Jamie, in the last two weeks, because he didn't want to know. But he did want to know.

"Is that the truth?" he asked.

"Yes," she said. "I need to get through Christmas alone. Margot's coming, and my mother. I'm a different person with you and with my family, and it's too hard to be both those people at once."

"I like the way you are with me better."

"I know."

"I think you do, too."

"December twenty-seventh," she said.

"And meanwhile you stay with Jamie."

"You sound like you don't trust me."

"Of course I don't," he said. "No one should be trusted alone with someone they've slept with. I would have to be insane. And if a girl ever needed a chaperone, it's you."

"Then why did you let me go?"

"You really want to know this?"

"Yes."

He answered carefully. "It was a gamble. I took the short-term risk of you being alone with Jamie, who can't *legally* steal you away, over the long-term risk that you wouldn't stay with someone who kept you from going."

She was silent.

"That's true, isn't it?" he asked.

"It might be."

"But I thought we were talking about a week."

"There's nothing going on," she said: again, the present tense. "I'm not that girl anymore."

"Everyone has limits, Abby. I have limits."

"I know," she said. "It's really fine. I sleep on the couch."

"In a better world," he said, "I wouldn't need that consolation."

77

TEDDY AND YVETTE'S house was packed when Abby arrived with T.J. and Jamie. Margot, Clarissa, and Jamie were staying in their old rooms, and Teddy and Yvette were in theirs. Owen was on one of the living room couches, and neither he nor Margot seemed sure how to talk to each other. Bennett was on the other couch, and Danny had brought a sleeping bag for the floor. T.J. got the spare twin bed in Jamie's room, and Abby got the spare twin bed in her mother's. Saffron and Martin and the baby, Liam, plus her uncle Freddie the healer in a bolo tie and black snakeskin boots, were in a bed-and-breakfast up the street.

The roles of the sisters seemed reversed. Margot was pale from the hospital, and overwhelmed. Clarissa, confident, happy, and tanned from sailing, had brought the movie she'd made for her film class. After dinner the first night, she gathered the family to watch it.

"A movie?" Yvette asked. "Is that why you had a camera here?"

"It's not going to be embarrassing, is it?" Jamie asked.

"No!"

"Really, Mom, is it?" Abby asked.

"Look who's talking," Jamie said.

"You guys!" Clarissa said. "You never take me seriously."

She started the VCR, and the screen was black, and then there was a shot of the front of the house.

"Hey, that's here," Saffron said.

The image wobbled slightly. Clarissa's voice, on the tape, said, "This is the house I grew up in, in the fifties. My father fought in the war, my parents were Eisenhower Republicans, and I wore white gloves to Mass."

"Oh, boy," Jamie said. "I think we're in for it."

There was a shot of the church, with Clarissa in front of it. "This is the church where I was confirmed," she said. "I used to make up sins for confession when I couldn't think of any. Talking back to my sister—that was a standby."

Everyone laughed.

"Margot the unwitting oppressor," Jamie said.

"Oh, she could be witting," Clarissa said.

Margot, who had been rocking the baby, looked hurt. There was an awkward silence, and then she handed the baby off to Martin and left the room.

"You kids are acting like nothing's happened to your sister," Yvette said angrily. "You have to be careful with her." She went down the hallway after Margot.

They had missed what Clarissa had said while standing in front of the public pool, and now she was in front of the house again. There was a breeze, and it blew her hair a little, and blew against the microphone, making a low roar. "I came here to tell my parents that I was a lesbian," she said. "That was my plan."

Del's voice from behind the camera said, "You just said *was*."

"Because it was a past-tense idea," Clarissa answered on camera. "I *came* to say I *was*. Now I'm not sure I can do it."

"What did she say?" Teddy asked Saffron.

"I think she said she was a lesbian," Saffron said quietly.

"She *did*?" Teddy said.

The image of Clarissa careened to one side of the frame, and Del spoke again, unseen. "See, this is the problem with this movie. You can't even say 'I'm a lesbian' to *me*. So why would you want to say it to your parents?"

"Is this a fictional movie?" Teddy asked Saffron.

"I don't know," Saffron said.

Jamie said, "Clar? This is the movie you wanted us to watch, right?"

"Yes," Clarissa said, as if uncertain now. "But you're not really watching it."

Abby sat frozen on the couch, waiting for the rest of the film.

The camera had gone inside the house and found Teddy in his recliner in the living room. It was like a trick mirror, reflecting the room they were in, but Teddy was alone there, telling stories. The room fell silent, listening. He talked about a Prussian officer who told him America would go to war, and about laying mines across a bay in the Pacific.

When Clarissa came on the screen again, explaining something, Jamie said, "Wow. You should be in war documentaries, Dad."

The baby started to fuss, and Martin jiggled him. "Is there more of Teddy?" he asked.

"I think that's it," Clarissa said. On-screen, she was giving a tour of her old bedroom down the hall. "It's almost over." Abby could see that it was not her dream reception, as director and star.

The baby started to cry, and Martin handed him off to Saffron. People turned to try to help.

"I think he's sick," Saffron said. "I think he has a cold."

Clarissa ejected the tape before the credits and left the room.

Abby followed her mother, who stopped outside her bedroom, glaring down the hall at her family. "They've *never* paid any attention," she said. "They've never *seen* me."

"I'm sorry."

"You don't understand what it was like being the younger daughter. Even in that book you didn't."

"I'm sorry," Abby said.

"How can they love me if they don't *see* me?"

"They do."

But the movie was already forgotten; all attention had turned to the baby's congested sobs.

By Christmas Eve, Martin and T.J. had sore throats and runny noses, too. Jamie said all babies should be banned from Christmas.

"That would go against the spirit of the holiday," Yvette said. "It's about the birth of a child."

"That's why the joke is funny, Ma," Jamie said.

"Oh—" she said.

The sick and the heathen stayed home from midnight Mass to play cards, and the faithful and the curious went to hear Yvette read from Isaiah. Abby and Jamie slid into a middle pew next to Margot and her family. Bennett had announced at dinner that he was an atheist—to only mild surprise—but Owen and Danny were there, and Teddy. The church filled up with parishioners in red and green sweaters.

"It's good to get out of that house," Jamie said. He stretched his arms over his head. "But it's weird not to have a kid in tow. Isn't it?"

"Sort of," Abby said.

He let one arm come down on the pew behind her.

"Don't get fresh," she said.

When it was Yvette's turn to read, she stood at the lectern and spoke from memory, in a clear voice:

> For a child is born to us, a son given to us;
> Authority rests upon his shoulders; and he is named
> Wonderful Counselor, Mighty God,
> Everlasting Father, Prince of Peace.

She sat down again, and a warm and friendly-seeming priest gave a sermon about the first reenactment of the Nativity, as staged by Francis of Assisi. He said that when Francis embraced the doll representing Jesus, the doll hugged him back. "We know that babies are difficult and wonderful," the priest said, "that they're rewarding and they're a lot of work. And loving Jesus, embracing Jesus in your life, is like that: both difficult and wonderfully worthwhile." There were wet coughs throughout the congregation: other families had colds, and not all the sick had stayed home.

Then a teenager in a black dress, her long red hair in ringlets, stood near the piano and sang "O Holy Night," from the beginning. She sang:

> *Truly He taught us to love one another*
> *His law is love and His gospel is peace*
> *Chains shall He break for the slave is our brother*
> *And in His name all oppression shall cease.*

Abby whispered to Jamie, "That prophecy didn't work out so well."

"I think she means eventually."

"I'm not holding my breath."

Margot gave them a look. The soprano went on, the song getting higher and more insistent:

> *Christ is the Lord, Oh, praise His name forever*
> *His pow'r and glo-o-ory ever more proclaim*
> *His pow'r and glo-o-ory ever mo-o-o-ore proclaim.*

When it was over, the girl collected her music and nodded slightly in the strange absence of applause. The Mass was finished, the candles were lit, and the congregation sang "Silent Night" and spilled out of the church. The night was cool and clear.

"Let's walk home," Jamie said. "I don't want to squeeze into that car."

They said good-bye to the others and walked past the line of cars waiting to leave the parking lot. There were roses blooming between the slats of the neighborhood fences as they started down the street.

Abby hummed "O Holy Night" as they walked, and Jamie sang, "*Christ* is the Lord, Oh *wor*-ship him or we'll kill . . . you!"

Abby laughed. "Careful. His pow'r and glory might strike you down."

"With a bad head cold?"

"Someone's next. Margot looked pale at church."

"My money's on Bennett. He's been weakened by stress."

"And Margot hasn't? Do you want odds?"

"No, I've got a feeling. Two dollars on Bennett. You take Margot."

They shook hands on the bet, and Jamie held on to hers.

"Oh, Abby, it's so weird," he said. "There's no one I'm at *home* with like I am with you. That's not a come-on, I swear."

She took her hand back and kept walking.

"Are you going to tell Peter what happened?" he asked.

"Maybe. If he wants to know. Right now he doesn't."

"Just admit that it's weird for you, too."

They passed a hedge of winter jasmine, and the air smelled headily sweet. "It is weird," she said.

"It's hard to tell. You've been so disciplined and clear."

She laughed. "For exactly two weeks. What you call disciplined and clear, the rest of the world calls dissociated and insane."

"You haven't had any attacks."

"Are you trying to trigger one?"

"No," he said. He caught her hand again and swung it as they walked. "I'm all for disciplined and clear."

78

MARGOT SAT AT midnight Mass between her husband and her younger son, thinking how strange it was to be doing what she had done every Christmas of her married life. She didn't recognize this woman, the adulteress who had suffered a nervous collapse, and it was jarring to see herself in the cozy old surroundings. Owen had no idea how to treat her: he seemed caught between anger and concern, and dealt with it by not speaking. She felt utterly unresolved, singing, "All is calm, all is bright," with Danny's cheerful baritone on one side and Owen mouthing the words on the other.

Then, in the backseat on the drive home, Owen's knee brushed hers, and she felt a shock run up her thigh, like she was nineteen again. She looked at him, but he was frowning at his seat belt. He hadn't meant to touch her; he wasn't letting her back in so easily. At the house, he went inside without holding the door. In another country she might be stoned to death for what she had done. She guessed she was getting off easy.

In the house, the others were still up playing rummy at the dining room table: her sister and crazy old Freddie, and the unhealthily beautiful Saffron.

"There was a call for you," Clarissa said. "It's by the phone."

On the message pad, in her sister's nun-trained cursive, she read, "Sgt. Tyrone called, please call station," with a Santa Barbara number.

Coats were being hung up, inquiries made about the sick, the kettle put on the stove. Margot felt a clammy sureness of death and wondered if Dominick had done it himself or if there had been an accident. The mad uncle was watching her, so she took the slip of paper to the phone in her parents' room.

"Mr. Jay asked me to call you," the sergeant on the line said. "He wants you to post bail."

She felt her shoulders relax a little, and relief held judgment at a distance. Dominick had been charged with possession and disorderly conduct. The sergeant said they found marijuana on him, but he seemed to be using something else. There had been an altercation on State Street, and only Mr. Jay had been taken in. He'd used his first call on someone else. The sergeant gave her the name of a bail bondsman, who was brusque at first but then decided he was speaking to a lady and became deferential and polite. She gave him her credit card number to get Dominick out that night, and said she would find a place to receive the faxed forms in the morning.

Then she hung up and sat on her parents' bed wondering how to start her life again. She felt she had bought her way free from something, in a real way.

Freddie came to the door. "Do you know where your mother keeps the dinner candles?" he asked.

"In the top drawer by the phone desk, in the kitchen."

He disappeared again.

Margot heard Saffron in the other room saying, "You can't leave! We need someone to play your hand. Where are Jamie and Abby?"

There was a short silence, and then Yvette said, "Oh, you guys. They're just walking home. *I'll* play Freddie's hand."

Freddie came back, holding two candles and two silver candleholders, and motioned for Margot to follow him. She got up as if hypnotized—she needed *something* to happen—and he led her to the laundry room. He set one candle on the old yellow Maytag washing machine and one on the dryer, and lit them with a lighter from his pocket.

He switched out the light so the room was lit by the small flames, and he positioned Margot on one side of the washer, in line with the two candles, looking over the top of them.

"I want you to focus on one candle and then the other," he said. "The far one and then the closer one. Can you see them both?"

Margot nodded, thinking she would stop this nonsense any minute.

"Now I want you to focus on the exact point between them," he said.

"That would be easier if I were facing them sideways."

"But that's not how it works," he said. "That would be simple, as if you could see your whole life laid out on a time line, like a stranger's life in a history book. Healing the past isn't easy."

"Oh, *healing*," she said. "Is that what we're doing here?" But she didn't leave.

"Sure," he said. "Finding the point between the candles is like living in the present moment. It's so easy to focus on the past or the future—those are solid and glowing in our heads, right? But they're just ideas, they're just recordings and projections. This moment, now, might be dark and uncertain, but it's the only thing that's real. So this is an exercise for focusing on it, visualizing the act of inhabiting it. You see? This moment, now, is like the point between the two candles. We have to train our minds to stop obsessing about things that don't exist anymore, or don't exist yet."

"Did you make up this exercise?" Margot asked, trying to guess, given the laws of perspective, where the exact midpoint would be.

"Do you see the spot in the middle?" he asked.

"I'm not sure. But I think so."

Freddie put one finger into the invisible line between the candle flames, exactly at the spot where Margot was concentrating. "Was it here?"

"Yes!" she said. She was flooded with joy and satisfaction, and then felt foolish for caring.

"I knew you'd be good at this," he said. "You seem like a good student."

She beamed at him, in spite of herself.

"Okay, find the spot again," he said. "This is only the first exercise. It's important to learn it before we move on."

Margot lost track of time and stopped worrying about what the others would think while she concentrated on the candles. There was a stack of index cards on the sewing table, the kind her mother used for recipes, and Freddie wrote words on them: PATIENCE and CLARITY. She sat on the floor, and he asked her to study the cards while the candles burned down. He said this was just the first part of the exercise, to sit with the cards and experience what the words made her feel, and to breathe deeply and evenly. They could work more tomorrow.

When Margot stood up, her knees were a little stiff, but otherwise she felt wonderful. Freddie put his hand on her face.

"You're a fine girl," he said.

When she got to her bedroom, her husband was waiting. "So you have a new Svengali," Owen said.

"No," she said. She didn't want to examine, through Owen's logic, the change in how she felt.

"Did he make a pass at you?"

She sat on the bed, exhausted. "No."

"I don't really want to talk, yet," he said. "But I want to sleep in here. I feel ridiculous on the couch, and it hurts my back."

"Do you want me to move out there?"

"No. We'll just sleep."

"Okay." She slipped off her shoes. It wasn't the romantic reconciliation she might have imagined, but it was a move in the direction she had chosen. She watched him untie his shoes and take them off. Owen's mother had liked to tell a story in which a nine-year-old Owen, asked what he wanted for Christmas, said, "A pair of brown socks." People laughed at the story, but Margot understood: it wasn't the only thing he wanted, but it was a thing he needed, so he set about getting it. It was illustrative not of his oddness but of his deliberate practicality. He was sleeping in her room because the couch hurt his back and his pride, but they would move on to the other reasons.

79

JAMIE WOKE ON Christmas morning in his parents' house with what felt like a killing hangover, but he hadn't even had the pleasure of being drunk. His head felt like a solid block. T.J. was still asleep on the other side of the room, and Jamie got up quietly. He put on his old flannel bathrobe over the sweats he had slept in and ventured out to see who else had come down with the plague. He didn't want to have lost the bet by getting sick first.

In the kitchen, Clarissa was doing a crossword puzzle, looking healthy. She seemed to have resigned herself to her family's inattention. Danny was making eggs.

Owen came from the direction of Margot's room and gave Jamie a look that suggested he wanted no commentary.

"I'm getting Margot some juice," he said. "She has this cold."

"I have it, too," Bennett called, in a stuffed-up voice from the couch.

Before Jamie could establish who had gotten it first, Yvette came out of her room in a bathrobe, in a fury. She passed Owen easily on the way to the refrigerator and pulled the door open so roughly the bottles and jars rattled.

"Ease up there, Mom," Jamie said.

"Oh, I'm just so mad," she said. "It's no one's fault. It's not the baby's fault, and it's not Saffron's, because she didn't know he was sick. But what an awful thing, at Christmas."

"Is Dad sick?"

"He can't even get out of bed. We have to rethink this whole thing, getting together when there are all these germs."

"That sounds a lot like banning babies from Christmas."

"I don't think we should gather at all," Yvette said. "Did you hear the coughing in church last night? Everyone in town must have it by now. I'm just so disgusted."

Abby came in wearing pajamas, and Jamie told her they had a draw: Bennett and Margot had both woken up sick.

"Oh, you kids," Yvette said. "How could you bet on that?"

"Can I pick Yvette?"

"Daniel!"

The doorbell rang and Saffron came in, wearing tight velvet jeans, a hood trimmed with white fur, and the baby in a sling. Jamie wondered what business a creature like Saffron had getting married and becoming a mother. She seemed to be dressing to show off the breasts that had come with the baby. There had been one moment alone in the hallway when she had thanked him for inviting her and kissed his cheek in a lingering way, the new breasts in a sweater brushing his chest, but then T.J. had come running through and she had pulled away and laughed. Now she sat down next to him with the baby in its rig.

"How's Patient Zero?" he asked.

"He's sleeping," she said. "Thank God."

"These terrible kids are betting on who gets sick next," Yvette said. "Danny picked me. Isn't that awful?"

"It's all my fault," Saffron said.

"It's nobody's fault. I'm going to take this to Teddy, and then we can get Christmas started." She left with a glass of orange juice.

"I feel so terrible," Saffron said.

"You've been officially absolved by my mom," Jamie said. "And she was blessed by the Pope."

"She was not," Abby said.

"In your book she was."

"God, those eggs smell good," Saffron said. "They have these horribly early breakfasts at the B-and-B. Who eats breakfast before eight-thirty?"

"Anyone with a job, I think," Jamie said. "Or a child."

"My baby sleeps in."

"Lucky you."

Yvette came back from the bedroom. "Jamie, honey? I want you to get dressed and take your father to Dr. Harris."

"It's Christmas Day," he said. "Dr. Harris is at home."

"To the emergency room, then," she said. "It's not an emergency"—this was said to the whole room—"I just want to get him looked at."

"I'm dressed," Saffron said. "I can go."

"No, you stay here. The baby shouldn't be on the road."

"I'm well," Clarissa said. "I'll take Dad."

"Jamie, *go*," Yvette said.

Jamie dressed quickly and caught up to his father, who was walking with Yvette's help to the front door.

"I'm all right," Teddy said. "A little tight in the chest, that's all."

Jamie threw food wrappers and music from the front seat of his car to the back, then tried to help his father get in.

"I'm all *right*!" Teddy said, impatient now. "Let me do it myself!"

But once they started driving toward the hospital, Teddy fell silent, as if consumed by the task of breathing. Jamie listened to his father wheeze. It sounded like there wasn't any room in Teddy's lungs.

"You all right, Dad?"

"I'm just fine," Teddy managed, between breaths.

In the emergency room, the nurse put Teddy in a wheelchair and wheeled him down a hallway while Jamie filled out information on a clipboard at the front. He hunted through Teddy's wallet for the insurance information and found photographs: one of the young and beautiful Yvette, smiling over her shoulder, and one each of

Jamie and Margot and Clarissa as kids. The photos were well handled, worn at the edges, and loose in the wallet, and they weren't ones Jamie recognized. Margot was sweetly demure in hers. Clarissa had a mischievous smile, like she was sharing a secret with the photographer. Jamie had a happy, oblivious grin.

Jamie tried to remember being so uncomplicatedly happy and couldn't. He guessed that by the following year his expression in pictures had started to darken and become recognizably him. He told himself that you wouldn't want to keep that oblivious grin through your whole life; it wasn't an adult expression. They would put you in a home if you looked like that. But he wished he had held on to it a little longer. Margot would say he had kept his childhood intact all his life, but he hadn't. It was there in the picture, unrecoverable.

"When you're done with that form, you can fill out this one," the receptionist said, and she handed Jamie another clipboard.

Jamie put the photographs away and started to fill in the names and numbers that would call up, for the receptionists and adjusters and actuaries, his father's life.

80

TEDDY WOKE WITH the claustrophobic feeling of being attached to things—tubes in his nose and an IV in his arm—to hear his wife talking. He listened with his eyes closed, to save his energy for answering, and then he realized Yvette was talking not to him but to God.

"He isn't ready yet," she was saying softly. "You know I'll let him go when he's ready, and I'll follow him. I'm not afraid. But he has things to do here."

Teddy thought automatically about the garage door opener that worked only sometimes, and the peeling wallpaper in the bathroom. There was something else he couldn't remember—not the dishwasher, he'd just replaced the dishwasher. Was it a porch light?

"He has further to go with his children," Yvette said.

Oh, *that,* Teddy thought.

"He can't leave now, when they're just coming back to us— Margot from that man, and Clarissa from that woman, and Jamie from his marriage. They've had such dark times, and they feel they've disappointed him, and that he disapproves, but they're coming back. He needs to acknowledge it and accept them, or they'll always feel incomplete."

Teddy opened his eyes now, to show her he was awake, but she was looking down at her lap. He couldn't believe that she had known about Clarissa's girlfriend and hadn't told him. How could she not have told him? What else hadn't she said?

"I know people go when they aren't ready all the time," Yvette went on. "But let him finish here. When it's my turn, I promise to go without an argument. Let him stay."

Teddy wasn't sure he could get the air in his lungs to speak. "Yvette," he said weakly. "I'm still here. Talk to *me*."

She opened her eyes and looked surprised. "You were sleeping," she said.

"I'm not now," he said. "Talk to me."

"You aren't supposed to go yet," she said. The anger in her voice gave way to tears almost as soon as she said it. "That wasn't the deal. You're supposed to stay."

"I'm not going anywhere."

"You can't!" she said. "You'd better not."

His lungs were too tired for him to promise again.

"I've just been sitting here worrying about you," she said, "and I can't *do* anything."

He didn't know how to make her stop worrying, with tubes coming out of him, and he didn't have the energy to talk, so he said, "Sing." He hoped it would distract her.

Yvette wiped her eyes with a tissue, and blew her nose, and frowned.

"Please," he said.

So she started to sing one of her French songs, a war song from his childhood:

> *Au jardin de mon père*
> *Les lauriers son fleuris*
> *Tous les oiseaux du monde*
> *Vont y faire leurs nids.*

Yvette stopped, and she seemed calmer already. She said, "My father's brother, who was a soldier, used to sing it for my sister and me in Canada. He was the one with shrapnel in his back. *In my father's garden, the laurels are flowering, and all the birds of the world make their nests.*" She thought for a second, hummed, and shook her head. "I can't remember the next verse. It's something about the white dove singing for the girls without husbands. But not for me, because I have a lovely one: *Car j'en ai-t-un joli.* And then the bird asks, But where is your husband?

> *Il n'est pas dans la danse*
> *Il est bien loin d'ici*
> *Dites-nous donc, la belle,*
> *Où donc est vot' mari?*

She sang the chorus, which he knew, and then she remembered the next verse:

> *Il est dans la Hollande*
> *Les Hollandais l'ont pris.*
> *Que donneriez-vous, belle,*
> *Pour qu'on vous le rendît?*

"*The Dutch have taken him, what would you give for them to send him back?*" she translated. "And the girl, the wife, says,

> *Je donnerai Versailles,*
> *Paris et Saint-Denis,*
> *Les tours de Notre-Dame*
> *Et l'clocher d'mon pays.*

"*I would give Versailles and Paris,*" she said, although he had understood, "*and the towers of Notre-Dame, and the church tower of my own little town.*"

Teddy started to say, "That's the attitude that got France occupied—" But then he ran out of air.

"Oh, but Teddy, it's about the women at home. Why would

they want their husbands to go off to war? They wouldn't, they never do."

"Sometimes there's no choice."

"But we don't have to like it," Yvette said. "I'd give Versailles and Notre-Dame to have you out of this damn hospital right now! I really would."

"And the church tower?" he wheezed, to tease her.

"And the damn church tower!" she said. "Just don't leave me here."

Teddy tried to smile and then closed his eyes, just for a minute, exhausted by her need.

81

CLARISSA WALKED THROUGH the house, barely seeing. She felt like a cartoon character after a safe had fallen on her head from a high building. She thought her body must be accordioned from the blow, her head surrounded by stars, and her walk a stagger. But when she looked down at her body, she was upright and unbent. And her father was dead. They had given him massive doses of antibiotics, but the pneumonia had gotten into his heart. His heart. She couldn't understand it.

She hadn't even kissed him good-bye when he went to the hospital. She'd been so sure he would be back. She had walked to the door and called "Bye, Dad," as they helped him out. He'd been so focused on getting to the car. But how could she not have had a sense, a feeling, and hugged him tight?

She picked up the phone in her mother's kitchen, to call Jimmy Vaughan, and heard her daughter's voice on the line.

"No one expected it," Abby was saying. "Jamie's a wreck, he feels like it's his fault."

"Why does he think that?" a woman's voice asked. It wasn't a voice Clarissa recognized. She stayed on just a second longer. She could apologize and hang up when she knew who it was.

"Because he brought the people who got sick first," Abby said. "Saffron and the baby. But no one was sick then. And the pneumonia probably came from midnight Mass. Everyone was sick there."

"So it isn't Jamie's fault," the woman said.

"Of course not."

"Do you feel like it's yours?"

Abby said nothing.

"Did your grandfather say anything about your book?"

"He asked if there had been more printings. And he told me again that he likes books without negativism in them." Abby made a funny noise as she finished the sentence.

"In which people don't die?"

Abby started to cry, on the other extension. "Not of pneumonia from a baby at Christmastime," she said. "Jesus."

"You didn't cause the pneumonia," the woman said.

"Saffron came with the baby because of the book. She wanted to meet them."

"Oh, Abby."

"It's your job to say it's not my fault, but it is," Abby said.

A therapist, then. Clarissa knew she should hang up, but she couldn't. She hadn't known Abby was seeing anyone. If she *had* known, she would have hung up at once.

"It was the fault of a virus or bacteria," the therapist said. "People get sick, this time of year, and some die. I'm not being callous. I'm *so* sorry it happened to your family and to you. But you didn't do it."

"I don't know," Abby said, and Clarissa thought that probably it *was* Abby's fault, for bringing the book and the baby on her father. He could still be alive, and instead he was gone. She was about to say it, but the thought of Abby knowing she'd listened stopped her. Abby would be furious, and she couldn't give her the advantage like that, so she silently hung up the phone.

82

ABBY DROVE HER grandmother to the church to finish the funeral plans. Yvette had put on lipstick, but she hadn't been out of the house since coming home from the hospital, and she was trembling and ghostlike.

"I haven't been to visit my shut-ins," she said in the car. "I have to go see Teddy's, too. There's no one else to do it."

"They can wait," Abby said, stopping at a yellow light.

"It helps them so much," Yvette said. "Some of them don't know anything, they don't know their children's names, they're in nursing homes, and then they take the Host and you should see their faces light up. They know exactly what it is."

The light turned green and Abby pulled through.

"Thank you for driving me, sweetheart," her grandmother said.

Father Kevin was the priest who had performed the Christmas Mass, and his office was small and simple, with a desk and visitors' chairs and a tall bookshelf. The passage about love from 1 Corinthians was framed on the wall, in calligraphy. Abby guessed a parishioner had done it and guessed there were some crushes on the priest, among the congregation. "Love is patient; love is kind." His beard up close was flecked with gray. They went over the readings and music together. They would sing St. Francis's prayer:

> *Make me a channel of your peace.*
> *Where there's despair in life, let me bring hope.*
> *Where there is darkness, only light.*
> *And where there's sadness, ever joy.*

Abby thought about the likelihood of that, even for one person, even for a saint.

Yvette said, "Teddy loved that song." She hummed a little bit, then was quiet. "I don't know what to do about the shut-ins," she said. "I feel so weak and sad."

"Someone else can take them for a while," Father Kevin said.

"But there are the ones Teddy visits, too," Yvette said. "It's so many. I want to do it, I'm just afraid I'll fall apart."

"I could go along," Abby offered.

Yvette shook her head. "You aren't baptized, honey. She isn't baptized," she told the priest. "If I need help, she can't give the Host."

"I'd still consider you to be the conduit," he said. "She'd just keep you company."

"But if I did need help."

"She'd be an attendant, like an altar boy."

"Altar boys are baptized," Yvette said firmly, "and have had communion." Her voice was stronger now that she had some focus.

"Well," the priest said, "the baptism would be easy to take care of."

"Wait a minute," Abby said.

The priest held his hands up. "I just wanted to present it as an option. Obviously it's a separate issue. But I think it might be good for you, Yvette, to continue with the lay ministry. And I know it's good for the people you visit. Is there someone you'd rather have with you?"

"The kids are all a wreck," Yvette said, bitterly. "I knew they would be."

There was a silence, and Abby felt a question in the air. The room felt so much like a shrink's office that she said what she was thinking:

"My mother always said I'd go to limbo, like the pagan babies who didn't get baptized. I think she was joking. But I used to think as a kid that limbo wasn't a terrible option. You lost your chance at heaven, but you definitely couldn't go to hell."

"Oh, honey, you don't want to go to limbo," Yvette said.

"I don't want to go to hell, either," Abby said, lightly. "Maybe limbo's not so bad."

"Maybe I should talk to Abby alone for a minute," the priest said.

Yvette stood up, taking her handbag. "I'll go think about flowers."

When she was gone, the priest said, in a reflective way, "I've thought a lot about the infants I baptize, the fact that they have no choice in the matter. They may eventually decide it doesn't mean anything to them. But I think they usually find that it does." He studied Abby's face. "I sense baptism doesn't mean much to you."

"Actually it does," Abby said.

He looked encouraged, and encouraging.

"I mean, it would *have* to mean something, for me to do it," she said. "I'm not an infant."

He sighed. "We have an aging parish, so I see a lot of grieving people," he said. "From my perspective, from that experience, I think it would be good for Yvette to keep her routine."

"But I don't have to get baptized for that to happen."

"No," he said. "I know. The whole topic is just something I've been thinking about. The funny thing is that the parents of the babies rarely come back to church again. I guess they don't have time."

Abby couldn't tell if he was lonely and wanted to talk about the decline of the Church, or if they were still arguing politely about the possibility of her baptism. She felt that Dr. Tirrett would want her to make her position clear, so she said, "I can't inject youth into your parish. I don't live here."

"Of course not," he said. "I thought from your book that you might want the opportunity presented to you."

Abby wondered if her grandmother had asked him to read it and help her deal with it. "You're thinking about the girl with cancer getting baptized?"

"I was thinking about the whole thing."

Abby looked at her hands in her lap and again felt she was in a shrink's office. She wondered if people gave confession in this room.

"What if I just give you a blessing," he said, "so that Yvette can accept your help in the ministry?"

"I'm not going to tell her I've been baptized."

"Of course not," he said. "It's just a blessing." He smiled. "It's very noninvasive. You can still think whatever you want."

"How do you know she'll accept that?"

"I think she will."

Abby gave in. "Okay," she said. "All I wanted was to be her driver. I didn't think there would be all this."

The priest laughed. "I promise I'm not trying to trap you for the faith," he said. "It doesn't work that way."

The words came out before she could stop herself: "I know the book hurt them. I know I'm guilty of that. I didn't want it to, but that doesn't change that it's true."

Father Kevin was silent.

Abby felt close to tears and said, "Okay, let's get it over with."

The priest stood in front of Abby's chair, in his ordinary clothes, and folded his hands and seemed to pray for a minute, while she sat, feeling embarrassed. Then he put his right hand on Abby's forehead, so his fingers rested on her hair. She was startled by his touch, and by the warmth that spread from his palm into her head. For a second she thought, *Oh, well, it's supposed to feel like something is happening,* and then the grief overcame her, and she shook under his hand with involuntary sobs.

83

HOW DO YOU KNOW he wasn't secretly baptizing you?" Peter asked, lying on his old bed in Philadelphia. His mother had left everything exactly as it was when he was in high school: an M. C. Escher poster held up with yellowing tape, a Yes album cover, some photographs he had taken with his new Pentax on a family trip to Yellowstone.

"He wasn't," Abby said. "There wasn't any water."

"Maybe they don't need water. The Mormons baptize people who are dead and buried."

"It was just a blessing."

"So he says."

"He's not that kind of priest."

"You see? They've got you."

"Peter, please," she said. "It's hard enough here."

"Sing me the St. Francis song again."

"I can't sing."

"Come on."

"Oh, Master, grant that I may never seek," she sang, off-key, "so much to be consoled as to console, to be understood as to understand, to be loved as to love with all my soul."

"St. Francis must have written that when he realized that his birds weren't going to console and understand and love him like he hoped."

"It's such a sixties folk song, the melody," Abby said. "It's strange that it was Teddy's favorite. It makes me think I didn't know him well enough."

"You knew he identified with St. Francis."

"But why? Maybe he wanted to escape all of us and go live with the birds."

"Sometimes he probably did."

"Yvette thinks he's with God. The afterlife is a really good selling point, for a religion."

"You're just noticing this *now*?"

"I keep thinking I brought a curse on my family. I murdered my grandmother in a book, and I must be punished, but God has a sense of irony, so he took Teddy."

"Abby, I love you, but you're insane."

"The difference is that the novel is basically comic, and this just feels agonizing."

"Your novel is sad, too."

"But it's comic in structure. Everyone comes together at the end."

"Because of a death."

"But you know what I mean. People come clean, they're moving on, they make toasts."

"Why does everything have to be strictly comic or tragic?" he asked, in his best teaching voice. "What about *Hamlet*? What about *Duck Soup*?"

"*Hamlet* is a tragedy and *Duck Soup* is a com— Oh, God," Abby said.

He was already laughing. He loved having caught her.

"That's so mean," she said. "I'm not prepared for jokes right now."

"I'm sorry," he said. "Will you hurry up with the consoling, and come seek to be consoled?"

84

THE FUNERAL WAS in the church, which was filled. Yvette was surprised how many people were there. They had come from all different parts of Teddy's life, from the church and the YMCA and the café where they had breakfast on Saturdays. Yvette saw their favorite waitress, in a flimsy black dress. There were nurses and attendants from the assisted-living homes. A big Samoan woman named Joey was red-eyed from crying.

The owner of the hardware store was there, with his daughter who worked at the counter. And there were some of the catechumens who had come to the house, and a young Navy pilot Teddy had met recently. There were old friends, too: some from the service, some from when the children were young—but Yvette was struck by the new ones, the near strangers, the people who must have responded to something in Teddy, in this quiet, kind man.

They had come because Teddy was gone. That was hard for Yvette to fully understand. She woke each morning on her own side of the bed, saw that he wasn't there, and thought how quietly he must have gotten up. Then consciousness and memory came back, and she had to catch her breath at the pain. She prayed to be able to accept it, to be graceful until her own time came, but she felt unsettlingly healthy.

It might be a long time. It didn't seem fair. She wanted to be quick to follow him, to feel that her body would not last long without him, but she knew it would. She was angry at God, angry at Teddy, angry at the doctors, angry at that damn baby with the cold.

Things happened that she wanted to tell him, just little daily things. She wanted to tell him about the priest talking to Abby about baptism, and maybe planting a seed. And about the way Margot seemed better every day now, after falling apart at first, and how even the grief seemed to bring her back to herself. She hoped Teddy somehow knew, and she told him in her head; it was like prayer. If God could hear, then why not Teddy?

Jimmy Vaughan turned up for the funeral, leather-skinned from the sun. Yvette cried out in surprise when she realized who it was— a boy who couldn't have grown a mustache the last time she saw him. He kissed her and said how sorry he was, and Yvette understood the comfort he would bring Clarissa. Teddy had disapproved of Jimmy when the children were young, but the boy had stood up to him. In that way he was like Teddy: he had quietly refused to give up what he wanted.

Father Kevin gave the eulogy, and Yvette spoke as long as she could before the tears came. Then Margot walked to the lectern. She wore her hair pulled back and looked like her elegant self, a little thinner.

"I wasn't going to speak today," she said, adjusting the microphone. "I've been having a difficult time, and I didn't think I was up to it. But this is my one chance to say good-bye to my father in public, and I realized I needed to do it." She took a breath and seemed to gather herself.

"Some of you know that my niece, Abby Collins, wrote a novel," she said. "And if you've read it, you know that it's fictional, but that my parents are very much alive in it, their voices are in it, even though their characters do things that they would never do. I'm in it, too, as the insufferable older sister."

The people in the room laughed, and Yvette glanced at her granddaughter next to her. Abby looked pale.

"I've been having a difficult time recently," Margot said, "that coincided with seeking out a part of my past that Abby's novel brought up for me. It had nothing to do with the novel, but the existence of the novel reminded me."

The room went silent.

Margot said, "My father died before I had really recovered—I'm still recovering—and I regret that I spent my last days with him so intently focused on myself. I regret that I caused him pain, at the end, and worry. He was a private man and wouldn't want me to say this so publicly, but I did cause him worry, we all did.

"I think I speak for my sister and brother, too, when I say that he was not always perfectly understanding about the things we did. He was an old-style Catholic father, and a good Marine, and it could make him rigid. It was difficult for him that Jamie hadn't settled down in the way he expected, and that my sister's life was not what he wanted for her. I was the good daughter for a long time, but in the end I gave him trouble, too. We knew in all of these cases that he hoped things would turn out differently. I think if he'd had more time, he would have seen that we were each finding our own way, but he didn't have that time. I want to be honest here."

Yvette didn't like the way this was going, but she felt that nothing was real, and she was lifted above the scene, looking down on it.

"I think I see, from being a mother myself," Margot said, "that you do want so much more for your children than life will ever offer them. And that's what he wanted for us. He wanted life to be understandable, and morally unambiguous, and not filled with strife. The defining event of his youth was the war, but he wanted what the song we're going to sing asks: to be a channel of peace. He wanted to trust in God and sow faith and love like St. Francis. Which is difficult always to do.

"So I wanted to say that I loved my father dearly," Margot said, "and I think you're all here because you saw the faith he had, that there is something of God in man. We're not always deserving of that conviction. Most of the time we're not. But he believed it of everyone he met. He believed it of each of you."

By this point people were crying, throughout the church; Yvette could hear them rummaging for Kleenexes and blowing noses. Yvette wondered if she herself were made of stone, because she had no intention of crying now. She knew everything Margot was saying and didn't think it needed to be aired here.

Then Margot stopped. "That's all," she said, in a small voice. "Thank you."

She left the lectern carefully, as if unsure of her legs, and headed for the back of the church. Saffron's uncle, Freddie Tucker, stood from a pew and followed her. People turned in their seats to watch them leave the church, and even the priest seemed distracted.

Finally Jamie stood up and addressed the startled congregation.

"My sister will be fine," he said. "We'll all sing St. Francis's peace prayer now, which is in your programs. It was a song my father liked."

The organist started up and vamped until people got their programs out, and then everyone began on Jamie's cue.

85

ABBY STOOD IN HER grandparents' crowded living room with a glass of wine she'd been handed, watching people talk, trying not to get drawn into conversation. Bennett was talking to the priest, and Owen was talking to Cara Ferris's mother, and everyone else was talking to someone.

She went to get rid of the wine and saw her mother on the back porch, sitting with Jimmy Vaughan on the deck chairs. He was singing—Abby could hear him through the screen—one of the teenage songs he'd written for her:

> *And when I go out in the rain*
> *I hear myself calling your name.*

Her mother was laughing or crying, or maybe both at once.

Abby put the wine on the kitchen counter. Saffron, in an expensive and low-cut black suit, was in the kitchen directing the caterers like a conductor. Margot came in crying, with a smear of mascara under her eye.

"Will you take me to Santa Barbara?" she asked Abby. "It's Dominick."

"You don't have to take care of him," Abby said, though she thought her aunt had been right to post bail. "Especially not now."

Margot shook her head. She looked puffy and strange. "That isn't the point anymore," she said. "Can we go in ten minutes?"

Abby went to her grandparents' room for her coat. Yvette was sitting on the bed in her black dress with the curtains drawn. The room was dim.

"Oh, honey," Yvette said. "I still can't believe he isn't here."

Abby sat beside her, and Yvette took her hand.

"Do you remember when you came down here to stay, from Santa Rosa, when you had chicken pox?"

"Sure," Abby said.

"You were so homesick and sad about your parents, and at night you would cry. And I would ask, 'Do you want to go home?' And you would say, 'Grandma, I want to stay here, and I want to go.'"

"I don't remember that."

"Oh, it used to break my heart," Yvette said. "But that's how I feel now. I want to stay here, and I want to go. I can't believe he left me."

"We want you to stay," Abby said. She felt how small Yvette's hands were, bent and knobby from arthritis.

"Did you see how many people were there today?" Yvette asked.

Abby nodded.

"I want to tell you, honey," Yvette said. "Life is so fragile. You have to remember that, when you love people. Because you can't be ready for what this feels like."

Abby nodded.

"Oh," Yvette said, her face crumpling again. "He was a part of me, and now it's gone."

She cried a little longer, then touched up her lipstick and went to brave the living room. Abby called Peter, who was back in San Diego, from the bedside phone.

"Are you finished yet?" he asked.

"Almost. I'm driving Margot up to Santa Barbara. Something happened to Dominick Jay."

"Some Christmas you're having."

"I hope this is the last thing."

"Do you think he's dead?"

She knew when he asked it. "Yes."

Peter was silent. "I hate that you're getting on the freeway for a dead guy."

"It's for Margot," she said, and she wondered if they were going to the morgue, and if Margot would then go back to being Owen's wife in Louisiana. That made her wonder about the rest of them: if Yvette could carry on without Teddy, with her friends and her shut-ins and her God. And if Jimmy and Clarissa would grow old together, or if there would be fights and infidelities and disillusion-ment, a drawn-out breaking up, and a repeat with someone new. If T.J. would lapse back into his sadness, and if Jamie was up to another dozen years, and more, of good-fatherhood.

"Hello?" Peter said. "Are you there?"

"I'm here."

"Are you coming home?"

She was surprised by the word. "I have to go to Santa Barbara."

"I mean after that."

She turned the word over, but nothing else fit. Not her father's house, made unrecognizable by the renters. Not her mother's house, where boyfriends and girlfriends would come and go. Not Jamie's couch, or Yvette's bedroom, with a hundred years of pictures on the wall. But Peter's apartment—was that home? The question wasn't about the makeshift desk in the living room, or the bedroom window shaded with trees; it was about the place where Peter was.

"Yes," she said.

"Good," he said. "Come soon."

ABOUT THE AUTHOR

Maile Meloy was born and raised in Helena, Montana. She is the author of the story collection *Half in Love* and the novel *Liars and Saints*. She received a Guggenheim Fellowship in 2004, and her stories have been published in *The New Yorker* and *The Paris Review*. She lives in Los Angeles.